MW01644317

all this time

Time After Time series, volume three

MEL HENRY

All This Time

Time After Time series, volume 3

Cover design by Kim Crecelius

Editing by Jacquelyn Ayres

Formatting by Champagne Formats

ISBN-13: 978-1523255214

ISBN-10: 1523255218

This book is dedicated to my husband, Nathan.

For all the nights you sleep alone while I stay up late with Josh and Carly. For the tears you dry and the ledges you talk me down from. For every hour you work away from home so I don't have to . . . I am eternally grateful. Not only do you tolerate it, you *encourage* me to do it. I'm sure this wasn't the life you signed on for, but I appreciate you letting me live it.

You are my *happily ever after*.

Prologue

Diary entry

April 1994

MY LIFE IS A MESS. EVERYTHING I THOUGHT I KNEW was wrong and I don't know where to begin rebuilding. As much as I'd like to blame the South Station phenomenon for the chaos, I know it has nothing to do with that. The fans are nuts—don't get me wrong—but they aren't the downfall of my relationship with Josh. I could even blame that blonde bitch Jenna if I wanted to, but I can't. If Josh tells me there's nothing going on, then I believe him. After all, I've been behind the scenes, and I see how things can be twisted by the media. Pure and simple, we are at different places in our lives. While I sit here in my dorm at NYU, he's on a tour bus somewhere in Australia. Or is it Asia? Hell, I don't even know. I don't know why I thought it could work, anyway. I was fooling myself.

I just reread the last letter Josh sent me over and over again, looking for obvious clues I missed the first sixty times I read it. Just like the last time, I didn't find any. The letter is full of "miss yous" and "I can't wait 'til we're together agains" and he signed it, "Love, Josh." He talked about the tough tour schedule and he mentioned looking for new management, but where "we" are concerned, everything looks fine.

My relationship with Josh McCarthy was something that pretty much fell into my lap. I was on a college visit at Northwestern where I ran into Josh and his bandmate, Marc Reyes, at a club, when I was with some friends. He invited me to a baseball game the next afternoon, and things bloomed from there. We spent the last year loving each other from a distance and up close.

My best friend Alejandro was one of the few people who supported our union. Alex Cruz was a big fan of South Station Boyz, too and loved that one of us was dating a member of the group. In fact, when Josh wanted to surprise me at prom, he and Alex worked together to make it happen. From that point on, they became best buds. Together, we were inseparable.

My mom was excited for me, but was cautious, of course. She'd never met anybody famous, so she was worried about how relationships worked in the public spotlight. She was a romantic and knew if our hearts were in it, we could make it work.

My stepdad was another story, however. At first, he thought someone was playing a joke and making a fool out of me, but after I showed him pictures of Josh and me together, his doubts turned into criticism. He told me Josh was just using me, that it was a publicity stunt, and then, when we didn't break up right away, he said that I was just a groupie and didn't mean anything to Josh. His favorite prediction was that I would end up pregnant right out of high school, like my sister.

My older brother, Terry, was also an opponent of my relationship with Josh. He was a lot like my stepfather with his never-ending doubt and criticism. He repeatedly told me that I was just one of many conquests Josh had sought in various cities throughout the country, maybe even the world, and I was an idiot for trusting him. He said it so frequently that I started to believe it and questioned Josh about it once. It took a while to work through that rift and I finally just had to tune my brother out.

South Station Boyz had a loyal following, affectionately known in the media as "Trainwreckz." There were many of them who lived up to that moniker. Even at my own school, I was taunted by girls claiming that Josh was *their* boyfriend, and that I better step off if I knew what was good for me. For obvious reasons, I went out of my way to lie low where my adoration for Josh and the band was concerned. He reminded me more than once that we knew the truth and that's what mattered.

Josh told me later that he noticed me the minute I walked into the club that night . . . that his eyes gravitated toward me. He'd watched me for a while before he decided he had to meet me, claiming that my smile intrigued him. The whole night was a blur, but I will always remember what it felt like to be in his arms on that dance floor.

I've forgotten the first song we danced to, but I remember him holding me close to him. Not so close that he couldn't make me melt with those baby blues of his, though. Josh was all smiles. Eyes and smiles. And a smooth tenor voice that sang along with every word of the songs we danced to. It was a triple threat of sexy, if there ever was one. He complimented my outfit—a carefully constructed ensemble my friends had put together before we left my hotel that night. He commented on my hair, twisting a stray brunette curl around his finger at random. He nearly purred in my ear when he mentioned how good my perfume smelled. We danced to that song and every other song after that until his bandmate Marc literally came and pulled him away.

We agreed to meet up the next day, and from there, I was hooked. I had my doubts, of course. My self-esteem had taken quite a beating over the years (at the hands of my stepdad) and my confidence frequently waivered, because of it. I wondered what Josh saw in me and, while I didn't often vocalize my fears, I questioned his decision to be with me. But as time went on, I learned to trust him, and I began believing the compliments he gave me. He was good for my spirit, and our relationship was all I'd ever dreamed it could be.

But, something changed.

We don't talk on the phone anymore. He hasn't mentioned coming to see me when the tour is done next month or talked about me visiting him. He hasn't brought up spending any time together this summer. In fact, he hasn't mentioned anything about us in a long time. I feel like a war bride. I keep waiting for someone to show up with a telegram to tell me our relationship has been killed in action. To quote that John Cusack movie we watched one time, "I gave her my heart and she gave me a pen." I'd given Josh my heart (among other body parts) and in return, I got to say I dated a member of

South Station Boyz. Yeah, that was a fair trade. I grunt in disgust at myself and the situation. Looking down at my diary, I continue writing.

The thing is, even for as crappy as I feel, I can't help thinking that I lived a dream thousands of girls would die for. I don't hate him. Hell, I'm not even angry at him. I miss him; don't get me wrong. My heart aches like it's never ached before. But, I can't help feeling like this isn't the end. Am I just being naïve? I guess time will tell.

Until then, I have to put my energy into school.

Chapter 1

September 2010

I SKIMMED OVER THE DOCUMENT IN FRONT OF ME AND sighed. It read just as I wanted it to—my attorney had made sure of that. This didn't make me feel any better, of course, but at least there hadn't been an argument. My pen poised over the line above my name, I briefly considered what it meant once I signed.

My marriage to Trey Foster was over.

The last five years would be just another page in my history book. There were no children involved. My defunct body had guaranteed it, despite several attempts. Trey and I were relatively diplomatic about our separation. We split everything equally and overall, we were walking away unscathed. We had come to the decision to get divorced as easily as we'd come to the decision to get married in the first place. We approached it with logic and reason, each of us having our own views on why we thought our marriage failed, another miscarriage—earlier this year—being the final straw for us both. We'd mutually decided to end things before it got ugly. Hell, Trey and I hadn't really fought the whole time we were married. It was only natural that we end it civilly, too.

I scrawled my name on the line and took a deep breath. The documents stated that I would return to my maiden name once it was filed, so I took pause as I looked at my name signed as "*Carlene Foster*" for the last time. My heart felt heavy and I took a deep, shaky breath as it all sank in. I slowly slid the paper across the table and looked up at my soon-to-be-ex-husband. I offered a half-smile/half-frown—one of those "I shouldn't smile, but I don't want you to think I hate you" kind of expressions. We'd both become good at those over the last year or so. He returned the gesture as he picked up the pen and signed his own name. He looked over at me sadly then handed the paper to his attorney, who picked it up and went into the hallway to make duplicates before the clerk took it to the courthouse to be signed by the judge. My lawyer followed him out of the room, leaving Trey and me alone. The second hand ticked on the clock above the door.

"We tried," I said, breaking the silence.

"We did." He nodded in agreement, his lips flattening in a slight scowl.

"I'm glad we can stay friends."

"Me, too," he agreed.

More silence. I picked at a snag on my skirt and stared at a smudge on the, otherwise shiny, board room table.

"I'm sor—" he began.

I held up my hand and shook my head. "No regrets, Trey. Remember? No regrets, no woulda-coulda-shouldas, no apologies. We agreed."

Trey and I had talked about our pending divorce for a couple of months and worked out all of the details ahead of time instead of paying our attorneys to create fights where none existed.

"I think it's over, Trey," I said softly as I picked at my dinner with my fork.

He looked up at me from over his wine glass, swallowing a mouthful of Riesling. He set the glass down and wiped his mouth. "It?"

"Us. This marriage. You and me. It's over."

He laid his napkin next to his plate and crossed his ankle over his knee, leaning back in his chair. He rested his chin on his fist and looked at me. Our eyes locked for what seemed like several minutes and he finally inhaled and nodded.

"I think you're right."

"I mean, it isn't that I don't love you. I do," I started to argue.

"As I do you," he agreed. "But you're right, this just isn't working."

I nodded solemnly. "Do you think counseling would help?" I offered, though knowing in my heart it wouldn't. Counseling wouldn't bring back our lost babies. Or the tension brought to our bedroom with every miscarriage. You couldn't relight a fire under cold embers. No amount of counseling could fix that.

He shrugged, "We could, but I don't know that it would help."

"It's not like we haven't tried. I mean, we have," I reasoned.

"We've definitely tried." And we really had. We took a trip to Hawaii in February for our anniversary. After the last miscarriage, in April, Trey made arrangements with a co-worker to

borrow his cabin on Lake Michigan for a weekend. We went to New York for a week in June for his mother's sixtieth birthday. We tried to scale back our work days and we purposely took weekends off with the intentions of spending them together.

All of it was futile, though. When you're married to a cop, there is no such thing as time off. His cell phone rang non-stop and his hours were always long. If it wasn't a case occupying his time, it was training or recertifying.

And I wasn't blameless in the matter, either. My phone was constantly pinging with new emails from work, too. Photographic editors weren't always as busy as I was, but when your boss was the female version of Hugh Hefner, you didn't get to ignore emails. Besides, I loved my job with Beguile. *We were two workaholics and I didn't see that changing for either one of us any time soon.*

"Maybe if we gave it a little more ti—"

"Babygirl, we've been living like roommates for months," he said. "How long do we really wanna pretend it's gonna work? Let's face it, there's just nothing left anymore."

I'd spent so much time worrying about how hard he'd fight me on this that I wasn't really prepared for his acquiescence. Tears I'd spent months shedding in solitude, rushed to my eyes; my face grew hot. I hoped for at least some small argument—something that told me I was wrong—that he did *still believe in us and we just needed to work on it some more. His immediate agreement indicated otherwise, and that stung worse than admitting out loud that we had problems.*

Ever the peacemaker, he stood and took my hand, pulling me to my feet. He wrapped his arms around me and rubbed my back as I let the tears spill.

We decided that he would keep our loft on Superior. It

was only six blocks from his work and since I worked by the lake, it would make more sense for me to find a new place closer to the office. We'd bought our condo in 2007, when we relocated to Chicago from New York, and we both worked so much that it was mostly just a place to sleep and change clothes between meetings and travel. Trey insisted I stay as long as I needed to, in order to find a decent place. He felt there was no reason to stop being nice just because our marriage failed. I agreed but moved into the guest bedroom that night.

Our attorneys returned and handed us a copy of our divorce papers explaining they'd send us each a notarized copy of the finalized decree sometime in the coming week after the judge signed it.

That was it.

We shook our lawyers' hands and turned, walking out of the meeting room together.

"So that's everything," Trey stood in the bedroom doorway, lights from the Christmas tree behind him silhouetting his shape. I didn't even want to think about how miserable this holiday would be. I hadn't really felt like putting up a tree, but, in the end, decided some normalcy might make things easier. I was wrong.

Hands on his hips, Trey looked authoritative, but I knew he was hurting inside as much as I was. The paperwork was one thing, cardboard boxes and packing tape were another.

Last night, as we went through the office, dividing up books, CDs, and DVDs, the gravity of it all had sunk in, and we nearly ended up in each other's arms—as if intimacy could stop a speeding train. Our divorce had been official a month earlier, but our weakness for each other knew no legal boundaries. Tear-filled and with a fear that I'd burn the divorce papers in the fireplace, I finally retreated to the spare bedroom shortly after midnight. There was no denying our attraction for one another. There had never been a problem with that. It was always a matter of putting that attraction first. We'd do okay for a couple weeks, then I'd get pulled away on business or he'd get put on a big case and we'd lose touch again emotionally. I refused to fall back into the routine we'd established for ourselves long ago.

"Did you get—" I started to ask.

"The box in the bathroom? Yeah. It's in the truck," he finished my sentence.

I stood in the center of the room, hands in my back pockets, doing a final scan of the open closet. Trey came up behind me and put his hands on my shoulders. I felt myself choke up, and I bit down hard on my lip to try and keep from crying.

"Carly, you got everything," he said quietly. "But if you didn't, you can always come back and get it. I'll be here."

With my back still toward him, I nodded because I knew I couldn't say anything without my voice cracking and making it harder on both of us.

He sighed and I knew the expression on his face without even having to look at him. He wrapped his arms around my shoulders and lowered his face, burying it in my neck as he hugged me against him. "We're doing the right thing, Carly."

I shook my head, "I don't know, Trey."

"Well, if not, we'll know soon enough. I mean it," he said as he turned me around to face him. "I'm not going anywhere. Okay?" He tipped my chin up and swiped his thumbs across my cheeks, wiping away the tears that began to fall. He kissed my forehead and hugged me again. A few moments later, we carried the last load to the truck and he followed me to my new place downtown.

"Jesus, I had no idea you had so much shit, woman!" Alejandro helped me haul box after box upstairs to our top-floor loft. Trey stayed long enough to help unload the heavy stuff, but I insisted we could get it from there. I was thankful Alex was there to help me move in. Not because his brute strength was something I couldn't live without, but because with him there, I'd be less likely to drive straight to Trey's and beg him to take me back.

Alejandro and I had been best friends for almost twenty years and he was my rock in times of despair. He'd once told me, "My wrist may be limp, but my backbone's stiff, honey. Cry on my shoulder." He'd taken his share of teasing over the years and learned to be strong early in life. I was grateful for that strength. Unfortunately, his outspoken opinion usually came with it, but I was used to taking the good with the bad, so it didn't faze me much after two decades of friendship.

When I'd broken the news to him about my pending divorce, he immediately offered me room in his apartment and wouldn't take "no" for an answer. After a nasty break-up last year with his partner, Nick, he'd bought and remodeled an apartment on Michigan Avenue that was far too big for him (his words, not mine). The place was amazing, and it didn't take much to convince me. At least I wouldn't have to be alone as I recovered from the failure, formerly known as my marriage.

"Yeah, because you have so little," I shot back at him, pointing to the floor-to-ceiling bookcases that were mostly full. "You realize we'll have to get another six feet of shelving to fit all my books, right?"

"Already done. It will be delivered Friday. It's up to you and the blue-eyed one to put it together, though." He was nonchalant in his mention of Josh, but I could see him watching me out of the corner of his eye to gauge my reaction.

Alejandro had always been a "Marc Girl" himself, but he and Josh had forged quite a bond over the years, as well. And when Josh drifted back into my life in 2002, he and Alejandro became almost as inseparable as Josh and I were, even if it was from a thousand miles away. We were a modern-day Three Musketeers—or at least we had been.

It had been seven years since I'd broken my engagement to "The Blue-eyed One" and put him on a plane to Los Angeles. I'd seen him only twice since then, though he and Alejandro had remained close friends through the years. In fact, it had caused quite a rift between Alex and me after the break-up. It wasn't easy trying to get over the heartache knowing my best friend was still buddy-buddy with my ex-fiancé. Eventually, I was able to move beyond it. And, through the years, I've been grateful for the vicarious little glimpses inside Josh's, otherwise private, world. It wasn't that I'd hung onto the hopes that we'd get back together—two journeys down that path were more than enough, and Josh was married, anyhow. But, it was nice to hear updates now and again. Alejandro was always careful not to divulge the intimate things, but his insight to Josh's life helped me move on.

Mostly.

Now here I was, realizing just how stupid I'd been not to

get closure all those years ago. Alejandro had invited Josh to Chicago for the weekend (his way of getting all three of us to a place where we could leave the baggage behind and move forward). I wasn't eager to see him again, but lacked the energy to say no. I was raw from my divorce from Trey, and while I didn't want to deal with the awkwardness that was bound to happen with Josh and me in the same room again after all this time, I couldn't put it off any longer.

"I'm sure I'll figure it out. I'm pretty handy. And let's face it . . ."

"Josh isn't." We both said in unison then snorted with a chuckle.

"I know you're nervous about seeing him again, but it'll be fine," he sensed my unease. "A lot of water has passed under that bridge and I promise, the weirdness will go away after the first glass of wine or six, and you'll be fine."

"Thanks for the confidence," I replied with a roll of my eyes.

"Anytime. Now, are you going to help me with this box or are you nursing me back to health after my hernia operation?" He squatted in front of one of my boxes of coffee table photo books, and I rushed to help him.

Several hours later, everything was moved in and a lot was even unpacked. We were sprawled across the living room furniture. He lay with his ankles crossed over the arm of the couch and his head hanging over the front edge, eyes closed. I'd collapsed with my legs over the arm of a giant poufy chair that I'd picked out when we went shopping a few weeks before I moved in. It was black with leopard print piping and looked like it belonged in a brothel. I loved it. Alejandro?—not so much. But, he resigned to it being the one piece of trash furniture I was allowed post-divorce. He told me to enjoy it because it will either get reupholstered after a year or the whole chair would end up in the street, eight stories below. I told him to leave my chair alone or I'd alert the Gay Council about his distaste for animal print and they'd take his card away. A good chuckle was shared, and he ended up buying me a leopard print pillow to complement the piping.

We each had a cold Corona in our hand and the stereo was cranked. It was probably a good thing the apartment directly below us was vacant because we'd, no doubt, piss off our neighbors, if we kept this up. Although, right then—at that moment—I needed this.

Chapter 2

January 2011

Alejandro called me from the airport to let me know Josh's flight was delayed. He wasn't expected to get in until after midnight. I was more than slightly relieved by this news. I knew I couldn't get out of seeing him, obviously. He was staying here with us, after all. But, having one more night to mentally prepare myself was certainly welcome.

Oh, who the hell was I kidding? I was a chicken shit. Plain and simple. It wasn't that I was still harboring feelings for the man. I'd gotten over that heartache years ago. I was just afraid of all the uneasiness I was sure would be there. I didn't like situations that allowed for confrontation, no matter how minute the chances might be.

I glanced at the clock—it was almost eight. Before bed, I'd have time for a bath and some wine. Going to my bathroom,

I turned on the faucets, then returned to the kitchen for the bottle of Moscato I'd put in the chiller earlier. Uncorking it, I returned to my room and closed the door behind me. Within a few minutes, I had stripped down and climbed into my claw foot tub. I drank straight from the bottle, something I was sure Alejandro would get in a snit about. He was fanatic about using the right stemware for the coordinating wine. Oh well. What he didn't know wouldn't hurt him.

Sucking back half the bottle in fifteen minutes, I closed my eyes, sinking into the cloud of bubbles. I began wondering how I'd ended up with a gay man as a roommate instead of a husband as I headed into my mid-thirties. I was supposed to be blissfully married with children by now. At least, that's what I'd planned. Tears trailed down my cheeks and dripped into the tub. I sniffled, wiped my nose with the back of my bubble-covered hand, and then sneezed, sending puffs of vanilla-scented foam everywhere. *I was such a classy drunk.*

I finally emerged from the tub two hours and one empty wine bottle later. Careful not to lose my balance in my slightly-inebriated state, I dried off and pulled on yoga pants and my NYU sweatshirt. I'd owned it the better part of fifteen years, but even in its tattered state, it was my favorite. It had gotten me through a broken heart twice before. It would be there for me again. I shuffled to the kitchen, dumping the bottle into the recycling bin. I left the light on over the stove and made my way back to my bedroom, kicking the door shut on the way through it. In a hazy fog, I pulled the covers up around me and was asleep in minutes.

A few hours later, I sat straight up in bed, my hand at my throat. I gasped for breath and took a moment to get my bearings. Blinking several times, my eyes darted around. Still getting used to this new place, it took me a minute to remember where I was.

Ahh, yes. The new apartment.

I sighed and ran my hand over my face, rubbing it briskly. I didn't have to think hard to remember the nightmare that had brought me out of my slumber. That particular dream was never far from the forefront of my mind, unfortunately. It had taken up residence five years ago. It was like the villain in a horror movie—I never knew when it would stumble into the light, but when it did, it always scared the shit out of me. Throwing the covers back, I flung my legs over the edge of the bed and shuffled to the door, opening it with a quiet creak. I let my eyes adjust a bit before starting down the hall.

"Coop? Is that you?" A familiar voice came from the guest room doorway. Josh had shortened my last name, Cooper, to a nickname almost upon meeting me. It had always been his term of endearment for me and even now, I got butterflies. "*Ah* you alright?"

I closed my eyes momentarily as that familiar Boston accent filled my ears again. Clearing my throat, I nodded, though I was sure he couldn't see it. I spoke in a gravelly voice, "Yeah. I'm fine, Josh. I'm sorry if I woke you." Looking in his general direction, I noticed his shadow pass across the hall into the kitchen. I followed him and braced myself against the island as he opened the fridge and got us both a bottle of water.

The fridge light illuminated his bare chest and the patch of light-colored hair that trailed from his bellybutton into the top of his loosely-tied lounge pants. *Fuck me.*

"I was already up," he said. "Nightmare?"

I nodded again, "Yeah. I'll just take this back to my room

and be out of your hair so you can get back to bed." The sooner I got away from Josh, the better. Temptation wasn't an option tonight.

"Nah, it's fine. I'm still on west coast time anyway." He unscrewed the cap and took a large gulp of water. "Wanna talk about it?"

Not if my life depended on it, I thought, recalling my last conversation with Josh in New York.

A masked smile crossed my face. "There's no point in rehashing it. Happy thoughts, right?" I reminded him of what he used to tell me when I'd wake up from a bad dream back when we were together.

"Something like that . . ." He gave me a slight smirk and took another drink. "Are you sure you don't wanna talk?"

I didn't know what good it would do, but clearly he had things he wanted to say. Temptation aside, I knew the sooner I got this uncomfortable conversation over with, the better our weekend would go.

"All right, but let's talk in my room so we don't wake up Alex." A tired Alex was a crabby Alex, and I didn't want to start out the weekend on a sour note.

Josh followed me down the hall and I paused long enough to use the bathroom before returning to my room. He'd turned on the lamp and stood near the foot of my bed looking at the pictures on my bookcase. In his hand, he held one of the few indulgences from my past that I'd allowed myself to keep—a picture of us in Boston the weekend of his parents' anniversary party, over fifteen years earlier. I watched from the doorway as he ran his fingers down the glass and smiled to himself.

His silhouette was just as handsome as it had always been

and I envied the wife who waited for him back in Los Angeles. His mop of curls was gone and a shorter, more-tapered cut had taken its place. The blond highlights he'd worn, when I last saw him, were gone. His chest was more sculpted now, too, but free of the small patch of hair between his pecs I remembered him having. The rest of him looked exactly the same and there wasn't a question in my mind why he'd always been my biggest weakness. From somewhere deep inside, I strangled the magnetism I felt pulling me toward him. Josh was off-limits. Period.

I cleared my throat softly and stepped through the door. He set the frame back down and turned his smile toward me.

"I can't believe you still have that," he said, taking a drink and motioning toward the picture.

"It's one of my favorite pictures. Takes me back to a happier time." I looked over at the picture reminiscently, hoping my glossy eyes wouldn't spill over. In an effort to hide my emotion, I slid between the covers and propped myself up against the headboard.

"You look really good," he said with an appreciative gaze.

"You, too," I said. "California's been good to you."

Josh sighed and sat down on the foot of the bed, opposite where I was sitting, leaning back against the footboard. "Carly, I wish I could . . ."

"Stop it."

He looked up at me, surprised.

"I mean it." I shook my head and let out a long breath, then drew another one in before speaking. "Alejandro showed me wedding pictures of you and Abby. You've got a beautiful wife, Josh, and I don't want you to spend one second regretting anything with me. If you were still with me, you wouldn't have her."

Josh fiddled with the cap on his water, not looking at me. "I just wish I could have been there, Carly. I should've been given the choice." He looked up at me and his blue eyes glistened with unshed tears.

Dammit, McCarthy, don't you do this to me. I hugged my knees to my chest and fought tears, myself.

"No. You shouldn't have. I let you go, Josh. It wasn't up to you anymore." I shook my head. "Besides, there was nothing you could've done. You'd have just felt guilty for not being there when it happened, and you'd have spent the last seven years blaming yourself and being trapped in a relationship with me when I wasn't in any shape to be in one."

He bit his lip and brought his knees up, propping his elbows on them. "Alex told me about your divorce. I'm sorry." His sincerity was obvious.

I shrugged nonchalantly as if it didn't matter, even though, down deep, I ached over my failed marriage. "Life goes on. Everything happens f—"

"—For a reason," he finished with a roll of his eyes. "God, how many times did you feed me that shit when I'd fuck up an audition or blow a note? C'mon, Coop. This is me you're talkin' to, remember? I know you better than that."

Remembah. Bettah. You could take the kid outta Boston, but you couldn't take Boston outta the kid.

"It hurts, Josh."

"I said I was sor . . ."

"No, you moron," I chuckled with a sniffle. "I meant my divorce. I still love him. And I let him go." I groaned into my hands as I covered my face.

"Not to rub salt in the wound, but that seems pretty apropos for you." Josh never was one to mince words, but I cringed just the same.

"Ouch."

"Sorry, but it's the truth."

"If I hadn't forced you to go to LA, you'd probably still be stuck in New York, struggling to make it on Broadway," I argued. "Besides, Hollywood's been good to you, Josh—professionally and personally. You've done really well for yourself." I spoke with more bravado than I felt. Abby had walked off with my first love and there would always be a part of me who held resentment toward her for that, no matter who broke up with whom.

Josh leaned over on his elbow and put his hand on the top of my feet, "I dunno, Coop. I'm not so great. My wife is alone in California while I'm sprawled across my ex-fiancé's bed in Chicago." He smirked. "That's not exactly 'Husband of the Year' material."

I grinned, "Fortunately for her, you've got a moral code a mile long." I declined to comment on where my impure thoughts were taking me. Shameless really, but Josh and I had always been good together. We just weren't good at the right times.

"You give me far more credit than I deserve," he mumbled. "Not a day goes by when I don't wonder if I did the right thing. You think you're the only one with regrets?"

"Shit, I'll always wonder 'what if?'" I confessed and swiped my thumbs under my eyes, wiping away tears. "Trey never stood a chance after you. And now, nobody else will stand a chance because of him." A sob caught in my throat and I covered my mouth.

Josh set his water bottle down on the floor next to the

bed and crawled over to me. He opened his arms and I leaned into him, letting him hold me. I shouldn't have and I knew it, but I also knew I was grieving for reasons that had very little to do with him. My heart would always be caught up in every relationship I'd ever had, instead of whichever one I was in. I had nothing left to give to anyone and I didn't know how to fix that. I told Josh as much.

He tipped my chin up and dabbed at my eyes with the sheet, "You have a lot left to give, Coop. Your heart is so full and when you love someone, you love them completely. You hold nothing back. I always loved that about you." He smiled and tucked my hair behind my ear. "You're hurting now, babe, but this will pass. You'll be in the right place at the right time, and when it's perfect, it'll happen. And you'll look back at this and wonder what you were so worried about. Mark my words." He winked and kissed my nose.

I nodded and managed a smile. "God, it's great to see you again, Josh. I missed you," I said, giving him a giant hug.

"I missed you too, beautiful." His blue eyes were dark as he looked at me. "So."

"So," I replied, forcing myself to ignore his endearment.

"So? Other than that, how's the play, Mrs. Lincoln?" He winked at me as he threw one of my favorite quotes back at me.

"You mean other than the fatal gunshot wound?"

"Well, there's that," he said with a chuckle. He pulled me in for another hug and kissed the top of my head. It was remarkable to me how quickly and easily we fell into a comfortable place again.

He leaned back against the headboard, propping a pillow up behind his neck and pulled me with him. We lay there like the lifelong friends we were and chatted about everything we'd experienced since our break-up. I brought him up to speed about my job as photographic editor with *Beguile*, one of the top gentleman's magazines in the nation. He was impressed, as any red-blooded male would be. He told me about some musical stuff coming up soon for him. He said he couldn't go into details just yet, but that I'd be thrilled with the project. We laid there for at least an hour catching up.

"So, what happened with your ex?" he asked me as he brushed my hair away from my eyes and looked at me. I bit the inside of my cheek and sighed. Closing my eyes, I thought back to one of the moments that led to my divorce.

"I'm sorry. I will be home as soon as I can." Trey seemed distracted and I could hear radio static in the background. It sounded like he was in his car. "I've got a lead on a case and I have to jump on it."

"Fine. I'll see you later." I hung up the phone and sighed. "Later" more than likely meant tomorrow night. I'd be asleep by the time he got in and gone before he got up in the morning. This was typical for us these days. If he wasn't working late, I was. I just didn't expect him to work late tonight.

Of course, if his lack of attention to me lately was any indication, he probably didn't even remember what today was. In fact, I was certain of it. I fought the overwhelming urge to gather up the corners of the tablecloth – dishes and all – and toss the whole thing out the sliding door and into the street, seven stories below. Instead, I blew out the candles and watched the smoke curl up from the tapers I had lit just twenty minutes earlier. The table was set with our best china, crystal, and silver. I slowly picked up the table settings and put them back into the credenza.

Happy fucking birthday.

"He blew off your birthday?" Josh asked his eyes wide.

I just nodded.

"You know how crazy I am about my birthday to begin with, so I honestly don't know why I got so upset about him forgetting, but I suppose it was just one more special occasion that Trey skipped over."

"Surely that wasn't all that led to your divorce?" he prodded for more history.

I shook my head and shrugged, "No, it wasn't just my birthday. It was all the holidays—all the special events. I felt like we were roommates. Half the time, I was waiting for an envelope on the counter with his portion of the rent," I vented.

"It was really that bad?" Josh's expression was one of disbelief and sadness.

I nodded. "My birthday was just one of the final straws. We both threw ourselves into our careers, the minute we moved to Chicago, and we let the fire slip from the flame. Something like that is easy to do, of course, when half of our marriage was spent not having sex." It was out of my mouth before I realized I said it.

"Do I wanna know?"

"Every miscarriage meant six to eight weeks of doctor-ordered celibacy," I spoke with no inflection in my voice.

"Oh."

I didn't really feel like talking about my reproductive situation with Josh, so I went on. "We had no social life, either. I had my friends, he had his. We never did anything together, anymore. His mother's meddling didn't help." I frowned at the memories of those conversations.

"Your mom called today."

Trey looked up from the TV, "Oh? What'd she have to say?"

I gave him a look, "Like you don't know?"

He frowned and if I hadn't known better, he would've seemed condescending, "C'mere." He patted the arm of the chair, inviting me to sit down. "What'd she have to say?"

I chose the ottoman in front of him instead. "Oh, she just called to go on and on about how your cousin Eric brought the new baby over and she said all she 'could do was cry' because she doesn't have a grandbaby of her own." I, of course, imitated her voice and the hand gestures I knew she'd been doing when she said it.

"Babygirl, why do you let her get to you like this?" he asked as he took my hands. I pulled them free and stood up, pacing the room.

"Trey! For Christ's sake, open your eyes. She's never liked me. And unless I produce a grandchild for her, she never will. I'm like some used car you settled for instead of the top-of-the-line Cadillac she had picked out for you." I sighed and waved my arms around as I spoke.

He stood and came over to me. "Heyyy," he rubbed my upper arms and didn't continue until I looked at him. "I love you whether you're a clunker or a luxury car. You are my wife and whether or not we give my mother grandchildren is completely irrelevant. I love you, no matter what."

I snorted dramatically.

"Nah, now stop that. Look at me." He held me by the shoulders. "To be fair, we haven't really started trying again after the last incident." Incident *was always the word he used. Miscarriage was too clinical for him, I guess.*

I pulled away, "I can't believe you're siding with her!"

"Whoa! Baby, I never said . . ." He shook his head in denial, but it was too late. The damage was done.

"So, you can't have children, then?" Josh's question snapped me out of my flashback and I wiped my eyes again.

I guess we were going to have this conversation after all.

"I don't know." I shrugged in reply. "Every pregnancy has ended in miscarriage. The longest I've carried was eight weeks and that was last year."

He sat up a little. "Aww, Coop."

"Don't." If he gave me pity, I'd be sending his dismembered parts back to California in a garbage bag. I *hated* pity. "After that, we just stopped trying. The pressure Trey's mom put on us didn't help, as if any of it was something within our control."

"Did you guys talk about it at all? The last miscarriage, I mean?" The fact that he said the word out loud—unlike Trey—did not go unnoticed.

I shook my head, picking at a loose thread on my comforter. "No, not really. There was no point."

"That's fucked up." He shook his head and clucked his tongue in response.

"Gee, thanks for not getting all judgmental, Josh."

"No, I just mean . . ." he growled under his breath. "I just mean you should be able to talk to your spouse about the big stuff." His eyes shifted away and his voice drifted off a bit at the last of what he said, but I heard his message loud and clear.

I nodded with a frown.

He settled back into the pillows and was quiet for a while before he asked, "Is it possible to start over?"

I shrugged with a shake of my head. "I can't think of a

reason I'd even want to."

"Well, I mean, you still love him," he said as more of a statement than a question. "He probably still loves you. Talk stuff out. Kids aren't the be-all-end-all of a marriage. Look at Abby and me—we've been talking about having kids for . . ." his voice changed pitch and he detoured of the conversation. "My point is, you guys fell in love for a reason. Isn't that worth trying to make things work?"

"Shit, Josh. You were kind of the reason we got together in the first place," I reluctantly admitted. His smile faded and he didn't say anything. And there it was—the awkwardness I had feared. I sighed, "Okay, let's get this over with."

He looked at me, feigning confusion, but I knew he knew what I was talking about.

"Look, this isn't a pleasant thing to talk about, but if we don't, it'll be dog shit on our shoes all weekend."

"Nice metaphor." He smirked. "All right, but I can't talk emotions and feelings and the 'mushy love stuff,'" he said with a wink, referring to one of my favorite Julia Roberts movies, "without junk food. What'cha got?"

"Sweet or salty?"

"Uhh, hello? It's me? Both!"

"Pretzels are above the microwave. The Boys are in the freezer," I said, referring to his favorite brand of ice cream, Ben & Jerry's. "Bring me some, too."

"Yeah . . . still me here. Not sharing." He made a funny face as he opened my bedroom door and headed for the kitchen.

"Jackass," I called after him with a chuckle.

He returned a couple minutes later with a bag of Rold Gold, what was left of a carton of Cherry Garcia, and two spoons. "You knew I was coming and you didn't stock the freezer? You've lost your touch, Coop."

I just rolled my eyes, took a spoon, and grabbed the bag of pretzels while he cracked open the lid on the ice cream.

"Jesus, do they freeze this shit on the moon or what?" He struggled to get his spoon into the ice cream. "Doesn't *mattah* how long you've had it in your *freezah*, it's always rock *hahd* when you go to eat it." He laughed and greatly exaggerated trying to dig into the frozen concoction. His accent always got thicker when he was tired. It still made me smile.

"They totally freeze it on the moon. Give it here." I grabbed it out of his hand and swiped a pretzel across the top of it, scraping just enough ice cream to coat it. Popping it in my mouth, I closed my eyes and groaned a little.

"God, that's as good as I remember."

Josh mirrored me and had the same reaction. We'd invented the combination, one snack-craving night, during a Celtics game, when we lived in New York. We'd run out of Chubby Hubby, so we made our own version with a bag of pretzels, a jar of Skippy, and a carton of plain vanilla ice cream. Over time, we broadened our horizons and ended up leaving out the peanut butter and introduced new ice cream flavors. I hadn't had it in years, but it tasted just as good as it did that first night.

"Good shit, man." He grinned as he popped another one in his mouth. "You know, Abby would no more let me eat ice cream straight outta the *cahton* than she'd let me use her toothbrush. You're the best."

"Meh. I can hold my own." I shrugged. "Don't think of using my toothbrush, though. That's just gross, dude."

He winked at me and laid back into the pillows next to

me. Pulling the covers up over us both, we laid there for a while, like teenage girls at a slumber party, snarfing on ice cream and pretzels.

"So, Coop," he started, looking over at me.

"So, McCarthy."

"So . . ." he urged.

"God, you still suck at conversation openers, don't you?" I teased.

"Yup." He flashed his pearly whites and I laughed at the smear of chocolate across his, otherwise perfect, smile.

"So, what do you know about Trey?" I asked him.

"Pretty much nothing. I only met him that once," he said, reminding me about his father's funeral. "And I never had the balls to bring it up with Alex."

I glanced over at the clock on my nightstand, "It's three a.m., Josh, are you sure you want to start this conversation now?"

"Now's as good a time as any," he said as he tossed another ice cream-covered pretzel in his mouth.

I swiped a large spoonful of the creamy goodness and picked at it with a pretzel as I figured out where to begin.

"Okay, so you know he's a cop, right?" At Josh's nod of acknowledgement, I continued. "Well, he was one of the detectives who investigated my attack." He winced, but allowed me to go on. "We built a friendship throughout the investigation and, when they finally caught the guy who did it, I guess we just mutually decided that we didn't want to say goodbye."

"So, you started dating?"

"Eh. Yes and no." I flipped the spoon over and scraped the ice cream off of it with my bottom lip. "We talked every once in a while. Then one night, when my friend ditched me at a club, I left and happened to run into him at Starbucks. We ended up talking all night long."

"So, how does that have anything to do with me?"

My mood became somber as I started wading in murky waters. "The night you . . . when I told you . . ." I searched his eyes praying he wouldn't make me say it out loud.

He didn't.

"I was a mess when you left, so I called him. I knew he was the one person who would understand. He was there when nobody else was. He was the only one who knew the whole truth."

"About the 'accident?'" He made quotation marks with his fingers.

"About the attack, about the baby, about everything."

Josh got quiet for a minute, then reached over me, setting the, now empty, ice cream carton and pretzels on the nightstand. I watched him carefully, not sure what his silence meant. He turned out the light and settled back into the pillows. "*C'meah*," he said and held out his arm.

I shook my head, "Josh? No."

"Are you going to jump me?"

"What?" I pushed myself up from the bed. I still found him insanely gorgeous, but there was no way I would make a move on him. He was a married man and therefore off-limits, no matter how handsome I thought he was. "No, of course not!"

"Then *c'meah*, dammit," he repeated and pulled me into his arms.

I could hear his heartbeat—a sound I wasn't entirely unfamiliar with, of course. Hesitantly, I lay my cheek against his bare chest and tried to relax. I was certain his wife was not happy with us spending the weekend together; she'd lose her mind at the thought of us sharing a bed like this.

"You're right, she wouldn't understand," he said, reading my mind. "That's why I'm not telling her."

I fought to sit up, but he held me close. "Josh, I don't think this is . . ."

"Coop," he cut me off, "Abby knows everything about us. She knows about how we started dating. She knows about how we broke up. She knows about our engagement, and she knows about the baby. I didn't go into details about your attack, but she knows you lost the baby . . . *our* baby."

I heard his voice crack and could tell it was tough for him to talk about, but I said nothing. I'd spent the last seven years processing my grief and it rarely brought anything more than emptiness these days. My tears had long been shed, but my heart ached for him—for *his* loss.

He continued, "But, Carly, she also knows that you gave me up when you had every reason to hang onto me. So, this? This moment, right here?" He paused to make sure I was listening. "This is to make up for me not being there that night."

"I don't know, Josh." I was undecided. My resolve was strong, but dancing with temptation wasn't smart.

"Nothing's gonna happen, so will you let me hold you? Please?"

I finally surrendered.

I was almost asleep when he spoke in nearly a whisper, "I missed you, beautiful."

"Missed you, too," I murmured in reply. He kissed the top of my head, and within minutes, he was softly snoring next to me.

Chapter 3

Much to my surprise, Josh managed to *not* screw up the bookshelves that were delivered on Friday. In fact, we even had time to head to Barnes & Noble to stock the new shelves. Apparently, I had fewer books than I thought I did. We ate a late lunch and spent the afternoon walking around the neighborhood. It was nice just hanging out.

We met Alejandro, after he got off work, and headed to our favorite neighborhood pub. We spent the entire night sucking back cocktails and grazing on appetizers. Laughter, tears, and hours of reminiscing completely set the mood for the weekend. It was just what I needed to get some of my mojo back. I even flirted a bit with Keith, our neighbor from two floors down. He stopped into the bar to pick up dinner and joined us for a drink. It may have been the six screw-drivers I'd had, but I invited him to go to a Bulls game with me the next night at Alex's insistence. Josh and Alejandro teased me something terrible after Keith left. I didn't care. I didn't have to marry the guy, but dammit, I needed to blow off some steam, and screaming at the Bulls for screwing up yet *another* game greatly appealed to me. Doing it in the male company of someone other than my roommate or my ex-fiancé was just a bonus.

I left Alejandro and Josh the next afternoon with a light heart. Keith was funny and fun to be with. I laughed my way through two beers and an order of nachos, not even paying that much attention to the game. Everything was great until Keith decided to kiss me when the Bulls made a three-point shot, tying up the game. It was one of those slow motion moments where you see two trains ready to collide, but you can't stop them. It wasn't that the kiss was bad. It was actually a really good one, as far as kisses go. I just didn't feel it. Keith was a nice enough guy—cute to0—but I wasn't quite ready to go there just yet.

"I'm sorry, Carly," he said, looking intently at his red foam finger. "I . . . I thought you were into me."

I tried to make an excuse, but he was right. I *wasn't* into him. "I'm having fun, Keith. I'm just," I paused, trying to think of how to put it nicely. "I guess it's just too soon."

He nodded and seemed to shrug it off, flagging down the beer guy, grabbing us two more cold ones. I sucked my third beer down in nothing flat. Tension, that hadn't been there before, now hung heavily in the air. We managed to get through the last half of the game, but despite the Bulls' win, it was a fail as far as dates go. Fortunately, Keith understood. He dropped me off that night with a hug, and I promised to call him when I was in a place to date again.

Kicking my shoes off, I tossed my purse on the counter.

A light peered out from under Alejandro's door. I figured he and Josh were still awake, chatting, but I didn't have the energy to play Twenty Questions about my date, so I just went to my room. Crawling into bed, I was asleep within a few minutes, memories of my disastrous date behind me.

I rolled over the next morning and lay there thinking about the night before. It had definitely been way too soon to even consider dating. God, Josh and I had been apart several months before I agreed to go out on a date with Trey. I'd been married to Trey for four years. It was ridiculous to think I could just wipe all that away without a second thought. I groaned and stretched. I could hear the tinkling of spoons in ceramic mugs and smelled coffee. The dynamic duo must be up. I reluctantly crawled from bed and threw some clothes on.

I knew they'd be filled with questions about my date with Keith. *Ugh.* I debated on crawling back into bed but decided "coward" wasn't on the menu this morning. Coffee, however, was. I opened my bedroom door and headed to the kitchen.

Josh and Alex sat at the island with their coffee cups, and I could feel them eyeing me as I pulled out my favorite mug from the cupboard. Pouring myself a full cup, I dumped in a heaping spoon of sugar and stirred my coffee. All the crap I was consuming over the weekend would kick my ass in the gym on Monday, but I didn't care, at this point. Taking a swig, I winced when the hot liquid hit my tongue, then I turned around slowly.

"So?" Josh wiggled his eyebrows at me.

I glanced over at Alejandro who was grinning like an idiot from behind his coffee cup.

"We're getting married," I replied without batting an eye. If these two nosy bastards were tactless enough to bug me about the gory details of my date, I was going to have fun with them.

"Bitch, please," Alex said with a snort. "C'mon. Just tell us how it went."

"You put out, didn't you?" Josh asked.

"Christ, McCarthy, what is wrong with you? Of course not!" I recalled the awkward kiss between Keith and me. "I've only been divorced three months."

"Dammit!" Josh exclaimed before reaching for his wallet and pulling out a twenty-dollar bill. He tossed it at Alex who laughed and promptly stuffed it in his front pocket.

"Duuuude," I groaned. "A bet? You two assholes were betting on my love life?"

"What love life?" Alejandro asked with a smirk on his face.

"Ahh, niiiiiice," Josh commended him with a fist bump.

"You guys suck."

Josh laughed and pulled me into a headlock before kissing the top of my head playfully. "You know we love you, Coop. We were just messin' around."

"Uh huh."

"Well, I know just the thing to take your mind off it," Josh teased. "Tell her, Alejandro."

I looked at my roommate, who was giving Josh a twinkling gaze.

"Aww shit! Do I need the Bailey's for this?" I asked, taking a step toward the cupboard where we kept the Irish crème. My gaze flipped back and forth between Josh and Alex until

Josh finally spoke.

"Well, I was gonna save it for dinner tonight," a slow smile spread across Josh's face, "but we're getting back together."

I wrinkled my brow and looked from him to Alejandro and back to Josh again.

"Um, I know I've been out of the loop a little, but when were you and Alex *together*?"

"Not us, you hag!" Alex admonished me with a loud guffaw.

"Then, what the hell are you talking about?"

"The guys . . . we're getting back together," Josh explained.

I nearly spilled my coffee. Giving them each lengthy blank stares, I sputtered, "The guys. The *guys*-guys? The *GUYS*?" I was nearly rendered speechless.

Josh nodded in confirmation and my face lit up.

"Holy shit! That's great news!" I threw my arms around him in a congratulatory hug. When South Station Boyz broke up in the mid-nineties and everybody went their own ways, nobody thought they'd ever get back together—not the media, not the fans, not me, not even the South Station Boyz themselves. This was big.

Alex smiled over his coffee cup.

"So, what does this entail exactly? This 'getting back together' thing?" I asked Josh as I took a sip from my coffee.

"It means getting back together," Josh said matter-of-factly. "Some interviews, photo shoots, an album, a tour. You know—the works."

"Wow! Tour? Album? Everything? How the hell, dude?" My excitement was genuine. I never thought I'd live to see the day when South Station Boyz would reunite. Every interview the guys had done individually, over the years, backed up my assumption. It had been a unanimous decision that they part ways, and it seemed unanimous that they'd never join forces again, either. I'd had some random curiosity over the years and Googled the guys once in a while to see what they'd been up to.

Dave Butler was married and divorced with three kids, and put out a solo album a few years back. His oldest son, practically an adult now, lived in Boston with his mother, but Dave had custody of the two younger ones who were nine and seven. Bobby Callahan had become an actor and was also married. He'd been the easiest to keep track of since he and his model wife were always in the spotlight. Marc had disappeared entirely from the radar. Although, I'd heard somewhere that he had become an attorney with a law firm in Boston . . . But now, they were back together. I couldn't hide my joy.

Josh laughed at me and my fan-girly enthusiasm, but his own eyes shone with excitement, too. "Yep. The whole shebang. Bobby found a sound and it just snowballed from there. It's crazy shit, but it's all good."

Smiling big, I gave him another giant hug. "This is awesome news, babe. Seriously. I'm so happy for you . . . for all the guys."

Josh hugged me back, "Thanks." He ran his hand through his hair and grinned, "Hell, this thing might crash and burn. It might just be you and Alex at the first show, but we're gonna give it a shot."

Alex piped up, "If it means finally meeting Marc Reyes, I'll be at *every* show."

"I'll see what I can do," Josh said with a laugh.

The corner of my mouth turned up in a smirk and I shook

my head. Some things never change.

“All right. I need a shower. Make us some breakfast, will you?” I gave him a quick peck on the cheek and headed to my bedroom, leaving him staring after me, trying to figure out how to argue his way out of cooking breakfast.

I emerged from my bedroom twenty minutes later in comfy jeans and an oversized sweater. Alejandro was setting the table and Josh had a dish towel thrown over his shoulder, scooping scrambled eggs into a bowl. A huge plate of bacon and a serving dish of crispy hash browns were already set out, and steam rose from the plates. Everything looked delicious. I'd forgotten how handy he was in the kitchen.

“Mmm . . . smells fantastic!” I complimented him.

“You're lucky I was hungry for real breakfast food or you'd have had a bowl of Cookie Crisp,” he teased, handing me the eggs to put on the table. We all sat down and hungrily dug in.

The rest of the weekend went off without incident and just as Alejandro had intended, the baggage on our broken relationships was left behind.

Chapter 4

September 2011

"SHAKE A LEG, YOU DIRTY WHORE! WE'RE GONNA miss our flight!" Alejandro hollered from the foyer as I struggled with my luggage. I knew I'd over packed, but this weekend was big. *Huge!* I hadn't seen all the guys in the same place since 1993. I didn't want to risk some fashion catastrophe by not packing the right thing.

As I pulled my suitcase off the bed, it crashed into my ankle. "Ouch!" I hopped on one foot, rubbing the sore one. "Sonofabitch," I mumbled under my breath before replying to my impatient roommate, "I. AM. COMING!" I threw my overnight bag over my shoulder and lugged the big bag out of my bedroom and down the hall.

Alex's eyes widened at my approach. He gave a disapproving look at my luggage, and then aimed it at me. "Not one word," I warned and followed him into the hall, dragging my wardrobe on wheels behind me. The cabby loaded our bags into the trunk of the car and we were off to the airport.

Once settled in the car, I rifled through my carry-on, going down my mental checklist. Tickets? Check. Wallet, complete with ID? Check. Lipstick, perfume, iPod? Check. Check. Check. "I hope I didn't forget anything," I muttered to myself.

"I don't see how that's even humanly possible," Alejandro said as he attempted to talk me off the ledge. "It's just a little shindig. Besides, it's New York, not a third-world country."

"I know, I know. I am just freaking out. It's been a while since I've seen the guys," I took a deep breath. "Sorry."

He was right, of course, but so was I. This was more than just some 'little shindig.' It was an album release party for the first music they'd recorded in almost twenty years. This was a *big. Fucking. Deal.* I'd been to plenty of celebrity events over the years. *Beguile* was known for their killer parties, after all. But, *this?* This was bigger than some centerfold soirée.

Aside from my own nervousness at seeing everyone again, I was nervous for the guys. I knew they were anxious to see how it all played out. I'd heard whispers and through-the-grapevines over the last several months. Josh would send me an occasional email and vent. Then there were comments I'd hear from Marc through Alejandro, of course. I was still shocked at that little turn of events.

Alejandro flung the door to my bedroom open the minute he got home from Boston, in the middle of March. I'd been battling a head cold for a week and was hunkered down in bed, working on some photo edits. Between the Nyquil and my exhaustion, my nerves were shot and he nearly scared the hell out of me.

"So I was standing in the middle of a meeting with Jack

and Gus and guess who walked in. Just guess!" He stood there with one hand on the door knob, the other one flailing about excitedly, tapping his foot.

"Uhh . . ." I didn't have the first clue who Jack and Gus were, but I suspected they were coworkers. Alex had gone to Boston for some meetings regarding a settlement between the Bulls franchise and a fan who'd gotten injured in the stands at a game.

"HIM!"

"Him," I said, blankly

"HIM!" His voice reached a pitch I'd never heard before. I was certain only dogs and dolphins could hear him speaking.

"Who, him?" I was so lost.

"HIM, him. MARC, him!" He was nearly hyperventilating.

"Marc who?"

"Reyes, you half-wit!"

I blinked.

I blinked again.

I was pretty sure my chin was resting on my laptop.

"I'm sorry. I must've taken too much Nyquil, because I thought you just said that you ran into Marc." I searched his face for a smirk or some twitch in his eyebrow like he always got when he was trying to pull one over on me. There was no smirk or facial spasm.

"Marc was at the meeting?"

He nodded.

"What the . . . how does he . . . why was . . ." My head was full of a thousand questions my mouth couldn't spill out fast enough. "Huh?" was all I could stammer out.

He started talking as he sat down in the chair opposite my bed, tucking his legs underneath him, spilling the story.

Not leaving a single detail out, he told me about how Marc's firm was representing the injured plaintiff and was there as his representative. Alejandro, being too blunt for his own good, mentioned how he already knew who Marc was from his music career days. Marc, apparently, was surprised but impressed at Alex's memory and recognizant abilities. When the meeting was over and a settlement was met, Marc invited Alejandro out for drinks, which led to dinner and a nightcap.

"So?" I was curious what this meant for him. For them.

"I dunno. But I'm pretty sure since he had his tongue down my throat that's a good thing, right?"

A good thing, indeed. Since meeting in March, Alex and Marc had spent countless hours on the phone, Skype, email, text, and God knows how many other social media outlets. Alex had flown out to Boston a couple times. Marc had come to Chicago once, when I was out of town, and they'd even spent a long weekend together in Barbados a few weeks ago. Things were definitely going well between the two and I was happy for them. It was no surprise when Marc invited Alex to see South Station perform on *Good Morning America*.

Which is why I was headed to the Big Apple. Josh said if Alejandro was going to be there, I couldn't very well stay home. Not that he had to do much convincing; I didn't want to miss seeing them perform for the first time in almost twenty years.

Our driver piled our suitcases in the back of the SUV and we made our way to Times Square. I wasn't keen on being anywhere near the busiest part of the city, but it was where the guys were staying, including Alex. After checking in to the hotel and getting settled, I headed down to Alejandro's room for a late dinner and some socializing.

Dave and his two youngest children were there, as were Josh and Marc. Bobby, apparently, was finishing up some business in Los Angeles and he wouldn't be in until later that night. Dave hadn't changed much. He was still handsome and, if it was even possible, better built than he'd been eighteen years ago. His long dark hair had been cut into an edgy, spikey, Mohawk-type style, and he sported a stubbly, short, goatee. He had more tattoos than he used to, but they suited him well. I gave him a brief hug, and he introduced me to his kids. Max was a smaller version of Dave, and Tori, who had his same dark hair and complexion, very indignantly pointed out that her name was short for Victoria. I grinned at her and told her I wouldn't forget such a pretty name. She smiled and leaned her head against her dad's arm, shyly. I glanced at Dave who reached down and tousled his daughter's hair. Not to be outdone, Max piped up that his name was short for Maxwell. I reassured him that I wouldn't forget his name, either. He puffed out his chest proudly, and I winked at him.

I turned and smiled warmly at Marc who greeted me with a hug. He looked pretty much the same, although the mullet he'd sported in his teen years were gone and there were flecks of gray at his temples, now. Laugh lines had developed at the corners of his eyes and he'd filled out a little from the slender kid he'd once been. Age had been kind to him.

"Long time, no see, stranger," I said.

"Yeah, it's been a while," he replied with a genuine smile. "How've you been?"

"Good. Very good," I said. "Yourself?"

"I'm good," he said with a nod.

"He's good, you're good, and I'm good. Everybody's good. Let's *eat*!" Alejandro declared, while handing the room service menu to me. I glanced at Marc who rolled his eyes playfully and made a face at Alex behind his back.

I scanned over the menu and passed it to Marc, as we all made idle chit-chat with one another, catching up on the past two decades. Having last been with the guys when we were all pretty much kids made it feel weird seeing Dave in the role of father now. I had read somewhere about him having children but I hadn't really visualized Dave, or any of the guys for that matter, as fathers.

My mind drifted back to my conversation with Josh in January about him and Abby having kids. I couldn't imagine what Josh would be like as a dad—and believe me, I'd tried. If fate hadn't been against us, we'd have a child in grade school right now. To avoid a meltdown, I quickly pushed the thought aside.

Alejandro wrote down everyone's order as Marc handed the menu to Dave who looked it over and pointed out a couple of suggestions to his children. Max shrugged noncommittally, and Tori had a slight frown on her face, then her eyes suddenly widened.

"Does that say 'octopus,' Daddy?" she whispered to him as she pointed to the menu. She was quiet and polite, but I could tell she wasn't impressed by the room service available to us. Honestly, I wasn't either. Over two hundred and fifty hotels in New York City and we picked the only one whose room service menu was nothing but seafood. I liked seafood, but I wasn't in the mood for it today.

"Yeah, honey. It's an octopus salad," he answered and then laughed out loud as she wrinkled up her nose in disgust.

"Hey, Tori? Would you and your brother like to split a pizza with me?" I offered with a smile. Her face lit up. I looked at Dave, hoping I wasn't overstepping bounds. He smiled and glanced down at the kids.

"I can't believe you're ordering pizza when you've got the best sushi and King crab this city has to offer!" Josh admonished me with a snort.

"You know what you can do with your sushi, McCarthy." I made a face similar to the one Tori had made and turned back to Dave and the kids.

"You guys want pizza with Carly, instead?" he asked his children. They both nodded with enthusiasm and he glanced over at me. "You sure you don't mind?"

I waved him off. "Of course not. I'm not much in the mood for fish. No sense in having a small pizza delivered when there could be two hungry munchkins to help me polish off a large."

He smiled and looked at the kids again. Their eyes shone with excitement at the new dinner plans. "You're welcome to join us," I suggested.

He glanced over the menu again with a wrinkled nose, "Count me in if you order some hot wings, too."

I grinned at him. A man after my own heart.

"You got it. I'll head down to my room and order it online." I stood up and headed for the door, "You guys wanna wait here and I'll call you when it comes or you wanna help me order it?

"You can order pizza on the internet?" Max asked, his eyes wide with surprise.

I chuckled and waved him over, "C'mon, I'll show you." I looked up at Dave again. "If it's all right with your dad, that is."

"Dad, can we?" Max asked, his hands clasped in front of him in a begging stance. Tori mirrored her brother's gesture.

"Nah, you guys can wait here," he said, shaking his head. "I don't want you getting in Carly's way."

"Really, Dave, I don't mind."

The kids' gazes were bouncing back and forth between their dad and me like a tennis match.

"I don't want them to be an imposition," he said. "They can stay here."

I could see the disappointment in their eyes and my pout must've matched theirs because Dave chuckled and said, "Wow, I can't fight all three of you. Fine. Go order dinner. Do you need me to come with?"

I smiled. "I think I can manage a pizza order with a couple of little people in tote."

Chuckling, he replied, "You're so new." Dave had the best laugh. I couldn't help smiling even if he was making fun of me. "Here, let me plug my number in your phone just in case, okay?" I rolled my eyes playfully, but handed my phone over, anyway.

"I'll catch up with you later." I waved at Alejandro as he waited on hold for room service. Josh gave me a quick hug goodbye and I gave Marc's hand a squeeze.

"You comin'?" I asked the kids.

They bobbed their heads excitedly and Dave handed me my phone. I told him I'd text him when the food got there, and the kids and I headed to the elevators.

As we waited, I made quick assessments of Dave's children. I reckoned they got included in a lot of what their dad did, but rarely got one-on-one attention from the adults in the South Station entourage. If their ear-to-ear smiles were any indication, they were enjoying this time with me.

Tori looked exactly like her dad and had the same sportiness about her that he did. Her hair was long, dark, and curly, just like I'd remembered her dad's being back in the day. Her eyes were wide and a deep chestnut color. Dave would have to beat the boys off her with a baseball bat when she got older. She was personable and affectionate, too. She took my hand the minute we left the room and didn't let go, even as we stood waiting. I took an instant liking to her.

Max was a bit quieter and more reserved than his sister, a trait I suspected he picked up from his dad. His hair was shaggy and hung a bit into his face, but it wasn't curly like his sister's. He, too, had deep brown eyes with full, dark eyelashes. He'd be a heartbreaker when he got older too, that was for sure. He stood by my side, hands clasped politely behind his back, watching the arrows above the elevator door, waiting for them to light up. He might be a tougher nut to crack, but I felt that he and I would get along well, too.

The elevator dinged quietly and we rode up the twelve stories to my floor. I keyed us into my suite and opened my laptop, which was sitting on the desk. The kids waited patiently on the couch. I got online and brought up the website for the best pizza place in my old neighborhood. When I got to the order page, I motioned them over.

"Okay kids, you're gonna have to help me out here. I don't know what you will eat or not eat. Let's pick some toppings, okay?" I smiled at them and together we ordered a hand tossed pie full of veggies and extra cheese. I also added two orders of hot wings for Dave and me. I wasn't sure how many he could eat, but I knew I was hungry enough to polish off an own order by myself. I threw some cheesy bread in, too and let Tori click the "Place Order" button. I turned on the TV and kicked off my shoes. I suspected the kids would beg to turn it to the Disney Channel or Cartoon Network, but they were too busy updating me to the status of our order to be bothered with the television:

"Somebody named Pedro just put it in the oven."

"Kym is doing a quality check."

"Skip is out for delivery!"

I was surprised at how quickly Domino's blew through our order. It took less than ten minutes for our order to leave my computer and get put in the delivery guy's bicycle basket. I texted Dave:

> Pizza guy should be here in a few minutes. We're in Rm. 3502.

Once the food was on its way, the kids' interest in order tracking had diminished greatly and they became engrossed in *Sponge Bob*. I skimmed the mini-bar for something to drink. "Do you guys want some sodas with your pizza?" I asked them.

"We usually just drink water," Max answered.

"Daddy doesn't let us drink soda" Tori chimed in.

Doesn't let them drink soda? Ugh. What the hell was pizza without a soda? I thought, but just smiled and nodded. "Okay, here's two bottl . . ." I was interrupted by a knock at the door, ". . . bottles of water," I continued, setting them on the coffee table in front of the kids while I went to answer the door. I opened the door and Dave stood there holding a large pizza box and three smaller clamshell boxes.

"Delivery for three very hungry peeps?" he teased. The children smiled and jumped up at the sound of their father's voice and ran over, each grabbing one of the smaller boxes.

"Does this negate the tip?" I giggled and he winked at me. "Thanks for going down to pick it up. I would've done it," I said, taking the other small box from him and closing the door behind him.

"It's no big deal. One of us would've had to go down anyway, and since you had the kids here and I was on my way through the lobby anyway. . ." he trailed off and shrugged with a smile.

We devoured our dinner, but even for as hungry as we all were, we still had a ton of food left. I did my best to cram the leftovers in the mini-fridge and grabbed another Coke for myself as I returned to the couch. Dave sat at one end and the kids were sitting on the floor, absorbed in the TV again.

Dave eyed my soda and smirked at me.

"What?"

"What, what?"

I unscrewed the cap, took a swig and swallowed. "That look you just gave me."

"What look?"

I raised my eyebrow and tilted my head at him. He just chuckled.

"It's the soda, isn't it?"

The corner of his mouth lifted a little. He took a big swig from his water bottle, but didn't say anything.

"Okay, so I have a vice," I argued. "I'm a Coke head." He laughed with a hyena cackle, and I laughed in return, kicking his leg with my foot. He just grinned and shook his head. "I'll give it up, eventually," I said, "but for now, my soda stays. I don't smoke. I don't do drugs. I work out religiously. I have to have one bad habit or I'll explode."

He conceded with a raise of his eyebrows and a smiling shrug, swallowing another gulp of water. He opened his mouth to say something, but his phone chimed, interrupting him. He reached into his pocket and hit a button on his Blackberry. Rolling the trackball, he clicked on the new message and growled as he finished reading it.

I didn't want to pry, but I was curious. "Bad news?"

"B's stuck in Chicago. A storm has grounded all East coast flights right now and he can't get in 'til tomorrow sometime. We're gonna have to cancel our *Good Morning, America* appearance. Son of a . . ." he growled again. "Sorry. This just isn't good."

I tried to think of some way to help, "If you need to go talk to the other guys, I'm fine with the kids staying here for a while. I'm up all hours and I've got some work I need to do, anyway."

He immediately shook his head, "I can't ask you to play babysitter, Carly, especially if you've got to work. I appreciate it, but . . ."

I looked over at the children, whose heads were bopping up and down to some music video. Motioning toward them, I smiled. "They seem pretty preoccupied. Really, it's not a big deal. Go. Deal with the mess. If they get tired, they can crash on the couch until you get back."

He got up and looked at his phone again as another message chimed, then another. He sighed, looking from his phone to the kids, then over at me. "Are you absolutely sure, Carly? I mean, I can call my dad and he . . ."

"Can drive the four hours from Boston to Midtown? I don't think so." I stood and tugged on his arm, trying to turn him around, giving him a healthy shove toward the door.

"Get outta here. I got this."

"I really owe you for this," he said to me, gratitude showing on his rugged face. He looked over the couch at his kids, "Hey guys, I need to go deal with some work stuff. Do you mind staying here with Carly for a little bit? I'll try not to be too long."

Their heads perked up with their typical smiling faces shining. "Hugs and kisses first, Daddy?" Tori said. Her chestnut eyes sparkled and I knew how much love she had for her father. My heart swelled as I watched their tender moment when she jumped up and ran into his arms. Max followed suit. He gave them each a kiss and hugged them tightly. I'd never pegged Dave as a sentimental type, but around his kids, there was no doubt he was a giant softie.

"Be good—all right, guys? Don't give Carly any trouble," he cautioned. They promised they'd behave and ran back over to their spots on the floor, quickly becoming enthused in their show again.

"They'll be fine, Dave. Really," I tried to put his worried mind at ease. "I've babysat before, and I'm willing to bet if I give them a pillow and a couple of beers they'll both be sacked out in a half-hour anyway." I laughed at the horrified look on his face. I winked, then looked over at them and caught Max covering a yawn with the back of his hand. "See what I mean," I whispered.

"All right. You've got my number. You'll call if you need anything, right?"

I nodded and walked him to the door, grabbing a keycard off the desk. I handed it to him. "I'm sure I'll still be awake when you get back, but go ahead and just let yourself in, that way a knock won't wake them up if they fall asleep."

"I appreciate this so much, Carly. Thank you." He smiled and squeezed my shoulder as he opened the door.

"Not a big deal, Dave. Really." I returned his smile and closed the door behind him.

I leaned my back against the door and glanced at his children, who were both yawning now. I knew they must be exhausted. With as disciplined of a life as they seemed to lead, I suspected their normal bedtime had been at least an hour ago. I grabbed a couple of pillows and the extra blanket out of the armoire in my bedroom and returned to the living room.

"Hey guys, wouldn't you be more comfortable on the couch? I've got pillows and a blanket you can share."

They looked at each other then back at me. I could tell they were struggling to find the polite, least intrusive answer. Their manners were impeccable and I thought that Dave should be proud of how well behaved they were.

I smiled widely and leaned over the back of the couch, resting my elbows on the cushions. "Kick your shoes off and hop up on the couch here, and we'll rent a movie. How's that?" I whispered as if we were keeping a big secret from any prying ears. They were totally game, quickly disposing of their flip-flops and climbing up onto the couch, their heads at opposite ends. Once they were settled, I covered their legs with the blanket and flipped through the movie rentals on the TV. They scanned the options and decided on some animated movie about a karate-chopping panda. I got the movie set up for them and as soon as it began, I excused myself and headed to my bedroom.

I washed off my make-up, took out my contacts and slipped into a t-shirt and yoga pants—my typical work-at-home attire for long, sleepless nights. We were gearing up for our Centerfold of the Year issue and the only way I'd been able to take any time off work was to bring it with me. I had to promise Susan, my boss and the senior photographic editor for *Beguile,* that I'd finish editing last week's shoot and get it back to her before I returned home from New York. It limited the time I'd have to spend with Alejandro, Josh, and the guys, but it was better than not being able to come at all. I returned to the living room and got to work, making sure my screen was facing away from the droopy-eyed children on my couch.

I had quite a bit of work to do, but my mind kept wandering. I'd gotten about five minutes of editing done in the half-hour I'd been sitting there. My mind constantly drifted to Josh, and I chastised myself for thinking about a married man.

I looked over at Dave's children, who were asleep, as I had predicted. I didn't want them to wake up, so I decided to try and work in bed. I clicked the TV off and turned on the low wattage lamp by the door, turning off the one by Max's head. They didn't so-much-as stir when I gathered my laptop and notes from the coffee table. I carried my things to the bedroom and set up shop again. I pushed Josh from my head and concentrated on getting work done.

About twenty minutes later, my phone chirped with a text message:

> Sorry it's taking so long. Be there to get the kids as soon as I can. - Dave

I smiled at his concern and replied:

> Not a problem. They're asleep anyway. Take your time.

I finished my work sometime after midnight and turned

off the light. I wasn't asleep long before I heard the beep of the front door being unlocked. It startled me, at first, then I remembered the children. I lazily pulled the covers back and padded out to the living room just as Dave was picking up a very limp Max. I grinned at the picture in front of me. I cleared my throat softly and smiled.

"Oh hey," Dave whispered in greeting. "We'll be out of your hair in just a minute."

I waved him off, "No biggie. Want me to help you carry Tori?" I asked softly, bending over and looping the straps to their flip-flops in my fingers.

"She's awfully big, I doubt . . ." he started to say as I reached over and gently lifted Tori's sleeping body, hugging her to me. I looked at him and raised an eyebrow at his surprised face. Dave just smiled and shook his head. I followed him out the door. We walked to the opposite end of the hall, past the elevators to the other side of the hotel. He keyed us into his room and held the door for me. His was one of the two-bedroom suites. He led the way to one of the bedrooms and pulled back the covers, laying Max on one side of the bed. I went to the opposite and carefully put Tori on the other side. The children barely moved as we covered them up and retreated to the living room, shutting the door behind us.

"Thank you again, Carly," Dave said. "You were a life saver."

"Don't be silly. It was no trouble at all," I replied, realizing I still had the kids' shoes in my hand. I set them down on the floor outside their bedroom.

"I can't believe you were able to carry Tori like that," he commented.

I flexed my arm with a smirk and he squeezed my bicep

then grinned in mock awe. "I've been workin' out. What can I say?"

He chuckled. "Pretty soon you'll be bigger than I am."

It was my turn to laugh, "Yeah, 'cause that'll happen. Jesus, Dave, cut down on the 'roids! They'll make your junk shrivel up like raisins."

"Yeah, I've pretty much got a breakfast cereal going on in my *draws*." Dave laughed out loud at that one, his contagious hyena laugh that got me going so hard, I had tears in my eyes.

"Dude, so don't need to know what you've got going on in your *draws*, but thanks," I replied when I finally caught my breath again. He snorted.

"You know, Carly," Dave said as his tone became serious. "You still look the same as you did all those years ago."

Now it was my turn to snort, "Whatever!" My scars and severed muscles had left me with a slight pouch above my panty line that prevented me from feeling confident in a bathing suit—it was why I'd begun working out so hard in the first place. And, I knew I needed more work on my upper arms. Years of desk work had left them flabby and less than sculpted.

"Don't kid yourself, girl." Dave leaned against the door frame and crossed his arms across his chest. I tried not to notice the bulging biceps and the He-Man shape he possessed. The man was a fucking action figure. "Do you remember the day we met?"

"That was a *long* time ago!" I said with a chuckle.

Dave grinned then turned a little more somber. "It was the morning after my girlfriend and I had a big fight. Josh, me, and Bobby were in the lobby signing autographs and shit, and you came strolling out of that elevator like you owned the fuckin' place. You wore one of those shirts that changed colors—pink and purple, I think—and a pair of white shorts that showed off your legs. You had white Ray-Bans on the top of your head, holding your hair back, a pair of white canvas tennis shoes, and a puka shell ankle bracelet."

I stared at him, stunned at his recall. "You remember that?"

"Babe, I remember everything about you that day," he admitted, sheepishly. "We've all aged a little, but you still look as beautiful as you did back then. No lie."

I mumbled a thank you and rubbed my face to hide the blush that had formed. "All right," I finally managed to say. "I'm goin' back to bed. That alarm comes awfully early."

He nodded. "Thanks again for taking care of the kids tonight."

"You're welcome. Thanks for picking up the tab on dinner," I replied.

"No problem." He smiled and opened the door for me. "Oh, here's your key," he said, handing it to me. I took it and waved goodbye. The door closed behind me, but not until after I was halfway down the hall.

I didn't know what to think about what Dave said. Had he been interested in me back then? If so, why didn't he say something? Josh, of course. Duh, Carly. Was there still interest now? I smiled at the thought.

I hung out my *Do Not Disturb* sign, turned out the lights, and crawled into bed. As I drifted off to sleep, thinking about what Dave had said, I hoped my dreams would be filled with memories of a summer, some fifteen years ago. I was asleep before I took my third breath.

I was awake early enough the next morning to hit the hotel gym. I threw on my workout clothes and pulled my hair back in a ponytail, tucking it under a ball cap. As much as I wanted to stay in bed, I knew between last night's hot wings and the cup of coffee I'd be sucking back after my workout, I would need to sweat off the calories before they began collecting on my ass.

I opened the door and was thankful to find the place empty. I set my water bottle and towel down and grabbed a mat hanging on the wall. I plugged my earphones in, cranked up my workout playlist and started my stretches. Fifteen minutes and two flexible hamstrings later, I hopped on the treadmill and began my warm-up. I was in my zone when I glanced up and saw Dave step onto the treadmill beside me. He flashed a smile at me as he punched buttons on the machine, firing it to life. I returned the smile but felt self-conscious, all of a sudden.

What the hell, Carly? I chastised myself for being nervous. *It's just Dave*, I told myself . . . the same Dave who called me beautiful the night before and admitted to thinking so all those years ago. I shook the thought loose and returned my focus to my workout.

Before long, I'd increased my pace to a steady 6 mph run. It wasn't the fastest I could do, but with three miles to go, it was the fastest I was willing to go if I expected to finish my workout without my lungs collapsing. Beside me, Dave hit the up arrow and it was like watching a movie in fast forward. He took off in a sprint that made my legs wobble just to look at. I continued my pace, but watched him in the mirror in front of us. Less than a minute later, he hit the down arrow and slowed to a pace similar to mine. I was puzzled. *That* was his workout? A thirty-second sprint? My thoughts were interrupted as Dave hit the buttons again and he took off at lightning speed. What the hell was he doing? I continued at the same pace I'd been moving as he repeated these increases and decreases about a half-dozen times. When my machine finally began to slow for my cool-down, I was grateful.

I may not have been doing what Dave was, but my own workout kicked my ass. I was covered in sweat and my heart-rate was definitely in prime cardio range. I took long cleansing breaths and slowly sucked back half my water in just a few thirsty gulps. As my treadmill came to crawl and then stopped entirely, I stepped off and wiped it down with sanitizer before I went back to the mats to stretch out. A few moments later, Dave joined me, doing a series of leg stretches. I pulled my ear buds out and waited for him to do the same.

"Okay, Fitness King, I gotta know—what the hell was that?" I truly was curious.

"What?" he replied with a chuckle.

"That run-jog-run-jog thing," I clarified, taking another drink of my water. "What was that?"

One of his eyebrows arched, and he shrugged with another laugh, "Uhh, my workout?"

I hit his arm with my towel. "I know that, smartass. What was it you were doing, exactly?"

He grinned and said that it was some sort of high intensity workout that he'd discovered a year or so ago. Although he went on to explain it in great detail, he lost me somewhere after the words "anaerobic state." Blah, blah . . . balance of lactic acid build-up . . . yada, yada and proper oxygenation of the blah, blah, blahs. My blank stare gave me away because he stopped mid-sentence and just laughed.

"You didn't hear any of that, did you?" he asked, sucking back a giant gulp of water and wiping his mouth on the back of his hand.

"Nope," I replied. "I don't speak 'Jock.'"

"Jock?" he blinked at me in surprise. "Jock!?"

The corner of my mouth curled up, "If it walks like a duck and talks like a duck . . ."

"I'll show you a duck, woman!" He jumped up and held out his hand to help me to my feet. "Tomorrow morning, five a.m. What are you doing?"

"I will be sprawled out across my bed, snoring, and it's probably a safe bet there will be drool involved." I chuckled.

"You'll feel better if you get up early and crank out some cardio before breakfast."

I snorted. "Dude, I'm not getting up at five o'clock, so you can try and disprove my duck theory."

"We'll see about that," he countered and held the door for me.

Chapter 5

I PEELED OFF MY CLOTHES THE MINUTE THE DOOR SHUT behind me and spent the next thirty minutes in the shower. Letting the hot spray beat against my neck muscles, I didn't move until I could turn my head without groaning. I normally didn't get this sore after a workout, but with little sleep and having eaten shitty the night before, it caught up with me. Wrapping a towel around my wet hair and a larger one around my body, I tucked the end inside the top to keep it in place. Returning to my bedroom, I flipped through the TV channels and ended up falling asleep, sprawled across my bed.

I awoke a while later to a text message:

`The kids and I are heading to lunch. Tag along?`

Dave.

The offer was tempting and I didn't have plans, but I also didn't want to send the wrong message. I knew Dave had been divorced for a while, but I hadn't been. And while the offer sounded innocent enough, I didn't know him well enough to be certain of that.

> Thanks, but I better stay here and work.
>
> Tell the kids I said hi.

I opened up my laptop and fired off a few emails with some of the work I had done the night before. I called room service and ordered a crab salad for lunch. Munching on my salad, I worked through some more of the edits I needed to finish. When those were done, I opened an email from one of my editors. Apparently, there were some photos that needed work done on them that he wasn't able to do. Personally, I thought he was just lazy, though incompetence was a possibility, too. I opened them up in my editing program and made faces at my computer as I flipped through shot after shot. Less than perfect wasn't acceptable and these didn't even rank *that* high. My editor wasn't incompetent—the photographer was. These really were horrible, and there wasn't much that could be done with them. They would need to be re-shot.

I was grumbling to myself about the shoddy photography of our newest contractor when my cell rang. It was Susan, my boss. She, too, thought the work of our new photographer was crap. She begged me to re-do the shoot myself. It was nice to feel needed, but the demand on my schedule was killing me. With her promise of some extra vacation days, I finally agreed to reshoot it when I got back Thursday, a day earlier than I'd planned on returning. Rubbing my temples as I hung up with Susan, I called my assistant, Geoffrey, to organize the shoot. I wasn't pleased that I had to do it at all, but I'd be damned if I was going to deal with the hassle of setting up the shoot, too. That's why he was hired to begin with: to do my grunt work. He had been eager when I interviewed him a few months earlier. Personally, I thought he was just hoping to catch a glimpse of naked centerfolds, but as long as he got the job done, I didn't care what he ogled in his free time. He was well-qualified, had great references, and he was cute to boot. Okay, I was single, not blind. Geoffrey assured me he would arrange everything, and he would email me the specs of the shoot later in the day.

Alejandro sent me a text mid-afternoon letting me know that he and Marc had plans that night for dinner and not to count on him for company. I was excited for the two of them and I smiled to myself. They made a cute couple, and I hoped whatever was going on between them was heading somewhere permanent. Alex deserved to be happy.

I finally gave up on work around six and decided to try and find some dinner. I've always hated eating alone, but my options were limited. I had called my old friend, Tisha, but she and her husband were in Connecticut visiting his family. I knew Marc and Alejandro were busy. Dave had the kids, and, again, I didn't want to send the wrong message. As far as Josh was concerned, I was pretty sure we had already pushed the limit back in January as to what Abby would be willing to put up with. Bobby still hadn't made it to town yet and honestly, dinner with him didn't appeal to me in the least. That left . . . well, me. Honestly, I didn't feel like going out, but I knew if I stayed in, I'd just order pizza again. The idea of spending an extra half-hour on the treadmill in the morning didn't sound like fun, so I got dressed and decided to see if the deli next to the hotel was any good.

I was waiting in line to order when two small people

tackled me in a hug. Realizing it was Max and Tori, I laughed and hugged them back.

"Sorry, I tried to stop them," Dave said, coming up behind us. "Guys, come on. Let go of her."

"It's fine, Dave." I'd hoped my wide smile indicated I wasn't too bothered by their affection.

"Carly, why didn't you come to lunch with us today?" Max asked.

I was about to answer when Tori piped in, "Don'chu like us?"

"Of course I like you!" I gave her another squeeze. "I just had some work I had to do, and I couldn't take the time to go.

"Can you eat dinner with us now?" Tori inquired, before turning to her father. "Can she, Daddy?"

"Please?" Max pleaded.

Dave just looked at me and smirked. "They'll keep begging until they get their way. You might as well give in."

I chuckled. "Is that so?"

As if on cue, they turned to me. "Please, Carly?" Max began. "We can eat in our room and we can play Monopoly when we're done!"

"Monopoly, huh? Hmm . . ." I teased, knowing full well these two already had me wrapped around their little fingers without even trying.

"I promise I won't beat you, Carly!" Tori vowed.

I glanced back and forth at the kids, then up at Dave. "Are you sure it's okay?"

"Of course," he said without hesitation. "I'd give anything for them to have someone else to beat at that damn game."

"All right. I give. But I get to be the shoe!" I demanded and the kids cheered.

"Oh, come on!" Dave groaned, "The shoe's mine!"

"Not anymore, Daddy!" Tori giggled as she took my hand in a sign of unity.

I just shrugged, "Sorry, Dave. Looks like the princess has spoken."

"Both of them," Dave muttered, winking at me and shook his head at his daughter in mock defeat.

As promised, Tori didn't beat me. Of course, it was only because she forgave me the $1,100 rent I owed her for landing on her hotel-developed Illinois Avenue. Max went bankrupt early on. As it turns out, he's not much of a good sport about losing, and Dave decided that bed was the best solution for his grumpy attitude. When he returned from getting him settled in, he proceeded to tromp Tori and me in about three trips around the board. After making me promise a rematch, Tori gave me a hug and reluctantly headed to bed. I began putting the game away while Dave tucked his youngest child in.

He came back out a few minutes later. "So, you gonna join me in the morning? That HIIT workout has your name all over it."

"That what?" If there was hitting involved, I didn't want to be at the end of his right cross.

"H-I-I-T," he spelled. "High-intensity interval training. HIIT."

That must be that run-jog-run-jog thing he did.

I laughed at his persistence and his assumption that I knew what the hell he was talking about. "If it needs an acronym, I'm not doing it. I'm especially not doing it at five a.m.!"

"I didn't peg you as a slacker," he teased, picking up the empty water bottles and tossing them into the garbage can by the desk.

"Then your slacker radar isn't working because there's no way I'm getting up that early."

"Uh huh. We'll see."

"Uh. No. There's no 'we'll see' about it." I raised my eyebrow in challenge.

"Ahh, you forget. I know your cell phone number and which room you're in."

"Uh huh, but what you don't know is that I can kick your ass," I warned. "Even the mighty Dave Butler doesn't stand a chance when you wake the bear."

"Oh, but I think he does."

"Oh, but I think you're delusional."

Our teasing continued for a couple more minutes until my yawning became too distracting to continue.

"All right, this girl needs sleep." I picked up my purse and walked toward the door. "Thanks for dinner, Dave. And tell the kids I had a great time."

He smiled and held the door for me. "I will and you're welcome."

I gave him a quick hug and kissed his cheek before walking down the hall to my room. I heard his door shut as soon as I opened mine.

As I got ready for bed, I debated on setting my alarm for 4:30. Dave's challenge weighed heavily on my competitive nature. Worst case scenario; I could always come back to my room to sleep later on. The only thing on my schedule was a spa appointment with Alejandro. My mind kept replaying Dave's "princess" comment, and I sighed in defeat. With a small grumble, I turned the alarm on and flipped the light switch, darkening the room. I was asleep within minutes.

Rolling over, I pressed my head between the mattress and the pillow, trying to muffle out the sound coming from the room above me. Loud talking and stomping had awoken me abruptly a few minutes earlier and I was trying to ignore it. Unfortunately, it wasn't working. *I hate inconsiderate people.* When another loud thump came from overhead, I growled and reached for the phone. I pushed the button for the front desk and made a sleepy complaint. The night audit clerk assured me she would take care of the problem immediately. When thirty minutes passed and the noise had not quieted, I decided the clerk was either full of shit or completely powerless. I'd just handle it myself. I threw on my sweatshirt and slippers as I tore through my room in a full snit. I grabbed my key off the table by the door and took the stairs to room 3602. Somebody was getting a new asshole.

I pounded on the door and waited for the occupant to answer. I had my fist raised to knock again when the door flung open.

"It's two in the morning! Who the hell . . ." his voice trailed off in a grumble as his eyes wandered over me from bottom to top. When his hazel eyes stopped on mine, I smirked. His hair was much shorter now. And darker. And formed into some ridiculous comb-over-slash-Mohawk thing. Clearly somebody was trying to hang onto his youth, if not his hairline. He'd also grown a closely-trimmed goatee since the last time I'd caught a glimpse of him. Back in the day, his bad boy attitude had turned me off and he'd always been my least favorite of the group. He'd also been the ringleader whenever Josh was teased and tormented by the guys in the group, so I leaned toward immense dislike for Bobby Callahan.

"Of course it's you. Why wouldn't it be?" I shook my head and sighed.

"Excuse me?" He didn't recognize me. Why would he? It had been almost twenty years since we'd last seen each other.

"Never mind, Callahan. Look, can you quiet the hell down? Some people actually sleep around here." I stared him down and bit back a chuckle when confusion crossed his face.

"Do I know you?" His gaze narrowed as he seemed to try and place why I seemed familiar.

"You did once," I said as I turned around and slowly made my way back down the hall. I turned back toward him as I opened the stairway door. "Seriously, though, dude? Quiet down, okay?"

The door clicked closed behind me and I returned to my room, no doubt leaving a very confused drummer still standing in his doorway, rummaging through his memory, trying to place me. To his credit, it was quiet the rest of the night.

I hit the snooze button on my alarm twice before finally turning it off the next morning. I had good intentions when I set it to get up at 4:30 and surprise Dave in the hotel's fitness center. That, of course, was before an inconsiderate Callahan took up residence in the room above me, keeping me awake half the night.

Ahh, Callahan.

I laid there with my eyes still closed thinking back to the night before. It was no surprise that Bobby hadn't recognized me. Although we'd met and interacted several times, with all the hazing the group had been doing to Josh at the time, it wasn't likely he had paid much attention to Josh's girlfriend. Not to mention my teased mall hair and acid-washed jeans were gone now. I still had unruly brunette curls, but they were tipped in blonde and longer than they'd been before. I'd gained about ten pounds since then and while my figure was still a good one—at least, according to Dave—I wasn't the slender teenager Bobby had last seen.

Of all the group's members, Callahan was the one I'd had the least desire to know. Other than the occasional white lie, I was a good kid. I didn't drink or use drugs. I didn't smoke or break the law. Hell, I didn't even break curfew. So when Callahan, with an arrest on his record and countless legal complaints against him hit the tabloids every other week, I was less than impressed. I thought he was a punk with a chip on his shoulder. And if I was being honest, my opinion hadn't changed much. Sure, he was a hell of an actor, but to me, he'd always be the thug he was back then.

I glanced at the clock again: 4:54. I had about five minutes if I still wanted to meet Dave in the gym. I threw back the covers with a grunt and swung my legs over the side of the bed. I was walking toward the bathroom when I heard a knock on the door.

Seriously?

I peeked through the peephole and just chuckled. "Good morning, Mr. Butler," I said, opening the door.

"I toldja you were coming to work out with me this morning."

"Indeed, you did. C'mon in. I was just getting dressed."

"No you weren't," he chuckled.

I tossed him my phone off the nightstand and told him to check the alarm as I shut the bedroom door to change.

All I heard from the other side of the door was a muffled, "I'll be damned."

I emerged three minutes later with my hair in a ponytail, donning yoga pants and a tank top. I tied my shoes, grabbed a fresh bottle of water out of the mini-bar and we headed downstairs together.

Thirty minutes later, I was more exhausted than I had been in months. Dave taught me an interval repetition that, up until then, I'd only read about in magazines. I'd been from the old school of fitness where you warmed up for ten minutes, ran hard for thirty, and cooled down for another ten. Some days I ran even longer than that to make up for an indulgent dinner the night before. It had never earned me much weight loss, but my cardiovascular system was in top-notch shape. This method, Dave assured me, would help me get rid of that extra ten pounds, around my middle, that I'd been carrying for so many years. I didn't know if he was right, but I did work up quite a sweat. Before we parted ways that morning, he promised to email me some links to websites that focused on interval training and breathing techniques to help my endurance levels (which he apparently identified as an issue I struggle with—who knew?).

I hit the shower and got dressed. Alex and I had planned a spa day later in the morning. The guys had an appearance on *Our 2¢ Worth*, a national talk show based here in the city, shortly and an album signing at Best Buy later, before the release party. We wanted no part of the noise and commotion that went along with those events—hence our decision to retreat to Elizabeth Arden for the day. Ol' Libby knew how to get a girl to relax and had taken care of New York's elite for decades. The Red Door had always been my favorite indulgence when I lived in New York. While I'd never gotten the full gamut of services, I did partake in a facial here and there. It took very little convincing to get Alejandro on board. I don't think he heard anything I said after "microdermabrasion." He wasn't the least bit feminine, like many gay men I knew, but he appreciated the importance of a good facial.

Apparently, three hours of lavender and eucalyptus aromatherapy combined with deep-tissue massage and high-end beauty products were exactly what our bodies needed. Thanks to Anastasia, one of the finest estheticians on the planet (ask her, she'll tell you), we'd been perfectly plucked and pampered. We left the salon refreshed and—dare I say—gorgeous? We had lunch in a little café nearby and spent a couple hours giving our credit cards a workout at Bloomingdale's. We finally hailed a cab around three and headed back to the hotel to get ready for the Release Party being held at a club, appropriately named "Trainwreckz", that night.

"So we're leaving the hotel," Josh looked at his watch, "in about three hours." We'd decided to grab a late dinner at the Galaxy Diner. It had been seven years since Josh and I last sat in the same booth, and while our lives had changed dramatically since our reunion that night in 2002, it felt like yesterday.

We hung up our coats and slid into a booth. The waitress poured us two steaming cups of coffee; that much had changed, at least. I nearly scalded my lips sucking back a swig. Josh leaned back and swung his arm up on the back of the booth.

"So . . ."

I smiled, "So."

"So? What have you been up to? Do you live here in New York? What do you do? Are you married? Do you have kids? Did you join a convent? What?" he prodded those eyes of his, dancing with curiosity.

I laughed, "Well, I went to NYU like I planned, but you knew that." We'd kept in touch for almost a year after I started school. "After I got my master's from Columbia, I spent the summer searching for a big girl job while I worked days at Bloomingdale's and bartended in Hell's Kitchen at night."

"Wait, you bartended?" Josh asked with a little snort.

I gave him a scowl, "I most certainly did and to this day, I still make the best "Fuck You Silly" on the planet, thank you very much!" I said quickly as if those last four words were really one very long one.

He raised his hands in surrender and chuckled, "I bet you do."

The same camaraderie we shared that warm August night, as we brought each other up to speed on our lives, was what we shared now.

"Dave and Marc are riding together—Alex, too, I assume—so I figured we'd go with B, if that's all right."

I started to nod then remembered last night's little encounter with Mr. Callahan. I decided to bring Josh up to speed.

"Funny you should mention Bobby."

"Funny?" he asked, then took another bite of his sandwich before mumbling something that slightly resembled,

"How 'shtho?" Abby clearly hadn't broken him of talking with food in his mouth.

I told him the story about Bobby waking me up and he just laughed and shook his head. "You realize he's probably already figured out your name, address, and the fact that you could hook him up with a centerfold, right? If he doesn't know the answer, he knows somebody who does. B's the most determined son of a bitch I've ever known."

"Yeah, I'm sure his wife would love that centerfold thing." I rolled my eyes. He was Callahan to the core. I'd been right in my thoughts that he hadn't changed his player ways.

"I'm pretty sure Eve doesn't give a shit." The look of confusion on my face must've been too obvious. Josh continued, "Oh, I didn't tell you?"

"Tell me what?"

"They've been separated since January. She filed for divorce a few months ago."

I was surprised, yet, at the same time, nothing about Callahan shocked me. I didn't know what to say, though, so I said nothing.

"Ooh! I know! You two should . . ."

"Don't even think about it, McCarthy." I knew what scheme he was concocting in that curly-haired head of his, and I didn't even want to entertain the thought. Bobby and me? Good Lord!

"I'm just sayin' *strange-ah* things have happened," Josh said with a shrug as he pointed his fork at me. "Who knows, you could be the rebound girl."

"Fantastic," I said dryly. "It's my life's ambition to be Bobby's rebound girl." With a roll of my eyes, I shoved a bite of salad in my mouth.

"Oh c'mon. He's a good guy," Josh began pleading Bobby's case as if he was trying to sell me a used car. His sales pitch was good, but let's get real—this this was Callahan we were talking about. If his ego was anything like it had been back in the day, I didn't possess the patience to deal with it. Besides, while I was finally coming to terms with my own divorce, I didn't know if I had the strength to help someone else through theirs. Callahan was a definite *no*.

"You won't have one drink with me?"

"Um, Bobby? I've already had four."

"Nah, girl, I meant one more." He grabbed the bottle of Cristal out of the ice bucket on the table in front of us and poured a heavy splash into my glass. I learned about two hours ago that nobody tells Bobby "no."

He lifted his champagne flute. "To new beginnings," he toasted as his glass clinked with mine. I repeated the toast and smiled.

After his brief shock at seeing me again, after our little 2:00 a.m. meeting, he was nothing short of humble and apologetic. He vowed to make it up to me somehow. Josh, who felt he needed to catch Bobby up on our history together, took great pleasure in bragging about how we'd dated back in the day and that we'd been engaged just a few years ago. Despite the suggestion he'd started to give earlier, I suspected Josh was trying to place some invisible claim on me to challenge Bobby, and I wasn't comfortable with that. Aside from the fact that I wasn't interested in hooking up with anybody, much less Callahan, I was irritated about the territorial circle Josh had pissed around me. I made a mental note to talk to him about it later. Until then, I would just try and enjoy the evening.

By the time we had made it inside earlier, the flashes of a thousand paparazzi cameras had blinded me and I could hardly get my bearings. Josh and Bobby had herded me straight through the velvet ropes toward Dave, Alejandro, and Marc. I'd lifted my hand in greeting, but they were a bit preoccupied with the fans to notice my arrival. My dates deposited me next to a stocky guy who Josh introduced as Antonio. I didn't know what his official title was in this entourage, but he quickly stepped in front of me, blocking me off from the hundreds of screaming women whom I was certain were there to ensure my demise. My hair got pulled, and I know I heard the word "whore" muttered at least twice as I walked by. These bitches were a special kind of crazy.

Much to my surprise, I actually enjoyed Bobby's company. Even with champagne and Grey Goose in his system, he was attentive, flirtatious and, dare I say it?—charming. He hadn't wandered far from my side most of the night and the few times I'd made the social rounds, he tracked me down again. I wasn't sure what Callahan wanted with me when there were dozens of women, half his age, to flirt with at the club, but I refused to second-guess it tonight. I looked good, I felt good, and I was enjoying myself despite my earlier irritation with Josh and the apprehension I felt about being in VIP.

I'd never liked being in the limelight and I avoided it if I could. Years ago, when Josh had to sign autographs or pose for pictures, I'd drifted into the background. I did the same thing when it came to work events. You'd never see photographs of me at any *Beguile* function, social or otherwise. I liked invisibility. However, there was no such thing as invisibility when you walked into an album release party on the arm of not one, but two South Station Boyz.

I spent most of the night in the fishbowl otherwise known as VIP. I'd been backstage plenty of times and had gone to numerous parties both with Josh and through work, but nothing could've prepared me for this weirdness. The club could hold about six hundred people, but I could swear that five hundred and ninety of those people were standing around the velvet ropes, waiting for those of us inside the ropes to balance a beach ball on our nose or something equally lame. They squealed at everything the guys did. Bobby must have managed to sneak in a nap at some point, because he seemed well-rested and in rare form. At one point, his drink slipped from his hands and he caught it with the other one, barely spilling a drop. The crowd erupted in shrieks and applause. Being the ham he is, he bowed deeply and raised his hands in the air like it was some elaborate magic trick. I caught Alejandro's gaze and we both rolled our eyes and made funny faces. The whole night was like that. Dave or Josh would crack a dumb joke and girls would laugh hysterically. After a few drinks, Marc even grabbed the mic and sang along when the club played "Ice Ice Baby". Alejandro nearly laughed himself into an asthma attack and I was too much in awe to do anything but stare with my mouth hanging open.

The fans? Ate. It. Up.

The guys were enjoying the attention, but some of them had focused their energies elsewhere. Marc, for example, was oblivious to the pretty women and stayed close to Alex most of the night, and Bobby seemed to be pretty caught up in me, which is what had led to our toast.

He leaned into me and pushed my hair to the side, speaking softly into my ear. "Come back to my room."

"Get real, Callahan," I snorted, laughing off his suggestion.

"I'm serious. We can't talk here, and I think we got off on the wrong foot last night." His voice lacked the confidence he usually carried. It caught me off guard, which is probably why I decided to join him—a mistake I'd most likely come to regret in the morning. But, at that moment, it seemed awfully damn appealing.

Bobby picked up my hand the minute we got out of the car at the hotel and he didn't let it go until we were in his room. Once inside the door, he pushed me against it and covered my mouth with his. His breath smelled of peppermint and faintly tasted of cigarettes. His kiss trailed from my lips, along my jaw, and over to my ear. I gripped his collar and whimpered. It had been too long since a man had touched me like this.

With his mouth at my ear, he began whispering breathily. "You like that, baby? Hmm?"

I held my breath. *What the hell did he just say?*

"Feels good, doesn't it?" His tongue flicked at my ear and while that would normally turn me on, his words brought nothing but a giggle.

I could hear him smile and he whispered again, ". . .'s that tickle?"

By now, my giggle had turned into a low rumble of a laugh, and I couldn't stop.

He ran his hand down my side and rested it at my hip before he finally pulled away, "What's so funny, girl?"

"Dude, you *have* to quit with the porn voice. I'm begging you."

He flashed his typical Callahan smirk and leaned in, whispering "You mean it doesn't get you hot?"

I let out another honk of laughter. But when I saw his expression, I quickly bit it back. "I'm sorry, babe. No. It doesn't get me hot."

Now he looked insulted and I felt bad for laughing.

"Just forget it. This was a mistake." He stepped back, adjusted his jacket and pants and reached for the door. "Goodnight, Carly."

I raised my eyebrow. "There's that Callahan ego! I knew it would show up, eventually."

He flipped his coat back and propped his hands on his hips in a defensive stance. His forehead wrinkled in irritation. "Excuse me? What's that supposed to mean?"

My mouth hung open in surprise, "Are you kidding me?! You really don't know?" I waited for his answer and when I was met with stubbornness, I continued. "I tell you that what you're saying doesn't turn me on and instead of finding out what *does* turn me on, you get pissy? Really?!"

"How am I pissy?"

I was appalled. "You know what? You're right. Forget it." I sighed loudly. "Goodnight, Callahan." I paused for a moment, giving him the opportunity to say something. When he didn't speak and instead opened the door, I rolled my eyes and walked out. The door slammed behind me.

Jackass.

Chapter 6

BOBBY EVENTUALLY CALLED ME LATER IN THE WEEK and apologized for that night. He started to hint at a second chance, but I cut him off, distracting him with questions about the upcoming tour. He immediately became absorbed in telling me the details and insisted that I join them. I reminded him that, while it sounded like a blast, I had a big girl job and couldn't just drop it to go gallivanting around the country like some groupie. He whined until I committed to seeing a couple of shows.

Josh, too, called me and I chewed him out for the gauntlet he'd thrown Callahan in New York. As I suspected, he didn't remember what he'd said but he did manage something resembling an apology. These boys were lucky they're cute.

Alejandro and I flew to Atlanta for opening night, which was nothing short of amazing. We'd both made it clear to the guys that we wanted to go into the show with no spoilers and they, thankfully, obliged. He and I stood hand in hand that first night with tears streaming down our faces the minute the opening montage began. As pictures of them from back in the day meshed with current photos, my heart fluttered in my chest. One by one, the members of the group were featured in the video and fans exploded with screams as their favorite came on the screen. As the lead singer of the band, Josh came up last and I wiped tears as my first love's face flashed in front of us. I was so proud of him—all of them.

When the spotlights came up, pyro geysers roared to life and smoke machines began to hiss. The group ran on to the stage from some stairs in the floor and the crowd went insane. The deafening applause didn't let up until the last confetti cannon went off during their encore. It wasn't until I saw the show that I wished I had a job that I could do remotely. I would've loved nothing more than to be at every show to experience that excitement over and over. Of course, it wasn't an option, so Alejandro and I settled instead for the Chicago show a month later. And since I had a business trip to Los Angeles the week of Thanksgiving, I caught the last show of the tour, too.

The holidays were relatively quiet. Bobby, relentless in his pursuit, invited me to join him and Dave in Las Vegas for New Year's Eve. I hadn't seen either of them since the night of the LA show, but we'd exchanged emails frequently. I talked with Dave more than B, though. I'd Skyped with the kids a couple times (chatting with him was an added bonus) and I got the occasional text from him from the road. I had come to cherish our friendship. Dave was the one I seemed to turn to most often when I needed a listening ear or a dry shoulder.

Attending the party in Vegas would allow me to see Dave face to face again, something I had been looking forward to since the trip to New York in September. I'd seen him at the shows, of course, but we hadn't been able to talk much; it was just too hectic.

I suppose I was curious about Bobby, too. We had one hell of a first exchange and I hoped that uneasiness between us would be gone once I saw him again. I didn't want a relationship, but I didn't want tension, either. We were all supposed to be friends, after all.

The New Year's Eve party didn't disappoint. There were fewer fans at Ebony than there was at Trainwreckz for the album release party, but Lamar, another bodyguard in the security brigade, kept me behind the walls of VIP, just to be on the safe side. It wasn't without good reason. Some snotty girl got a little big for her britches at the show in LA back in November and I set her straight. Antonio intervened with that situation before it got too bad, but to say I wasn't his favorite person was an understatement. Lamar and I got along okay, though. Tank, their third and largest bodyguard, was neutral but Antonio outright refused to deal with me. He said that I was a loose cannon and I needed to "remember my place." Whatever. I totally could've kicked that girl's ass.

New Year's Eve wasn't free from drama, either. Bobby had overtaken the DJ booth at midnight and I became a little irritated. I didn't like being ditched. I never had been good at hiding my feelings, so when some brunette with pink highlights started shit with me, I didn't hesitate to give it back to her. She mumbled something to a friend of hers. The friend looked at me and began snickering. I slammed my drink back and stood up, ready to yank the weave from her snarky scalp, but Dave intervened, suggesting we get some air. He ended up walking me to my room—with Lamar's observing eye not far behind us, of course. Lamar left and while I assured Dave he could leave, too, he said he was partied out.

"Suit yourself, but I plan on getting naked in about four seconds, so consider yourself warned." I grinned and began by kicking off my shoes.

"And you're telling me this because a naked woman is supposed to scare me?"

"This one should." I reached behind me and unzipped my dress. I shimmied the fabric over my shoulders and paused.

Son of a bitch! He was calling my bluff.

"Don't stop now. I'm enjoying the show." Dave's smirk was playful and daring, but *even I* wasn't that brave.

"Perv! Go ogle the tits down at Skin," I snorted, referring to the topless pool in the hotel. "Mine are off limits."

"Are they, now?" He turned and looked at me, one eyebrow raised.

I met his stare with one of my own. "Uh," was all I could seem to stutter.

"You know what your problem is, Carly?"

"I have a problem?" I took advantage of the question to regain my composure as I hurried to the bedroom. I shut the door most of the way and stepped out of view to change while I waited for his answer. When he didn't answer right away, I peeked out to see if he was still there.

"You're no goddamn fun." He had turned away from me now and was standing by the open curtains, staring out at the Strip. I could tell by the outline of his jaw he had a smirk on his face. With his hands in his pockets, he looked quite natural standing there—handsome, even. He turned his head and met my gaze.

"I beg your pardon?" I stood with my hand on my hip and the other on the door handle. "I'm a shit-ton of fun, thank you very much!"

He grinned.

"What?" I asked as I walked across the room, tying the belt of my robe around me before joining him at the window.

Dave raised his eyebrow at me.

"What is that look for?"

"What look?"

I wiggled my finger at his face. "That one!"

"I don't know what you're talking about," he denied, the smirk disappearing. He stood just a few inches away from me. His eyes didn't leave mine and I suddenly felt self-conscious . . . as if he could read my thoughts.

I opened my mouth to say something but nothing came out. After a few silent moments, I finally cleared my throat and broke our stare.

"Happy New Year, Carly," Dave whispered, before pressing his lips to mine. Just as I caught my breath again, he broke the kiss. He grazed my still-pursed lips with his thumb then turned and left, clicking the door shut behind him.

Chapter 7

THE NEW YEAR BROUGHT THE BEGINNING OF A European tour. I declined the offer to join the guys. I wasn't sure what happened between Dave and me in Vegas, but I didn't think I wanted to put myself in a situation where it could be repeated. I needed some time to sort things out in my head. I'd been led into things by following my heart too many times and didn't want to make that mistake again.

The beginning of the year also brought the announcement of the Party Barge Cruise, a concert cruise with several old school musicians and bands. The whole cruise idea sounded like fun, but, at the same time, I was horrified at the thought of being trapped on a boat with two thousand fans for three days. I'd last ten minutes before I started launching citrus fruit at people or tossing the nutters overboard. I'd end up like Leonardo DiCaprio, handcuffed to heating ducts in the bowels of the ship, in no time at all.

The guys did a lot of promo work in the spring, as well as

a few concert dates at smaller arenas, trying to reach as much of their fan base as possible. Unfortunately, I wasn't able to attend any of the shows on their mini-tour. *Beguile* had cutback hundreds of jobs which, for me, meant working sixty-hour weeks and doing the job of ten people. Dave and Bobby were both disappointed but in talking with Josh, he assured me that I wasn't missing anything new.

At the end of April, I flew to Los Angeles again for work. Cutbacks there meant on-staff photographers had been let go, so my schedule was packed full of shoots, edits, and meetings. But, it didn't stop Josh and Bobby both from hijacking my time. Bobby made me commit to a night of clubbing, and Josh wouldn't take no for an answer when he invited me to his house for a barbecue. Quite honestly, I didn't want to do either. Bobby was far too intent on pushing for a relationship and I could go forever without meeting Abby, as far as I was concerned. But, for the sake of keeping the peace, I agreed to both offers.

After a long day of meetings, all I wanted to do was soak in a hot bath and finish off a bottle of wine. Beverly Hills had great spas that I would've loved to check out too, but Callahan had other plans for me. First, he insisted on poisoning me with sushi.

"You just haven't had *good* sushi," he said when I told him that I didn't like it. We argued about that from the time we left the hotel until we got to Taku, the place Bobby proclaimed had the best sushi on the planet. I bit my tongue to keep from telling him I was certain that the people of Japan might claim otherwise. Humoring him, I let him order for me. I even refrained from telling him that I had already had the best sushi New York had to offer and still couldn't stand the taste or texture of it. Before the waiter left the table, I ordered the lamb chops just in case. Bobby shook his head in disgust.

When our plates were delivered, I caught a whiff of the seafood and grimaced. I held my breath and took a bite. Choking down a piece of unagi, I chased the eel with my entire glass of wine hoping to kill the aftertaste. I motioned for the waiter to take my plate away and I dug into the chops instead. Bobby soon changed his opinion and determined that it wasn't good *sushi* but rather good *taste* that I lacked. I simply smiled and dropped a big glob of wasabi in his sake when he wasn't looking. I laughed my ass off when he gagged on his drink a couple minutes later.

While dinner was a disaster, the club wasn't. Bobby took me to Swag, one of the most elite clubs in LA. There were a handful of fans milling around us all night, but they had the couth not to ask for autographs. It didn't stop them from taking pictures, of course, but at least the whispers of "bitch" and "whore" were left for another time. I suspected our pictures would make their way to the internet by midnight and a chorus of jealousy among fans would soon follow. Not that I cared what they thought, but for some reason, I worried that it would get back to Dave that Bobby and I had gone out. It wasn't that it was a secret, really. I just preferred him to find out about it from me rather than some fan.

"Hey, girl!" Bobby snapped his fingers. "You still wit' me?"

"Yeah," I blinked the thoughts of Dave away and smiled at him. "Still with you. Sorry. Guess I was more tired than I thought."

"Who is he?"

"Who's who?" A shot of adrenaline went through me and

I panicked that Bobby could read my mind. I took a large sip of my cocktail, hoping it would mask my nervousness.

"You're like a thousand miles away," he said with a frank look on his face. "It's gotta be a dude. Who is it?"

"Nobody," I replied, trying to reassure him. "Really. My mind's just on shit I need to do tomorrow for work."

Bobby looked at me skeptically but didn't say anything else about it. A few moments later, he took my hand and coaxed me out of my seat. "I didn't bring you here to think about work. Let's shake that ass, girl."

I smirked at him. "Half a bottle of Belvedere and you think you own me, is that it?"

"You know it. Now move!" He slipped behind me as we made our way through the crowd and kept his hands on my hips as we began grinding on the dance floor. The man may not have Josh's smooth footwork, but he could dance and I enjoyed every minute of it. We didn't return to our seats for almost an hour and by then, I was out of breath and had worked up quite a sweat. It was the most fun I'd had in a long time.

"Girl, why didn't I know you could move like that?" Bobby asked me as the waitress delivered a fresh bucket of ice and another bottle of vodka. She set a chilled carafe of cranberry juice on the table in front of us and gave a flirtatious smile to Bobby before taking away our empties. I skipped the Belvedere and went straight for the juice, downing half my glass in a couple of thirsty gulps.

"If you'd paid any attention to me at all, you'd already know that I could move." I grinned, cheekily. I didn't know why, but whenever I was around Callahan, I couldn't resist being a snarky bitch.

"Damn, girl, why you gotta be like that?" He pursed his lips, but they quivered in the beginnings of a smile.

"What can I say, you bring out the worst in me," I replied with a wiggle of my eyebrows. He just shook his head and splashed a healthy amount of liquor in my glass before taking a sip straight from the bottle himself.

We left shortly after midnight and since Bobby couldn't convince me that he was sober enough to drive, I took his keys and drove us back to my hotel, but not before we hit a 24-hour diner. I had burned the calories from dinner within thirty minutes at the club and what I didn't burn off, I doused in alcohol. I'd sobered up, but I was starving. Bobby looked like he could use something to sop up the liquor in his system, so we ordered two double cheeseburgers and fries. Devouring them quickly, we left with two milk shakes to go and sucked them back on the way back to my hotel.

All the food apparently rendered me stupid however, because I invited Bobby to come up to my room. In my defense, my intention was to allow him more time for sobriety. It was almost an hour from my hotel to his house. I didn't want him driving that far if he was still even remotely buzzed. His intentions, however, were a bit different as I found out a few moments after we stepped inside the room.

Once again, I declined his advances. To his credit, he didn't use the porn voice this time, but the taste of vodka and cranberries mixed with pickle and onion didn't do it for me, either. Neither did the thought of a night of fumbling in the dark with a drunken Callahan. He handled the rejection better this time, though. And by "better" I mean, he passed out cold on the couch. Reaching down, I pushed his tousled hair back into place and gave a small chuckle. The man would always be a twenty-year-old delinquent, I swear. After removing his shoes, I covered him up with a blanket and went to bed.

The next morning brought a string of apologies, which I accepted. But to dissuade any future bumbles, I decided I should probably make it very clear what my feelings were for him. I explained gently that I loved him dearly but that he would never be more than a friend to me. I didn't want to hurt his feelings or bruise his ego, but I didn't want to spend the rest of my days dodging his porn voice or wandering hands. He seemed to take it well. At least he didn't storm out in a huff. With Callahan, that was progress. I gave him a hug and a small peck goodbye. And, when he invited me to come to Miami for a bon voyage party in May, I promised to consider it.

Work ran me ragged all day and I had to postpone the barbecue with the McCarthys until the next day. Josh seemed disappointed when I called, but by the sounds of the yelling in the background, I suspected my absence was more welcome than he let on.

Before I turned in that night, I checked my email and smiled as I read one from Dave. He, too, invited me to the bon voyage party, filling me in on the details of the event. He also caught me up on what he'd been doing since the tour ended and sent some snapshots of the kids. I hadn't seen him since New Year's Eve, and while it had been something I couldn't explain, I did miss him terribly. I didn't have the time to go on the cruise, but I considered taking a couple days off and going to Miami for the party.

I finished my meetings early in the day and spent some time on Rodeo Drive. As I went in and out of snobby boutiques, I wished silently that Alejandro was there so we could rattle off *Pretty Woman* quotes. By the time I made it to the third or fourth store, I was ready to go. True to the stereotype, I—decked out in capris and a trendy little t-shirt—was ignored while the clerks fawned all over some tiny little blonde with a yapping terrier stuffed inside a Louis Vuitton purse. I snuffed in disgust, which drew the attention of the dog-owner who looked down her nose at me. I mumbled an impolite "Fuck this" and walked back out of the shop, firing off a text to Alejandro on my way to my rental car.

You work on commission, right? Big mistake. Big. Huge!

My phone rang a minute later with him rattling off, "I have to go shopping now," followed by a string of laughter. "Rodeo Drive, eh?"

"Where else would I be?" I replied with a laugh. "God, I hate Beverly Hills. Thank God I've got the search for a Lotus Esprit to keep me occupied."

"Right? Ugh. So how is LA, anyway?"

"You mean aside from hoity-toity bitches with their yippy Yorkies? It's fine, I guess." Pressing the button on my key fob, the parking lights on my car blinked in response as the locks released. I got in the car, tossing my purse into the passenger seat.

"Hoity-toity? Yippy Yorkies? Who the hell are you, Dr. Seuss?" He laughed at his own joke. "How are things with Josh and Callahan?" he graciously changed the subject. I could tell Alex had tucked his phone in the crook of his shoulder because his voice became a little muffled and I heard him typing loudly in the background. He was a multitasker, that one.

"Callahan's . . . well, Callahan. We had dinner the other

night and he passed out on me."

I heard a clunk followed by a muffled "Oh shit!" then a rustling noise as Alejandro picked the phone back up. "He passed out . . . *on you*? What the fuck does that mean?"

I rattled off the story. Alex, as usual, responded with appropriate commentary where fitting. He had never been a big fan of Bobby's, either. He knew Bobby and Marc had a few problems back in the day, and Alex wasn't one to forgive grudges very easily.

I continued my LA diatribe with a whine about having to finally meet Abby. Alex couldn't believe that I'd never met Josh's wife before. It wasn't without great effort on my part, I had to be honest. She'd been backstage in Atlanta and was there at the last show in Los Angeles before Thanksgiving, too, but I bowed out early and said my goodbyes at both shows, just missing the newest Mrs. McCarthy by mere moments. I rambled on with my explanation as I half listened to my GPS rattling off directions to Josh's house in its annoying British accent. I was halfway to Santa Monica when I realized Chauncey (every GPS device needed a name, didn't it?) had been "recalculating" for the last ten minutes. I said a quick goodbye to Alejandro, who had probably tuned me out in exchange for work anyway, and whipped a U-ie, finally heading east again. Chauncey stopped yelling at me and I pulled up in front of the McCarthy home a short time later.

After a few moments of chanting quietly to myself that I would, in fact, survive dinner, I drew the courage to head inside. I reached into the backseat and pulled out a bottle of wine I'd picked up the day before and locked the car. Inhaling deeply, I smoothed out my shirt and slung my handbag over my shoulder. With all the moxie I could muster, I rang the bell and waited.

Josh flung the door open two breaths later and wrapped me in a welcoming hug. "Hey, Coop!" he greeted me, jovially. "I thought you were gonna bail on us again." He ushered me inside and took the wine from me. "What the hell took you so long?"

"Blame Chauncey," I replied with a giggle, but no explanation.

"Chaun . . ."

"Tango! Come back here!" I heard a woman's voice holler from the other end of the house just as a black and white mop of a dog came tearing into the hall and jumped up at me. His tail wagged a mile a minute and his large, soulful eyes pleaded with me to pick him up.

I obliged with a cooing, "Aww," as I lifted him into my arms. His tongue took a swipe up my face before I could stop him, and I laughed in response.

A moment later, a slim woman with blonde hair rounded the corner carrying a dog leash and a rolled-up newspaper.

"Damn mutt," she said, ignoring me in exchange for the Shih Tzu mix she was referring to, whose little body shivered in, what I assumed was, fear of a swat for bad behavior. Josh took him from me and held his collar while she snapped the leash on and handed it to him. I wiped the dog saliva from my cheek and chuckled. Abby finally turned toward me as Josh cleared his throat.

Abby was exactly like I pictured her: head-to-toe gorgeous. Her pixie haircut reminded me of the actress, Michelle Williams. With her high cheekbones, flawless skin, and vibrant, green eyes, I'd swear she had just come off a cover of *Vogue*. Her clothes were freshly pressed and fit her like a glove. The woman was fucking perfect. No wonder Josh had chosen to marry her.

"Carly, this is my wife, Abby." Josh shifted Tango to his right arm and put his left one around her slender shoulders and gave them a squeeze. "Honey? This is Carly."

I smiled as warmly as I could muster, given the circumstances, and extended my hand. Abby, ever the example of poise and manners I pictured her to be, smiled politely and lightly took my hand in hers, giving it a lady-like shake. "Carly, it's a pleasure. I've heard a lot about you." Her smile extended only to the corners of her mouth and the glint in her eyes told me the smile was as fake as the tips on her nails.

Ahh, so we're playing that *game.*

"And I, you," I managed to reply, my own expression most likely giving my façade away, as well.

"And this dust bunny is Tango," Josh said as he made smoochy faces at the dog. Tango yipped in response and licked his chin.

"Ugh, Josh, that's disgusting!" Abby exclaimed with exasperation, grabbing the dog and mumbling something about kenneling him as the two of them disappeared around the corner.

I took a deep breath and chuckled nervously.

"Well, that was awkward."

"Wha? Nah," Josh shrugged it off and glanced behind him toward the direction his wife went. He turned back around and smirked. "Okay, so it was a little awkward, but it'll get better. C'mon in." He placed a hand on the small of my back and led me down the hall toward the family room.

It didn't get better.

When Josh went outside to put the chicken on the grill,

I made the mistake of asking Abby about her parents, who had just announced their separation a month earlier. Then at lunch, I had to spit a mouthful of salad into a napkin when I realized it had almond slivers in it, to which I'm highly allergic. Dessert went off uneventfully, but when we went outside later to sit by the pool, I accidentally shut Tango's back leg in the door, causing him to limp the rest of the afternoon. When I finally left around five o'clock, I had all I could do not to cry the whole way back to my hotel. It couldn't have gone any worse if I'd set out to ruin the day on purpose. Despite Josh's reassurance, I felt like an utter and complete ass. If I never saw Abby again, it would be too soon. I'm sure she felt the same.

Chapter 8

"THERE'S NO WAY I CAN GO TO MIAMI. I CAN'T JUST pick up in the middle of the week and go to Florida just because Josh wants us there." Alejandro carefully turned the steaks and basted them with a teriyaki glaze before he closed the lid on the grill again. He wiped his hands on a dish towel and turned to look at me. "He's acting like a whiney baby and I'm over it. At least Marc understands that I can't attend every event. Josh might as well throw himself on the ground kicking and screaming."

We lounged on our deck, enjoying the warm weather that had finally decided to stick around. With the sun casting long shadows across Grant Park nearby, it was the picture-perfect Chicago evening. Picking up his beer, Alex stretched out in one of the Adirondack chairs.

Alejandro was practically married to his job. He was always at the office by 7 a.m. and rarely left before six that night. I still wasn't completely convinced he didn't send a clone of himself to New York and Atlanta and he actually stayed in Chicago working. He answered personal texts and emails sparingly and was the same way with phone calls. "Yes. No. Call you later." This demeanor obviously worked for him, as he's only about two retirement parties and a funeral away from making senior legal partner within the Bulls franchise, where he'd been since he got his law degree. I was dedicated to my job, but I also took vacation days and knew how to disengage when it came to personal time.

Usually.

Alejandro? Not so much. It was no surprise that he refused to make this party in Miami a priority.

"So, I'll go and give your regrets. It's not a big deal." I took a sip from my bottle and set it back down on the arm of my chair.

"Tell *him* that."

"I'll get right on that," I snorted. "Because we know how much Josh loves it when I argue with him."

It had taken me a couple more days to come to the decision to attend the party in Miami. Josh insisted it was the "least I could do" since I "broke his dog." He was only teasing, but I cringed with guilt every time I thought about his poor dog. I also wasn't so sure Josh's tone was all that teasing. Maybe Alex was right about the whiner part. He did seem to be a little more demanding of us than usual.

Although Dave hadn't brought the party up to me again, Bobby was persistent. I finally texted him and told him to find me a decent hotel. An hour later, he emailed me with hotel reservations and flight information. I rolled my eyes. Callahan never did anything half-assed, I supposed. I sent back a quick thank you and printed off my itinerary. I'd smack Callahan around later over the hotel suite. A few more emails to Josh and Dave, as well as my boss, and plans were set.

When I exited my bedroom the morning of my flight, Alejandro stood there with his mouth hanging open as he stared at my overnight bag.

"You've got your Fendi loaded down and it's in the bedroom, right? I mean surely you didn't fit *everything* you're taking in just that little carry-on," his tone was one of disbelief tainted with sarcasm.

"Shut up," I said, chuckling at him. "I'm only going overnight and I *do* know how to pack lightly, you know."

"Two words: New. Fucking. York."

"That's three words."

His arched eyebrow made me laugh.

"Uh huh." He grinned, "Anyway, have a good time. Give everybody my best. Tell Josh to stop being such a baby."

I agreed to deliver his messages and gave him a hug goodbye. Picking up my purse and slinging it on my shoulder next to the other bag, I headed out the door. Two hours later, I was airborne.

Of all the places my travel had taken me, Miami had never been a destination. Joking with Alejandro, I told him I wasn't sure I would know I'd arrived in the right city if I wasn't met at the airport with the sound of steel drums and a personal welcome from Gloria Estefan. Unfortunately, my only personal welcome was from the clerk at the Hertz desk when I picked up my rental car. A convertible, of course, because hello?—it's fucking Miami! Sunshine abounds!

I plugged in my old GPS friend, Chauncey, and let him

get his bearings while I opened the windows and pulled back the roof, letting out the broiling heat that goes along with that abounding sunshine. I punched the hotel address into Chauncey's tiny keyboard and off I went.

As I tooled along Collins Avenue, I cranked the radio and let the city envelop me. Wind whipped through my hair as I let the weather give me a proper Floridian welcome. I was so glad I decided to come.

Later that evening, as I readied myself for the party, I began second-guessing myself. I was half nauseous with nerves and I couldn't figure out why. Just as I popped a Tums in my mouth, my text ringtone went off.

`I hear you came to send me off?`

Dave. I smiled involuntarily and replied.

`Maybe ☺`

A few moments later, as I was securing a bracelet around my wrist, there was a knock at the door. I opened it and was met with a grinning Josh McCarthy.

"Your chariot awaits!" He flashed his pearly whites and tapped his watch. "In *othah* words, we're late. Let's go!" Josh was dressed quite casually in just a gray t-shirt and dark jeans. He'd skipped shaving, apparently for a few days, based on the stubble that had formed on his chin, cheeks, and upper lip. It was a good look on him. The scent of his Carolina Herrera cologne drifted past me and old olfactory senses kicked in, causing me to recall a different time in our lives.

On the afternoon of Christmas Eve, Josh and I went downtown for last minute Christmas shopping. With our arms full of packages, we put them in the trunk of the car, stopped at Dunks for coffee, and then meandered toward the Common. While I'd visited Boston a couple of times over the years, I hadn't been here since the last time we'd strolled this same path ten years previously. Large, fluffy snowflakes dusted the park in a blanket of white powder. I'd never been a fan of the cold weather, but the setting was picturesque. We paused for a while at Frog Pond and watched the ice skaters. Josh teased me, recalling the time I spent on my butt the last time I got on ice skates with him. Needless to say, I wouldn't be donning blades anytime soon.

We finished our coffee and wandered some more, ending up on Lagoon Bridge. The clouds cleared away just in time for the sunset, which cast an orange glow across the snow in the park that had been falling most of the day. Giant willow trees draped their branches over the banks of the pond, providing shelter to the Canadian geese and rabbits that took up residence in the park this time of year.

"God, I wish I had my camera. This is beautiful," I admired and glanced back at Josh. He just smiled as he saddled up behind me, putting his arm around my waist. I leaned against him and watched some geese fly in and land on the little island refuge in the center of the pond, waddling under one of its protective trees. No artist could have painted a more magnificent picture than the one before us.

"I love you," Josh whispered in my ear. I closed my eyes and sighed. His breath was warm against my neck and I tilted my head against his. I caught the drift of his cologne as he put his other arm around me.

"I love you back," I whispered in reply, opening my eyes and looking down to pick up his hand. I saw the glint of sunlight off a sparkly stone . . . . a giant, familiar solitaire stone set in a platinum band. It was the Asscher Mr. Clemens had pulled from the display case at Cartier a decade ago. My breath caught in my chest. I looked from the ring to Josh, who had crouched down

on one knee and held the red box in front of me now.

"Marry me, Carly." He took the ring out of the box and held it between his fingers. "I let you get away once and it was the biggest mistake of my life. Please say you'll be my wife."

My heart hurt at the retrospect and I blinked away the thoughts. I quickly slammed the giant iron door on our past, hopefully locking out reminiscence like this for good. We were each in much different places now and no good could come of me wandering through old trunks of memories. There were new memories to make . . . with a new man this time. Dave and I had gotten close through our online conversations and I needed to concentrate on that.

"Not until you tell me how fabulous I look, Joshua." Playing off his flirtation, I focused instead on prodding him for a compliment as I twirled in the pale pink dress I bought specifically for the party. With a halter-style neckline and flowing knee-length skirt that flared around my upper thighs as I turned, I couldn't say no to this purchase.

"*Killah* dress. Let's goooooooo," he urged with a grand, sweeping motion of his arms toward the hallway.

"Nice, Josh. You know just how to shoot down a girl's confidence," I grumbled as I slipped on my strappy heels and grabbed my clutch.

As I squeezed between him and the door on my way out, he put his hand at the small of my back. I paused and looked at him. "You still take my breath away, Carly. You look gorgeous."

Motherfucker!

My breath caught in my throat and slow smile spread across my face. I exhaled sharply and pretended the murmured compliment didn't make my loins ache. The proverbial iron door creaked under pressure and I gave in briefly, standing on my tip-toes to kiss his nose. "Much better. Now let's roll, McCarthy. We're late!"

He winked at me, and we walked down the hall. Minutes later, we stepped into the elevator to take us to the bar downstairs where the party was being held.

Dave had been pulled in fifteen different directions in the hour I'd been there, but he and I finally found a quiet corner of VIP to share a drink. He looked just as amazing as he did the night in Vegas five months earlier.

He held a drink in one hand and draped the other over the railing behind me, resting it against my back—not in a possessive way, but more attentively.

"You look really incredible tonight, Carly."

"Wha? This ole thing? Thank you," I responded, coyly. "You know, you really know how to throw quite the party."

Modestly, Dave shook his head. "Nah, we've got party people who do this stuff for us. We just sign the checks." He grinned.

"Well, either way, the party's awesome and everybody seems to be having a good time."

Leaning in, his fingers brushed my spine, "Are *you* having a good time, Carly?" His voice was low—almost too soft to hear—but I caught every word. And was thankful for them. It took my mind off the sprint down memory lane back in my room with Josh.

"I am," I answered. "Thank you again for the invitation. I needed to get away."

"It wouldn't be a party without you. I'm glad you decided to come." He flashed a smile and leaned in, pressing his lips against mine. The stubble on his chin brushed roughly against my face and it sent shivers down my arms. With a flick of his tongue, he kissed me more deeply then pulled away. My knees went weak and, while the kiss on New Year's should've prepared me for this, it caught me by surprise and I had to brace myself on the railing.

Still standing inches away, he put his hand around my waist and leaned in. His whiskers now tickled the side of my neck.

Sweet Jesus.

"I want you, Carly." His breath passed over my earlobe and I prayed my whimper couldn't be heard out loud.

Before I had the time to respond, Bobby came up to us and tapped Dave on the shoulder. I took the opportunity to guzzle back half my drink to calm my nerves. After a brief whispered conversation with lots of nodding on Dave's part, Bobby pulled away, gave me a wink, and a quick kiss to the cheek before he walked away.

"Carly, I'm sorry. I need to go handle something that's come up." His eyes wandered up and down my form and I got the impression he didn't want to leave. "I wish I could . . ."

"Don't be silly," I interrupted. "Go and do whatever you need to do. I'll be around."

"Promise?"

I smiled widely. "I promise. But, just in case . . ." I reached into my bag and pulled out a keycard—no doubt the boldest move I'd ever made with any man. "You can take this." I told him my room number and gave his hand a squeeze. He pocketed the card and gave me a playful smile before turning and heading off to, no doubt, sign more checks.

I exhaled the breath I'd been holding and gave my head a slight shake. Here I had Dave telling me how much he wanted me when, for the last hour, I'd been thinking about the could've beens with Josh. What the hell was I doing? I had to stop living in the past and start living up the present.

I threw back another drink. That plan had to start somewhere. Perhaps the Gray Goose would have an idea.

"Coop, how much have you had to drink?" Josh asked me.

"Aww, leave 'er alone, Josh," Bobby urged, patting my knee and winking at me. "She's fine."

Josh flashed Bobby a glare of frustration and turned back to me. "Seriously, Carly. How much?"

His faces were swimming in front of me and I just giggled and shrugged. I rarely drank to excess but Callahan kept supplying me with a fresh glass and, for once, it felt good to let loose.

"Since when is the Irishman the voice of sobriety?" Marc joked. "C'mon, Carly. I'll buy you another drink."

"She doesn't need another damn drink, Marc," Josh admonished him and patted my hand to get my attention.

"C'mon, love. Let's *not* pickle our *livah* tonight? If I send you home dead, Alex will fucking kill me. Let's get you back to your room and get you to bed."

"Pickle *livah*," I giggled as I mimicked Josh. "Pickle *livah*. Pickle *livah*. Pickle *livah*. That sounds funny if you say it fast," I repeated myself again and hiccupped. "Hey, where's Dave?"

A snort and a chuckle came from behind me.

"I'm right here, babe." Dave put his hand on my shoulder to steady me as I whipped around. I grabbed his forearm for support. "Look, Josh's gonna take you back to your room and when I can get away, I'll come check on you."

"Knock really hard cuz it's *waaaay* loud in here and I dunno if I'll hear you."

Bobby laughed out loud at my humor and I thanked him for it.

"Christ, don't encourage her," Josh said, but Bobby just winked at me. Josh helped me to my feet and handed me my purse. We stumbled to the door as I waved goodbye over my shoulder at the rest of the guys . . . all six of them. *Damn, how much* did *I have to drink?*

I barely remembered the walk back to my room, but I had vague memories of blowing kisses to the concierge and giggling. There also may have been a staircase banister and sliding involved, but I confess to nothing.

"All right, Slash. Close your eyes, so you don't see me undressing you," Josh teased when we got back to my room.

"You're undressing me? Why for?"

"Because I'm sure you paid way too much for this dress to use it as a nightgown. Close 'em."

I covered my eyes with my hands, which only worked long enough to get the dress pulled up to my shoulders. After that, I popped my eyes opened, belched, and giggled uncontrollably until Josh scowled at me then clamped my eyes shut again while he lifted the dress over my arms. I kept them shut and swayed forward and back for a few moments as I heard the rustling of bed linens behind me.

"Waaaaaaaaait," I slurred. "I covered up *my* eyes but you didn't cover up yours! You saw my tatas!"

"And they're as beautiful as they've ever been. Now, cop a squat."

"Cop a feel? What?" With a drunken giggle, I reached out and goosed him. "Whadyoujussay?"

"Sit," he smirked and gave a gentle shove to my shoulders.

I flopped back on the bed and Josh knelt down, unbuckling my shoes, which was probably slightly more difficult than nailing Jell-O to a tree. Once my feet were finally free from their designer prison, he swung my legs around and tucked them beneath the blankets.

I sighed in intoxicated contentment as he wrapped me in a silky cocoon and kissed my forehead. He crossed the room and returned with a bottle of water, setting it on the nightstand next to my Blackberry, which he'd plucked from my purse.

"All right, beautiful, I'm taking your *keycahd* so I can check on you in a little bit. Your phone is here and there's a bottle of *watah*, too. I suggest you drink it before you fall asleep; *hangovah* prevention and all. And if you puke, you're cleaning it up when you're sober. I'm a nurse, not a *housekeepah*—got it?"

I mumbled in hazy understanding and he left shortly thereafter, turning off all but the hall lamp behind him. I sucked back half the bottle of water in a few guzzles and was asleep in minutes.

I don't know how long I had been asleep, but awoke a while later to the click of my door being opened. I squinted at the dark figure coming toward me then groaned in protest as the light next to the bed came on. Josh felt my cheek, then my forehead with the back of his hand.

"Are you dead?" he inquired.

"Mm hmm," I confirmed, flopping my head back on the pillow.

"Awesome," he replied with a chuckle. "Drink some more *watah*."

I obliged, managing to dribble only a few drops on myself.

"Atta girl. Now sleep. I'll be back *latah* to check on you," he said as he pressed his lips to my forehead again. "Goodnight."

"Guhnigh," I mumbled and rolled to my belly, burying my face between the pillows. He turned out the light and left again.

I was in and out of consciousness most of the night, awakening to the soft beep of the keycard in my door again sometime later. I managed to roll over, covering my eyes with the back of my hand so Josh couldn't blind me with the lamplight this time.

The bed shifted with his weight and I felt his lips against my temple. He let out a sigh.

"Dammit, why can't you be sober?"

Wow. Josh's voice sounded a lot like Dave's. I'd never noticed that before.

I flung my hand away from my face, propping myself up on my elbows and opened my eyes. I struggled to focus on his shape in the dark room. I rambled off something that resembled "Whatthehell?"

"I told you I'd come check on you," the well-formed silhouette explained. "How do you feel?"

"Oh yeah," I groaned in reply and collapsed against my fluffy pillows. "I feel' fine."

He chuckled and got up. He came back a minute later with a fresh bottle of water. He turned on the light and held me up with one strong arm while he balanced the water bottle for me in the other.

When I'd drunk enough water to drown a fish, I wiped my mouth with the back of my hand and settled back into bed. "Why d'you wan' me sober?" I asked, suddenly remembering his first words to me.

"It's not important. I'll tell you later," he said, capping the water bottle and setting it on the nightstand.

"Tell me now."

"Later."

"Nowwwwww," I whined in the most pathetic voice I could muster.

"I can't tell you when you're like this," he tried to reason.

"Uggghhhh," I grumbled, a scowl scrunching up my face. "Can you show me?"

"Show you?"

"Yeah. Like chardonnay."

"Chardonnay?"

"Yeah, chardonnay. You know! That game you play where you act out the words."

"You mean *Charades?*"

"Tha's what I said." I hiccupped and giggled.

He just shook his head, his body shaking with silent laughter.

"Pleeeeeaaaaase? Pleaseohpleaseohplease?" I begged. "C'mon! How many syb-a-lulls?

He laughed his infectious laugh, and I giggled in response.

"All right," he agreed, holding up three fingers.

"Three!"

He chuckled again and held up one finger.

"First one!" *I loved games!*

He nodded and pointed to his eye.

"Think! No wait, that's not right. See!" *This one was a toughie!* "Eye?" I guessed.

He touched his nose with a grin and held up two fingers.

"Second one!"

He drew a little heart over his chest.

"Boob! Heart! Nonononono, wait. Love!" I clapped with glee when he nodded.

Holding up three fingers, he was laughing so hard, I wasn't sure how I was gonna guess the third word. He pointed to me.

"Me?" I asked. He shook his head, pursed his lips and looked at me like I was stupid. "Hey, you're the one who sucks at this, not me. Gimme another clue!"

He sighed and pointed to himself.

I was more confused than ever. I rattled off everything that came to mind with every new gesture, "Chest? Shirt? Throat? Tantrum? Conniption? Christ, are you having a seizure? What the fuck?"

"*You!*" he shouted in exasperation, throwing his hands in the air.

I tilted my head, "Wait. What were the first two words again?"

He looked at me, shook his head with a smirk and sat on the bed again, leaning in closely. He tipped my chin up with his fingertip and covered my mouth with his. His breath was warm against my cheek as he exhaled and I slipped my arm around his neck, parting my lips slightly. His tongue slipped between them and ran along mine, before he withdrew it moments later and pulled away.

"You being here means so much to me, and I wish you

were sober so you'd remember this in the morning. God, I love you, Carly," his voice was barely a whisper as his eyes searched my face for reassurance.

Instead, hot tears filled my eyes and spilled over, running into my hair. I let out a little sob as relief flooded through me. I'd been fighting these same emotions for months and kept convincing myself it was nothing. "I love you, too," I finally managed to sputter.

His face lit up with a wide smile and he swiped the back of his fingers against each of my temples, wiping away my tears. He slanted his mouth over mine again and cupped my face in his strong hands. My fingers trembled as I ran them along his chiseled features. His kisses gave me butterflies and a yearning stirred within me I hadn't felt in a long time. I needed this man.

His mouth licked and suckled at the soft skin of my throat and collarbone as his hands pulled at the sheet, anxious to free my naked form from its linen prison.

"Too many clothes," I whispered in hungry anguish, as my wandering hands tugged at the hindrances.

He let go of me long enough to stand up and undress, something I watched every torturous second of. He kicked his shoes off and bent over, kissing me again. That familiar stubble brushed my chin and I moaned softly. He pulled his t-shirt over his head, tossing it to the floor at the foot of the bed. Hastily, he unbuckled his belt and yanked at the fly of his jeans, pulling them down over his hips in the process. The loose denim fell into a heap at his feet and he stood before me, naked in all his bare-skinned glory.

I gasped audibly. *Please dear God, don't let me be dreaming this.*

He laughed and leaned over again, "You're not dreaming, Carly."

Shit. Apparently I'd said that out loud. But before I could apologize, he consumed my mouth with his soft lips as he pulled back the covers and climbed into bed beside me. He hugged my body against him and rolled onto his back, taking me with him. I intertwined my legs with his as I lay across him, hungrily kissing his mouth. His large hands ran up the length of my ribs and I came alive at his touch. His skin was smooth and taut over his well-sculpted chest and I wasted no time in touching every inch of it. A low growl erupted in his throat when I raked my nails across his pecs and down his ribs.

I gasped in surprise when he slid his hands up my arms and quickly flipped me over, pinning my wrists above my head. Covering my body with his, he devoured my mouth again. I slipped one leg around his hips and pulled him against me, whimpering as his granite length pressed against areas of me that had gone ignored for far too long.

All it took was one pleading word and he slid himself inside me.

I let out a low moan and quivered as my long-neglected body adjusted to his size. He took his time and spent every agonizing minute with his eyes locked on mine as he began to rock his hips back and forth. After what seemed like only a few moments later, I began to tremble beneath his powerful frame as my climax overtook me. He locked his fingers with mine and covered my face in kisses as I reached the peak. I let out a strangled cry and buried my face in his neck. He came moments later and collapsed against me.

With sweaty skin and weary muscles, we replayed the moment several more times that night. We spent hours tasting and touching each other, exploring every mound and valley our bodies possessed. We made up for months of agonizing flirting and innuendos. As we lay there afterward, exhausted and sated, he hummed quietly in my ear and I ran my fingers lazily over his forearm.

I looked up at him from beneath sleepy, fluttery eyelashes and smiled as he met my gaze. When he lowered his face, I brushed my lips against his and sighed happily. He squeezed me tightly then relaxed against me as our tired bodies finally gave into sleep once again.

A few hours later, I woke up alone. The sun was high in the sky and cast short rays on the light brown carpet near the window. I knew the cruise ship had already left port. I picked up my phone from the nightstand and while I expected a text from Dave, the only one waiting for me was one from Josh.

> Sorry I didn't say goodbye. I'll call you when I get back. We need to talk. -jm

I didn't know what that was about, but hopefully it wasn't because of the situation with Dave. I knew the last thing any of them needed was tension within the group and I wasn't sure how my relationship with Dave might affect that. Our closeness in VIP hadn't seemed to bother Bobby, so that was a good sign, at least.

At the thought of Dave, I smiled involuntarily and nestled down into the covers further. With a catlike stretch, I moaned and breathed deeply, smelling the faint scent of his cologne still lingering on the sheets.

With the memories still fresh in my head, I ordered coffee from room service and drank it on the balcony. I knew in a few hours I would have to return home to Chicago, but until then, I would soak up the Florida sunshine without a worry in my head.

With the exception of why Dave didn't say goodbye.

Chapter 9

On the plane ride home from Miami, I began having second thoughts about getting involved with Dave. Regrets weren't my forte, but if I'd ever been close to feeling them, it was now. Aside from cursing my own intoxication, I wondered what kind of hornets' nest we had stirred up by doing what we'd done. Dave was friends with Josh after all, and there was still that elephant in the room every time Bobby and I were together. This thing had "cluster fuck" written all over it.

I nestled back in my seat with a heavy heart and turned my head, looking out the window as the sun set on the horizon. I closed my eyes and tried to catch a small nap since there'd been so little sleeping the night before, but I couldn't help fantasizing about the man who'd occupied my time instead. I heard the sound of his breath in my ear. I felt hands cupping my face as he kissed me. Everything about the previous night flooded my memory, and I couldn't think of anything else.

Except my nerves. Something didn't feel right.

I needed to learn how to be less scared.It had been months since my split with Trey and as much as I'd thought otherwise early on, I had accepted our divorce. Josh reassured me over a year ago that things would eventually fall into place and I was finally at a point where I believed him.

As far as Josh went, the less time I spent with him, the better. Temptation was too close for comfort, and I suspected if Abby hadn't already forbidden me from being friends with him, it wouldn't take much to push her over the edge. His remark when I fished for a compliment was probably a bit much *and* why did I even go fishing, for Christ's sake? I cringed as I recalled him undressing me when he took me back to my room. Distance was definitely called for. There were boundaries between us for a reason. Perhaps that's what his text was about . . . that he recognized it, too.

My head spun as I tried to come up with answers that continued to evade me. I finally gave up and drifted to a brief, fitful slumber; the hum of the airplane engine lulling me to sleep.

The loft was empty when I got home and I was grateful. Alejandro was probably at the office and, if I knew him, would be there for hours more. I hauled my bags to my room, tossed them on the floor, and closed the door with a click behind me. I kicked off my shoes and went to the bathroom, turning on the bathtub faucet at full blast. I dribbled a capful of bubble bath under the stream of water and let the tub fill as I got undressed. I dug the iPod out of my purse and plugged it into the speaker on the bathroom counter, then sunk into thirty gallons of bubbly heaven. Nothing felt better than soaking off the stink from traveling. There was just something emotionally cleansing about a hot shower or a long bath after a day of being stuck in an airplane. That was especially true now.

Emerging an hour later from the tub, I felt a little better about Miami. I was still scared and knew we would need to take it slow, but I decided to see where things went with Dave. I had no idea what might happen or what it would mean for either of us, but I decided worrying about it was pointless.

"I don't give a fuck, Geoffrey! I hired you to handle shit like this. Now*!*" I slammed the door behind me and flopped into the chair behind my desk, whirling around toward the window. I had a headache that stretched across my forehead, around the right side of my head, and into my neck. This job was great most days. Today wasn't one of them.

If I didn't fire my assistant by three o'clock, it would be a miracle. I had a huge meeting this week with Arturo, a well-known photographer that Susan had spent the last six months schmoozing to get him to do a guest pictorial in an upcoming issue. My meeting with him was "Crucial! Just *crucial*!" to landing the shoot, according to my boss. I'd worked with Arturo years ago, when I covered Fashion Week for the *Daily News* and admired the man greatly. I understood what needed to happen in my meeting and I was confident we'd get him without incident. That was until my assistant, Dipshit McDumbass, double-booked me to oversee a shoot with Big Stewie, a hot rap star currently surrounded in tabloid hoopla, whose interview was supposed to be featured in the holiday issue coming out in December. The shoot with Stewie was important to me as I'd fought tooth and nail with his agent to get the interview in the first place. Usually that sort of thing didn't fall under my responsibilities, but I called in a few favors when I heard he'd made the short list for upcoming issues. I couldn't afford to lose Stewie. Short of cloning me, I wasn't sure how Geoffrey was going to straighten this mess out, but with everything else on my mind lately, I lacked the focus required to figure it out myself.

As I willed myself not to murder my assistant, I looked out over Lake Michigan and the blinding glint of the sun on the water made me wish I was anywhere but at work today. Summer in Chicago was beautiful, and I normally loved my job, but these last few weeks were slowly picking away at my sanity.

Despite what happened in Miami, Dave hadn't returned my texts with more than a brief "yes," "no," or "I dunno." The only exception was a one-sentence text that simply said, "Gimme some time." It gave me a nauseous feeling in my stomach, and I had everything I could to keep my wits about me. Leaving without a goodbye was one thing—he could've been short on time, could've gotten busy with cruise stuff, anything—but to have second thoughts was something totally different. I never pegged him for a one-night stand guy, especially with his declaration of love. I hoped it was just stress about the upcoming summer tour, but seeing as how we hadn't gotten much chance to talk since the cruise, I couldn't be sure.

We had to talk. Soon.

Just as a new knot began to form in my neck, my cell phone vibrated on my desk and I reached for it without bothering to turn around.

Please let it be Dave.

I scrolled the trackball and clicked on the text message that had just come in. I sighed in disappointment.

`Still avoiding me? -jm`

I replied with the first thing that came to mind.

`Yes, but you won't go away. ;)`

A moment later my cell rang.

"I went away once. You're outta luck." I heard the creaking noise of a water bottle collapsing as he drank it dry.

"Twice, but who's counting?"

"Ouch! That stings, woman!" I heard him chuckle and then voices in the background interrupted him before he could say anything else.

"Who's that?" I asked.

"Bobby and Dave just came back in," he said. "Hang on a sec."

I could tell he'd covered up the phone, as I heard his muffled voice. I heard my name before there was a shuffle of the phone and Bobby's voice was in my ear.

"Hey, girl! Wassup?"

Disappointment washed over me again. *Why wouldn't Dave talk to me?*

"Work, work, and more work. How're you?" I tried to make small talk.

"Livin' the dream, baby. Livin' the dream."

"Hey, while I've got you on the phone, I wanted to thank you for picking up my tab for the Miami trip. The hotel was amazing." Since the vodka had other ideas that night, I hadn't gotten a chance to thank him for booking my plane ticket and covering the hotel expenses.

"No thanks necessary. Did you have a good time?" His tone was teasing, but I suspected he already knew what had taken place that night. He had been the only one to witness my moment with Dave at the bar, after all.

"I did. The party was great and the room was beautiful. Thanks again." I wasn't about to confirm anything with him about what happened. Thankfully, he changed the subject.

"So whatchu doin' talkin' to Josh? You got a little sum'in-sum'in I don't know about?" he baited me.

"Well, what am I supposed to do, Callahan? You don't answer your phone, anymore," I teased, in hopes that my joking tone would downplay the current situation.

"That hurts, girl. I'm wounded," he mocked a sniffle then whispered, "I'm bigger, you know."

I fought back a laugh, "Yeah, a bigger egomaniac. Give your boy his phone back, you letch."

"Your loss, babe." He made a clucking noise with his tongue then hollered to Josh. "Yo, Josh! She don' want me no more." When he handed over the phone, he said loudly enough for me to hear, "I dunno why, but she wants you."

I rolled my eyes as Josh got back on the phone.

"Okay, so since you're still avoiding me, I'll make it quick," he began. "Opening night for *One Night Stand* is now on June 4th. You'll be there, right?"

I nearly choked on my own spit at their choice for tour names. *Would Miami ever stop haunting me?* This man was going to drive me nuts, but if it meant being able to talk to Dave, then I would jump through fiery hoops. "Tell me where 'there' is and I'll be there."

"Dallas."

"All right." I scrawled a quick note on my desk calendar. "I'll do my best."

"Not your best, Carly. Be there," Josh commanded. "We

still need to talk."

Oy.

We hung up and I spun my chair back around, trying to focus on work again, my mind drifting in fifteen different directions, none of them associated with *Beguile.*

After a sleepless night, I rolled over and texted Geoffrey the next morning to tell him I wouldn't be in at my normal time. I was exhausted and overworked and while I hated the term "mental health day," it was exactly what I needed. The headache from yesterday had lessened to a dull roar, but I had the remnant nausea from the migraine threatening to strike any minute. I'd already clocked almost forty hours this week and it was only Wednesday. The rest of the week was scheduled to be slow and honestly, I could take the whole day off if I wanted to, but I needed to stay on Geoffrey until he sorted out the double-booking nightmare. He was a good assistant, but had a bad habit of doing things in his own time. I couldn't afford for that to happen right now. Going in later to be an annoying presence in his world, reminding him who was in charge, should be enough. Until then, however, I would try and sleep.

The sun began to blaze in the sky, casting a sharp stream of light directly into the mirror above the dresser, so I got up and pulled down my blackout shades. Alex left for work a half-hour earlier and, thanks to six-inch concrete floors, the apartment was silent. Every once in a while, an errant horn would drift upward from the street and vaguely echo between the brick and glass that formed our home. The noise may have bothered some people. To me, it was a lullaby. I crawled back into bed, pulled the covers around me and drifted in and out of sleep for another couple of hours.

A little before nine, my phone chirped. I blindly retrieved it from my nightstand and with one eye read the "good morning" text that had become habitual for Josh. I rarely responded because the texts usually came right about the time I was headed to work. Despite his matrimonial boundary, there was something I cherished about the fact that he took time to tell me good morning before he addressed the rest of the world on Twitter. Keeping things in perspective, I also appreciated Bobby's goodnight texts that came long after he bid the Twitterverse adieu.

I pulled another pillow behind my head, propping myself up a little bit in bed and opened my Twitter app. I didn't follow a lot of people, so it was easy to scroll back through my timeline to see what I'd missed overnight. Bobby had started giving people shout-outs in the wee hours of the morning. Josh mentioned he was heading to rehearsal and Dave just Tweeted a picture of himself holding up a giant smoothie. I smiled and ran my fingertip lightly down the screen. Whether he was having second thoughts or not, I missed him.

I stretched then snuggled down into my covers farther. I refreshed my timeline and snorted at Bobby's latest tweet where he called out the batshit crazies for having camped out all day yesterday at the arena. He did it in his own subtle way, of course, but did it nonetheless. A few minutes later, Marc replied to him with typical snark. Everybody was up and getting their day started.

Me? Not so much. I yawned, set my phone on the nightstand and drifted back to sleep.

I was awoken late-morning by a text from Geoffrey.

Big Stewie's ppl called. Postponed

`mtg til nxt Thurs.`

I glanced at the calendar and sighed. I didn't like it, but I was stuck.

`Fine. I'm taking the rest of today off. Let Susan know. Thx.`

The rescheduled meeting would mean I couldn't be in Dallas for the first show of *One Night Stand*. I told Josh I'd be there. So much for me trying to show him I wasn't avoiding him.

Josh called me when they broke for lunch around noon.

"Hey, beautiful," he greeted me cheerfully. "What's goin' on?"

"Oh, you know me. Just sitting here pining away and wondering when I'd hear from my favorite rock star," I teased, purposefully ignoring his old nickname for me. Keeping things light-hearted had so far been the best plan of attack. We still hadn't had the talk he'd been pressuring me about since Miami, so it seemed to be working. "I'm trying to enjoy my day off, dork. How're you?"

"It's hot. It's rainy. And I'm ready to kill my band mates for waiting 'til the last damn minute to memorize the set. Other than that, it's peachy."

"So then now probably wouldn't be the time to tell you I have bad news about opening night, huh?" I closed my eyes and waited for his disappointed grumble.

"No. No, no, no! Aww, Coop, please don't tell me you're cancelling."

"I'm sorry, babe." I really did feel bad. Now that I could hear his reaction, I was more torn up about my meeting than before. I did want to maintain some distance, but I hated that I couldn't be there opening night. I missed the guys and it hurt me not to be able to support them like I wanted to. "I wish I could be there, but I've got a shoot with Big Stewie that day and I can't get away."

He sighed and his voice grew soft. "It's all right. I know you've got work." He didn't even try to hide the disappointment.

"I'll make it up to you. I promise."

"I know," he replied. I heard someone holler in the background. "Look, I gotta go. Try and see when you can come out, okay?"

"Oka . . ." I began but heard the silence on the other end of the line and knew he'd already disconnected.

When I didn't get my "good morning" text the next day, I wondered if Josh had forgotten or if he was still sulking about opening night. Either way, there was nothing I could do. Besides, it wasn't like Josh was the only South Station Boy ignoring me. I sent Dave a text earlier in the week telling him "good luck" at rehearsal. He'd yet to reply. Even for as brief as his messages usually were, he always replied.

By mid-afternoon, I'd driven myself crazy with paranoid scenarios and texted Dave again.

> I think my phone has been acting up because I didn't get a reply from you the other day. Miss you.

I nibbled on my lip and ran my finger around the silicone phone case waiting for it to vibrate under my touch. I didn't have to wait long.

> Your phone's fine. I didn't text you.

What the hell? Dave was always the one to say whatever was on his mind. It was one of the things I appreciated most about him. So what's with the games now?

`Is everything ok?`

I waited a full ten minutes before I finally gave up and tossed my phone onto the desk. Whatever was wrong, it was clear he didn't plan on discussing it with me. Geoffrey interrupted my pity party a few moments later to remind me of a meeting with Susan. Out of stubbornness, I left my phone in my office. I may have been sitting in the board room, but my mind, however, stayed with the phone.

"He hasn't talked to me since Thursday, Alex. I can't sleep. I'm half-sick with worry, and the stress is killing me." I stabbed at the eggplant Parmesan on my plate. Alejandro slaved away all day as he tried to perfect one of Marc's favorite dishes. "*You never know when I might need to ply a man with Italian food,*" he told me earlier when I commented about the smell of oregano drifting through the apartment.

Alex leaned back in the chair, his arm crossed in front of him, swirling a glass of wine. He took a sip and set the glass down. "Carly, you can't keep getting freaked out like this. He's got a crazy schedule right now. Tour starts in four days. Give him 'til Friday and if he still hasn't changed his attitude, then we'll fly down to . . ." he pursed his lips as he struggled to remember, ". . . well, wherever the hell they are on Friday."

"Baton Rouge," I mumbled.

"Fine. We'll fly down to Baton Rouge on Friday."

I sighed. That was five days from now and I honestly didn't know if I could last another five days without hearing from Dave. There were bad moods and attitude. I was used to those. I had been best friends with a gay man for the last several decades, after all. But this felt like something else. I dragged the bite of eggplant I'd just speared through the tomato sauce, but didn't eat it. I tossed my fork to the plate and pushed it away.

"Oh hell no! You aren't wasting that! Give it here," Alex scolded me as he reached for my plate and scraped it onto his. "God, you really are a mess if you're not eating my eggplant. What's going on between you guys, anyway? "

"Apparently, nothing." I forgot I hadn't told Alex about sleeping with Dave in Miami.

Alejandro and I had a standing rule that we never discussed our sex lives (or, most of the time, lack thereof) with each other. I didn't care one way or another what he knew about me, but since he had issues with me discussing my vagina or the recreational activities in which it partook, he chose not to know who I slept with or how.

"You're gonna stress your way into a size four if you're not careful," he paused, looked at the heaping amount of pasta, eggplant, and cheese on his plate. "On second thought, maybe you're onto something." He smirked and looked over at me. His sense of humor was usually something I enjoyed the most about Alex, but tonight, I just didn't feel like laughing. He scowled at me, insulted.

"Oh, for Christ's sake, woman!—go book us two tickets to Louisiana. You're making me stabby!"

I looked at him, sighed, and decided he was right. Even if I did hear from Dave before Friday, I needed to get away. Other than the overnight trip to Miami, all the travel I'd done so far that year was for work. I needed some fun.

It had been almost a week since I'd heard from Dave. From any of the guys, now that I thought about it. That was out of character for them. Usually Josh would send me at least one text a day bitching about "the amateurs he was forced to work with," tongue-in-cheek, of course. I didn't ask Alex if he'd heard from Marc. I guess, down deep, if he had, I didn't want to know about it. It was easier thinking that there'd been some sort of cellular outage that affected only their four phones and I had nothing to worry about. I hadn't sent a text to Dave since Sunday morning. There was no point in sending them if he wasn't going to respond. I also tried backing out of the trip to Louisiana with Alejandro, but he wouldn't hear of it. Said if he'd had to put up with me acting like a bigger baby than Josh, then he was forcing me to go to the Bayou, as he so sweetly nicknamed our destination.

I got a call from Big Stewie's publicist Tuesday morning. They were postponing the shoot again. He, apparently, didn't want to come all the way to Chicago for a "ten-minute Olan Mills stunt and some small talk." To say that I was irritated with his arrogance, especially considering what it had cost me this week, was an understatement. I told Monique, his publicist, that we'd be more than happy to come to New York to do the interview and photo shoot. Ass kissing was a sport I greatly despised, but I'd had to do my fair share of it over the years. This was nothing new. She seemed emotionless about the hitch in plans, but I knew it couldn't be easy having her job. She assured me that she would be in touch as soon as she knew what Stewie's schedule was. I hung up the phone and growled loudly at the four walls of my office.

I decided to walk to the deli, a couple blocks away, to grab lunch. It was a beautiful day—normally one that would've led me to take an extra half-hour and do some retail therapy on the Mag Mile, but I'd been fighting some sort of bug for the last couple days. The last thing I needed was the hot summer sun leaving me dehydrated and urpy. As it was, I'd be lucky to choke down a cold drink.

I felt my forehead as I waited for my order number to be called. It felt a little warm, but I wasn't sure if that was from the walk or if I had a low-grade fever. I leaned against the divider and sipped the lemonade in my hand until my chicken salad was ready.

I grabbed a table near the window and nibbled at my salad while scrolling through my Twitter timeline. It was filled with tour excitement. I swallowed my bite and called Alejandro.

"Hey gorgeous," he greeted me. Normally, he'd fire off something about making it quick, but since Dave had started acting like a douche toward me, he'd softened his approach a little.

"Let's go to Dallas." I wasted no time in getting to the point.

"Are you kidding me?"

"Nope. I can't wait 'til Friday."

"Christ, woman, you're killing me," he sighed. "Wait. Does this mean I can return my banjo and skip the Bayou?" Alejandro's voice was bubbling with excitement. Or sarcasm. With Alex, it's hard to tell.

"Depends on how Dallas goes," I replied. "But you can probably ditch the banjo, at least."

"Thank God. Those damn strings would wreck my nails."

I love having a gay bestie.

Chapter 10

"Honey, you look like hell." Alejandro patted the back of my hand as I clutched the arms of my seat on the plane. I didn't doubt him. I *felt* like hell. Thunderstorms in Dallas had delayed us twice before we could even leave O'Hare and the turbulence had sent me racing for the lavatory the second the seatbelt lights went off. "Do you want me to get you a ginger ale?"

I nodded and Alex pushed the button above me to summon the flight attendant. I closed my eyes and leaned back against the head rest. A few moments later, I heard the crack of a can opening and Alex nudged my lips with the straw. Taking a slow sip, I opened my eyes and looked over at him.

"Thank you for taking care of me," I said, gratefully. "You're like my own little nursemaid. I could get used to it."

"Yep. I'm a regular Florence Nightengay, but don't you dare get used to it. I'm the diva, remember?" Alejandro winked at me then patted a cocktail napkin against my forehead and scowled. "Girl, if you came out here to woo a man, we're gonna need to hit a MAC counter the minute our feet hit that Texas dirt."

I smiled weakly, acknowledging his attempt at humor, but I was cut short as a wave of nausea hit again. I made it to the bathroom just in time as I lost the ginger ale and the crackers I'd been nibbling since we'd begun circling the Dallas skies ten minutes earlier. When all further threats of vomiting seemed to have subsided, I rinsed out my mouth and dampened a paper towel with cold water, pressing it against the back of my neck. I closed the lid on the toilet and sat down, pressing my face against the cold plastic wall next to the sink.

I hated being sick. In fact, I couldn't remember the last time I'd even been this sick. I wasn't running a fever, thank God, but that didn't do much to console my misery. I prided myself on how well I took care of my health. I ate well and the minute I felt myself get so much as the sniffles, I popped herbal immunity boosters and drank my weight in orange juice. I'd been doing that all week and none of it helped this time. Stupid stress! I had to face it; this bug was kicking my ass.

I made it back to my seat just in time for the seatbelt sign to come back on and the captain to announce that we'd finally been cleared for landing. Ninety minutes and two more mad dashes to the bathroom later, we checked into our hotel downtown. Lacking the strength to do much else, I kicked off my shoes and climbed into bed the minute we got to our suite. I let Alejandro take care of letting the guys know we were here.

A few hours later, I awoke to someone's fingertips brushing my hair away from my face. My eyes fluttered open and I was greeted with a pair of handsome brown eyes.

"Not feeling so hot, huh?"

Forgetting the last three weeks of hell he put me through, I flung my arms around Dave's shoulders and hugged him.

"Hey, hey, hey. It's okay. You're gonna be all right." His giant arms squeezed me briefly before he pulled away to look at me.

My eyes welled up at his reassurance and I managed a nod.

"You got the stomach flu? Or . . . what's goin' on?"

"I dunno. Been urpy for a few days. Thought maybe it was food poisoning or a reaction to stress, but the minute we were airborne, I couldn't keep anything down. I wanted to surpri . . ."

"Shhh . . . it's okay."

"You stopped answering my texts," I recalled solemnly, as I laid my head back down against the pillow.

Dave's eyes shifted away and he nodded, "I know."

"What's going on?"

He shook his head and frowned. After a small pause he spoke, "Miami. It fucked me up." He looked up again.

Propping myself up on my pillow, I sighed. "Dave, if our relationship is an issue, then we need to work on it."

A frown put a deep wrinkle in his forehead and he gave me a blank stare.

"What? Why are you looking at me like that?"

"That's an understatement," he replied somberly. "Look, I think you've got some stuff to work out on your own."

"On my own? Dave, what are you talking about?"

"You really don't know?"

"Don't know what!?" He was talking in circles and it was

pissing me off.

"Damn, Carly," he said, standing up quickly. "I dunno what's worse; you acting like you don't remember or the fact that it's not a big deal to you."

"What the hell are you talking about, Dave? Of course I remember. And it's a *very* big deal to me. Miami was amazing."

With a flare of his nostrils, he shook his head. "I can't do this."

I raised my eyebrows and blinked several times, trying to digest his words. "This? This conversation? This relationship? This tour? What?"

"Everything to do with you."

I felt like the wind had been knocked out of me.

When I didn't say anything, he held his hands up, "Carly, you asked."

"Indeed, I did. I gave you a way out, didn't I?" My nausea was gone now and I was filled with anger. "So, Miami? What was that? You told me you wanted me. Was that a lie?"

He dropped his eyes again.

"Really, David?" My tone was incredulous. I got up from the bed and began pacing. I was too mad to cry, but the unshed tears burned my eyes and I clenched my teeth to keep from exploding. I stared at him, waiting for an explanation.

"I *wanted* there to be an 'us,' Carly . . . but now?" his voice drifted off and I was met with a cold shrug.

"Awesome."

"I don't know what *you're* getting so pissed off about." His tone was defensive and I didn't understand why. He closed his eyes and huffed angrily, his nostrils flaring again.

"Leave, Dave. Just go."

"If I go, I'm not coming back. I don't have time for drama, Carly. I mean it. This?" he pointed back and forth between the both of us, "is why I don't date." He paused and waited for me to say something. When I didn't, he said softly, "If I leave, I'm gone."

I walked to the door and opened it. "You're already gone, Dave."

Alejandro looked up from his computer when he heard my voice. His eyes followed Dave across the room as he left without another word, shutting the hallway door behind him with a firm crack.

"Um. What the fuck just happened?" Alex asked with a rise of concern in his voice.

"Hell if I know."

"Did we just fly all the way to Dallas for no reason?"

"It would appear that one of us did." I replied, before I pulled a bottle of water from the minibar and flopped down on the couch next to Alejandro, who stared at me like I'd grown a second head.

My forehead was throbbing and my shoulder muscles ached from all the vomiting earlier. I took a couple sips of water before I capped the bottle and laid my head on Alex's leg, letting tears of humiliation spill down my face. Thankfully, he had the compassion not to push the issue and I fell asleep to him stroking my hair.

The sun was deep in the sky when I woke up. The room was quiet, and I suspected Alejandro had gone to see Marc. I stretched and sighed as I remembered my conversation with Dave just a few hours earlier.

Part of me was disgusted with myself for having trusted him. The other part of me knew he was stressed and I suspected our whole argument was a reaction to that stress. Both sides considered, I had just enough self-respect not to call him and beg him to work things out. If he wanted to be gone, then he could stay gone. I didn't have the energy to go chasing after anybody anymore.

I huffed in frustration as I threw some clothes on and texted Alejandro to find out where he was. A moment later, he walked in with a bag of food, his phone in his hands.

"Sorry, girl," he said apologetically. "I was gonna leave a note and forgot." He opened the bag and pulled out a couple cartons with little metal handles and red hanzi scrawled on the side. A small clamshell container came out next, followed by two plastic bowls with lids. He handed me one of them and a spoon.

"You feeling any better?"

Though my eyes were swollen from crying and I probably looked like a hell, I nodded.

"Think you can handle some soup?"

I closed my eyes and flashed a grateful smile. Alejandro was an angel.

"Yes, love. I'm starving. Thank you." I carefully peeled back the lid and took a small sip from the spoon, letting the warm liquid flood my throat. Food had never tasted so good.

He tipped his head in a "you're welcome" gesture and grabbed one of the take-out cartons, unfolding the top and digging in with a pair of chopsticks. With a mouthful of what I suspected was Mongolian beef, he started the inquisition.

"So, you gonna tell me what that thing was earlier?"

"With Dave?" I replied.

"No, with my mother," he snipped with a chuckle. "Yes, with Dave. What was that about?"

I recalled our rule about no sex talk and just shook my head. "You don't want to hear about it."

"If I didn't, I wouldn't have asked. Now spill it, girl." He took another bite of his dinner, retrieving a piece of onion on his lip with a flick of his tongue.

"It has to do with that icky vag stuff you hate hearing about."

Alejandro' eyes bugged out and he swallowed quickly.

"NUH. UH! When?!"

I sighed. "Miami."

"You slept with him? I didn't think things were *that* serious. Shit, girl!"

"Well Christ, Alex. Women get horny too, you know."

"Ew. Stop. Skip that part, please." He clamped his eyes shut and fanned his hand in front of him as if waving away a bad smell.

"You asked," I mumbled. "Anyway . . . it doesn't matter now."

"Right?" Alejandro said, recovering from his momentary gross-out. "Men are a dime a dozen. Go out and find you a new one. It's not like you're married to him or God forbid . . ." He stopped, dropped his chopsticks and turned to me, his eyes wide.

"What?"

"How long have you been sick?"

"What's with the theatrics?" I had acclimated to over-the-topness early in life having a gay best friend, but I was certain Alex was going to swallow his tongue in a second.

"How long!?"

"I dunno," I said, frustrated. "A couple days."

"And no fever?" He clamped his hand over my forehead, much to my irritation. "And you're fine now that it's nighttime? The trip to Miami was what, three weeks ago?" The inquisition didn't stop. "Girl, that's it!"

"That's what?"

"You're PG!"

"Oh for fuck's sake, Alex. Get real." I'd had five pregnancies and I'd never once thrown up. His suggestion was ridiculous and I told him so. "I'm *not* pregnant. Now, will you get off me?" I pushed him away.

"Ridiculous, huh?" He raised his eyebrow at me. "So then you used protection in Miami? And there's nothing to worry about then, right?"

I struggled hard to remember. Damn the vodka! Did we? Were we smart about it? I couldn't remember. My silence was telling.

"Jesus, Carly! You're smarter than that!"

I didn't argue.

"We have to go get a pregnancy test."

"What? Now? Here?"

"What, you wanna wait to see if a kid walks out of your . . ." Alex curled up his lip in disgust and pointed toward my lady bits in a swirly motion.

"We're like a thousand miles from home. Does it really have to be right now?"

"Well," he began, his voice dripping with condescension, "we don't *have* to do it now. I mean, you know, with the potential father nearby so you can let him know in person rather than, you know, while he's on the road in a different city with *his fucking band*." Alex's voice rose and he blinked repeatedly.

"Uh, I ain't tellin' anybody shit."

He blinked again and set the carton of Chinese food on the coffee table, turning toward me.

"He *is* the only possible father, right?"

"Of course! Ugh! I'm not even pregnant!" *I hoped.*

"Then explain."

"Explain what? He said if he left he wasn't coming back. He isn't gonna find out anything."

"Carly, you can't *not* tell him. This is a whole different scenario than some unreturned texts."

I set the soup on the table in front of me, sloshing a little bit over the side as I returned its lid in my haste. I sighed loudly and shook my head.

"I mean it, honey. There's a time and a place for stubbornness. This isn't it," Alex pointed out gently.

This wasn't about stubbornness.

Mostly.

"We don't even know if I'm pregnant, so just stop! Okay?" My frustration was obvious and I didn't care. "When I get home, I'll make an appointment if I haven't gotten my period and then I'll deal with it."

"So you *are* late!"

"Get your nose outta my uterus, Alejandro!" I got up, grabbed my soup and the other carton of food and retreated to my room, leaving Alex in the living room with his lip curled up at the mention of my feminine business.

I slept fitfully that night. I managed to escape the nightmares, unless you count the pregnancy dreams that peppered my sleep, but I woke up a little after nine the next morning much less rested than usual. With my eyes barely open I reached over to the nightstand to check my phone for missed messages and knocked a small paper bag onto the floor. I leaned over and picked it up. With curiosity I pulled out its contents and groaned in frustration.

I'd recognize that familiar pink box anywhere. Alejandro must've gone to the pharmacy sometime during the night and picked up the test. *So much for keeping his nose out of my uterus.* I tossed it aside and picked up my phone instead.

Scrolling through the messages, I took inventory of what had gone on in my absence the last twenty-four hours. There were three messages from Josh asking how I felt, two messages from Callahan—both impatiently telling me to get my "fine ass" to the venue, and an event notification from Geoffrey alerting me to a departmental meeting next week. The last text was from Alejandro – "Just pee and get it the fuck over with."

ARGH!

I threw the covers back and stomped off to the bathroom with the slender box in my hand. I muttered under my breath the whole time.

Fine.

I'll pee.

Then what?

Beg forgiveness?

Go on with my life?

Wait for my body to fail me again?

Stupid queen getting his nose all up in my Kool-Aid by buying me a fucking pregnancy test. Fuck him. Fuck him, fuck Dave, and fuck this.

There! You happy now? I peed.

I replaced the cap on the test, flushed the toilet and tossed the stick on the counter before stripping off my clothes and climbing into the hottest shower I could stand. With the spray beating on my neck, I let the tension of the last few days wash down the drain. Just as I rinsed the conditioner out of my hair, a strong wave of nausea swept over me and I barely reached the toilet before retching.

With my cheek against the cool porcelain of the tank, I flushed and wiped my mouth with a washcloth. When I could lift my head again, I glanced up at the counter and saw the tip of the test stick hanging out over the edge.

No time like the present, I thought.

Groaning, I reached over and pulled it down. I leaned back against the cool tile wall, sighed heavily and turned it over so I could see the little window.

One line.

And a very faint, very light, second one.

Fuck.

"So?"

Alejandro pounced on me the minute I walked out of my room. He was sitting at the table reading the newspaper and picking at a bowl of fruit.

I held up one finger, poured myself a cup of coffee and sat down beside him. I picked up a piece of toast off his plate and brought one knee up, propping it between myself and the table.

Alex watched every move I made, but to his credit, he waited patiently for me to speak.

I was halfway through my cup of coffee and gobbled

down a piece of toast before I indulged him with a simple nod.

He blinked several times and put down his fork.

"And it's Dave's?"

"No. It's another immaculate conception," I snarled. "Prepare yourself for the second coming of Christ."

"Really, Carly? This attitude isn't becoming," Alex chastised me. "I'm just trying to make sense of it all, okay? You're the one who's been holding out on all the details that you've been privy to all this time."

I mumbled an apology and took another sip of my coffee.

"You know, you should probably switch to decaf."

"And you should probably be thankful I'm not throwin' back shots of Jäger," I grumbled. "I'll do all the right things later but for now? The fact that I'm not in the bathroom clutching a bottle of booze and a straight razor should be a sign of my progress in the acceptance part of all this, 'kay?"

Alejandro pursed his lips and gave a small huff.

"Just gimme time, Alex. That's all I'm asking."

Before he could answer, my phone rang. Even from the other room, I recognized Josh's ringtone and my head rolled back as I closed my eyes. *Not right now.*

I let it ring.

I could feel Alex's side-eyed glare.

I ignored him. And the phone.

"You gonna answer that?"

"Nope." My eyes remained closed.

"Why the hell not? It could be Dave."

"It's not."

Alejandro crossed the room and reached inside my door, picking my phone up off the nightstand. Seeing Josh's name and picture on the screen for incoming calls, he looked at me pointedly and answered it.

"Goddammit, Alex!" I growled, getting up quickly.

"Yeah, Josh. Hang on. She's right here." He covered up the phone and pointed at me. "You *need* to talk to him."

I clenched my teeth and in a whisper, scolded Alejandro. "You need to learn to mind your own goddamn business. I don't want to talk to anybody right now!"

"This isn't about *you,* Carly," he said in a matching tone and with determination, he thrust the phone toward me. "Fucking talk to him."

I grabbed the phone and smacked the back of Alejandro's head as he passed by me.

"Hey, Josh."

"Jesus, Mary, and Joseph, woman! You're tough to get ahold of!" Josh exclaimed.

"I know. I'm sorry," I instantly felt bad. "I've been sick since we got here. What's up?" Ignoring Alex's snort, I went into my room and shut the door.

"Can you come to the arena?" he asked, anxiety speckling his voice. "We . . . we need to talk."

"Yeah, we'll be there by the time you guys get out of your fan meets," I explained.

"No, I mean earlier," he said. "Can you be here before lunch?"

"God, Josh. You're scaring me. What's going on?"

"Can you?" he persisted.

"Yeah," I said, glancing at my watch. "I'll change and take a cab over. Gimme an hour?"

"Thank you," he said with relief. "Call me when you get here and I'll send somebody to the gate to get you."

"Okay," I replied. "Are you okay, Josh?"

"Yeah. I'll be fine."

I hung up the phone and opened my door. Alex had retreated to his room and had his door closed. I crossed the room and pounded on the door.

He opened it and braced himself on the door handle. Before he could say anything, I let him have it.

"First of all, Alejandro, we need to get a couple things clear." I shook my finger in his face. "My uterus and all its happenings are *my* business. You got it? Whatever I do, don't do, or even ponder doing are up to *me*. Do I make myself clear?"

"Crystal," he responded.

"Secondly, what the fuck is going on with Josh? Why the sudden urgency to talk to me and what do you know about it?"

A flash of guilt passed over his face but he quickly covered it up. "You've been avoiding him and he *needs* to talk to you."

"I know *that* much. I'm talking about the whole 'this isn't about you' shit you flipped me before I got on the phone. What is going on?"

"Carly," he crossed his arms as he began. I hated when he started out a conversation like this. It almost always assured me I wasn't going to like what he has to say. "I know right now, you've got a giant pile of shit to work through, but sometimes you tend to get a little . . ." he paused and I knew the worst was about to come. "I dunno, narcissistic, I guess? And you forget that other people have problems, too."

"Narcissistic?" Alex had *never* referred to me like that before. I was taken aback.

He shook his head and put his hand on my arm. “Not all the time and not to an extreme, so please don’t take it wrong. It’s just that, right now, Josh’s got some pretty heavy stuff he’s dealing with. And honestly, he’s been dealing with it for a couple months now, and he’s tried to talk to you about it, but you haven’t been listening. You won’t call him or return his texts or emails, and when he tried to talk to you in Miami, you ended up getting drunk.”

I was silent. What could I possibly say?

“Honey, just get dressed and go over there. He’ll explain it all.”

I nodded and turned but stopped. With as much humility as I could muster, I apologized. “I’m sorry if I’ve neglected you or him, Alex. You’re right and I’ll try to do better.”

“I know you will.” He flashed a reassuring smile at me. “I’ve got tough skin, girl. It’s okay. Him? Not so much.”

I lowered my head and gave a slight nod, but I didn’t know what I could do to help Josh through whatever was going on. Being the ex-fiancé didn’t exactly put me in the best position to offer a supportive shoulder. Abby would, no doubt, have a lot to say about my involvement in whatever Josh was dealing with.

Chapter 11

"I'M HERE AND THESE ASSHOLES AT THE GATE WON'T let me in." My frustration with arena security was obvious when I called Josh. The rainy weather didn't help my mood. The gorilla assigned to this particular entrance glared at me with nostrils flared. I glared back from under my umbrella.

"I know," he replied. "They're takin' their job pretty seriously. Sorry. I'll send Lamar out."

The big bodyguard hurried across the parking lot a few minutes later and with barely more than a hello, he led me to the shiny Prevost bus Josh was calling home for the summer. Just as we got to the buses, the door flew open and Dave stormed out, slamming the door behind him and stomped off.

Uh oh.

As he passed me, our eyes met and he glared.

I froze in place.

"Oh good. You're here." Sarcasm dripped from his words like venom. He jerked his head away with a loud snuff and a roll of his eyes before he took off in a dead run toward the building entrance, water kicking up off his shoes as he ran.

What. The. Fuck?

A moment later, Josh opened his bus door and raised his hand in a wave.

"Hey, beautiful!" Josh called out, a smile painted on his face as if his band mate hadn't just stormed out the door in a full tantrum. With a kiss to the cheek, he welcomed me on board and dismissed Lamar, who left with barely a perceptible nod.

"Did I come at a bad time?" I inquired as I sat down on the sofa and he went to the counter and finished smearing mayo on his sandwich.

"Huh?" Josh pretended not to know what I was talking about.

"Dave. You know, tattooed, muscly guy . . . just blew through here like a tornado, leaving piss and vinegar in his wake?"

Josh shrugged. "Hell, it's always a bad time these days. Don't worry about it." He put the second slice of bread on the sandwich and took a giant bite.

"That'll guarantee I'm gonna worry about it."

"Well, don't," he reassured me. He swallowed the bite and offered the sandwich to me. I shook my head and he took another bite. "He's been acting like an ass since the cruise," he said, with his mouth full.

"You don't know what's wrong?" I asked.

"Not a clue. He stomps off when I ask, and he sure-as-hell ain't offering anything on his own." He looked at me then shrugged. Setting the sandwich down on the table, he reached into the fridge and grabbed two beers, offering me one.

Shit.

"Do you have water?" I asked, declining the beer.

"Huh? Oh. Yeah," Josh replied, putting the bottle back and grabbing a bottle of Fiji instead. "Sorry . . . forgot you've been sick."

Whew. Bullet dodged.

I uncapped the water and drank a few sips as he sat down at the table and picked up his sandwich again.

"Okay, so what's going on, Josh?" I questioned him, hoping to distract him from the fact that I turned down alcohol—something he'd never seen me do before. "Why did I have to come over here right this second?"

In an apparent recollection of our phone call, he scowled and stopped chewing, pushing his sandwich away. With a mouthful of lunchmeat and bread, he took a long drink from his bottle and swallowed hard.

He took a couple breaths and finally looked up at me. "Carly, when we broke up, was it solely because you wanted me to pursue my career?"

I was caught off guard and wrinkled my eyebrows in confusion. "Yeah. Why?"

"It didn't have anything to do with me being egotistical? Or selfish? Or an attention whore? Or anything else?"

"Josh, you're one of the biggest attention whores I know," I said, grinning at him, "but that isn't a reason to break up. It's who you are and part of the reason people love you. Besides, we all have our moments of selfishness." I crooked my head, "What's this about?"

He looked down and picked at the label on his beer.

When he met my gaze again, his eyes glistened with unshed tears.

"Josh?"

He cleared his throat and without a word, he stood up, reached into a drawer and pulled out a manila envelope. Handing it to me, he leaned back against the counter, crossed one ankle in front of the other and waited for me to open it.

I reached inside and pulled out the papers enclosed.

In bold letters that stood out from the page were the words, "**Superior Court of California, County of Los Angeles**." I scanned the pages and looked up at Josh.

"Is this what I think it is?"

He raised his beer in salute and gave me a wry smile before taking a big chug.

"Oh my God, Josh! When?" I was stunned.

He reached over and pointed at the date stamped at the top of the first page.

"Last week?"

"Well, that's when she filed," he explained. "They served me this morning, but she's been gone since the beginning of May."

"May?!" my voice squeaked in surprise. "You've known since May and you didn't tell me?"

"You haven't exactly been 'available to take my call,' now have you?" He did air quotes around the words in my outgoing voicemail message.

"But I was in Miami. We could've talked then," I countered, trying to relinquish a portion of my guilt.

"I didn't want to drop that on you that night. I wanted you to enjoy the party. It's what you came down there for. Besides, you were a bit preoccupied."

I felt an inch tall. I understood now why Alex had been so upset with me. He must've known all this time and didn't want to betray Josh's trust. I was such an asshole.

"Josh, I'm so sorry," I stood and pulled him into a hug. He wrapped his arms around my waist and held me tightly against him. I felt his body melt into mine as he let go of the pent-up pain.

After a few moments passed, he pulled back and wiped his eyes on the sleeve of his t-shirt. "You didn't know. You couldn't have known."

"Still." I recognized the pain in his expression and remembered what I went through with Trey. "Honey, what happened?"

"Who knows?" he gestured loudly with his arms and splashed beer on his arm. Without stopping, he switched which hand held the bottle and wiped his damp wrist on his shorts. "She threw out all the shit about being selfish and self-centered early on, but the last fight we had, before she moved out, she told me she was tired of not living up to my expectations. She was sick of living with a ghost, which I'm assuming referred to you."

"Me? What the hell do I have to do with it?"

"She's always had a problem with you, Coop." I could hear the heaviness in his tone and immediately felt guilty that I'd held such power over their marriage. "You getting our wedding invitation? That was her trying to lay claim to me. I would have *never* hurt you like that. You have to believe me."

Down deep, I'd always known it was her. It was nice to finally have confirmation, though, it didn't make me feel any better.

"She said she couldn't ever give me what I wanted."

I tilted my head, "She thinks you want me?"

"No clue."

"Or could she be talking about having kids?"

"I dunno. I mean, we talked about it a lot, but she never really seemed that broken up about not having them. Not as much as I was, at least. She always said it just meant it wasn't the right time, what with our careers being so busy." Josh had never hidden his desire for a large family, and I knew how much it must've hurt him for her not to want kids as badly as he did.

"What about the band?" I hoped I wouldn't have to carry all of the blame. "Did she have issues with the reunion?"

He answered with a shrug of his shoulders. "I always asked for her input before we did anything with the group. Always! Specifically made sure it was okay with her to do a tour and appearances and everything."

"And she gave you permission?"

"With almost everything."

"Almost everything?"

"Well, she hated the spring tour. She complained that it took me away from home for too long," he commented. "But she took time off, packed her bags and came along. We had a great time. Then we got back and it all went to hell from there."

"Fights? Name calling? What?"

"Nah. None of that," he said. He finished his beer, reached in the fridge for another and popped off the cap. "Just distance. She went back to New York to visit her folks in March. That's when she found out they were splitting up. That didn't help."

I recalled my faux pas back in April, when I visited Abby

and Josh, and brought up her parents in conversation. That aside, she'd definitely seemed a little disengaged from our conversation, but I had assumed it was more because of the present company than from something wrong in their marriage. Obviously, that was more the case than I'd ever suspected.

"Josh, I'm so sorry if I ever gave her any indication that I was a threat to your marriage. I would never do anything to—."

"—It doesn't matter, Coop. It's over." He shrugged, his shoulders sagging in defeat. "Besides, this has always been *her* issue, not yours."

I sighed and reached out, taking his hand in mine. He immediately linked fingers with me. His pain wasn't unfamiliar to me and I hated that he was going through this.

"Josh, what can I do?" I would do whatever it took to make things right.

He paused for a moment then brought the back of my hand to his lips and kissed it. "Don't go away again."

When we headed into the arena a while later, I was nervous about seeing Dave again. His nonchalance regarding what happened in Miami was one thing. His projectile vomiting of dickheadedness was totally another.

"Josh?"

"Yeah?" he answered from the other side of the table. The room was empty, save a few members of the catering staff.

"Are you sure you don't know what Dave's problem is?" I asked him as I started to grab a Coke from the cooler then decided on a Fiji. Good habits had to start somewhere.

"I . . ." Josh began then stopped as a familiar voice filled the room.

"Well hey there, gorgeous!" Bobby's voice echoed against the concrete walls as he came up behind me and nuzzled my neck in a playful greeting.

Callahan and his lousy timing were starting to piss me off.

"Hey B," I replied, glancing over at Josh who seemed oblivious to my irritation.

"It's 'bout time you came to see me," Bobby teased as he reached past me and grabbed a Red Bull from the cooler and a banana off the table. "What took you so damn long?"

"Oh, you know me. I just didn't have a thing to wear."

"Well, if that's all, you could've come in your birthday suit." He winked, wiggled his eyebrows, and swatted my behind.

"Well, I would've, but it was wrinkled and I didn't feel like ironing it," I quipped in response.

The conversation continued with Callahan's flirtations, my snark, and Josh's oblivion for the next few minutes as we walked to the stage where the other guys had gathered for sound check.

While normally I would go out of my way to avoid concert spoilers, I knew Josh needed me there. Aside from that, I preferred to know where Dave was so he didn't pop up out of nowhere, again. My anxiety couldn't take another Jackass-in-the-box moment. From the shadows, I watched the guys go through the set, song by song. For almost three hours, they fine-tuned every detail, every note, every burst of pyro, every flash of light. I drifted asleep in the chair and was blasted awake every time a firework went off. My nerves were shot by the time they got the last note of the encore perfected.

"So? What'dja think?" Josh asked excitedly, awaiting my answer. He had a towel draped around his neck and was wiping the sweat from his forehead.

"It's amazing." And, from everything I'd seen, it was. Well, except for all the jolting me out of my seat when the pyro went off, but I suspected if I hadn't fallen asleep, I'd have been okay. "I can't wait to see it tonight with wardrobe and everything."

"Well, you've got your choice—front row or side stage." He pointed in the two directions where I was able to view the show.

While I didn't like the idea of seeing it from the wings, the thought of catching Dave's eye during the show, throwing him off his groove and giving him an opportunity to blame me for something else ridiculously stupid and out of my control didn't appeal to me.

"Side stage."

"Cool. I'll set you up near the soundboard."

Chapter 12

"CARLY, YOU HAVEN'T BEEN YOURSELF SINCE Dallas," Josh's voice was filled with concern. "You're getting distant again after you promised you wouldn't. What the hell is going on? Does it have to do with my divorce?"

"No, Josh," I reassured him. "It has nothing to do with you and Abby."

It *so* had nothing to do with him. He had no idea.

With the exception of our minor confrontation outside the buses in Dallas, Dave stayed true to his word about staying gone, and I didn't push it. He hadn't sent a single text, email, or phone call since the afternoon in Dallas, two weeks before, nor had I. I managed to avoid seeing him backstage on opening night and as much as I struggled with the urge to call him, I knew it wasn't what was best.

His douchebaggery aside, I missed him. I missed him desperately. And with the life that had begun to grow inside me, I felt a connection to him now that I hadn't felt before. Despite his attitude opening night, I had my history with pregnancy to consider. I needed to keep my feet on the ground and my head out of the clouds. If—and that was a big if—there would ever come a time when I would tell Dave about the baby, it would come much later, when I knew my body wouldn't fail me.

My obstetrician, Dr. Reynolds, made it very clear that while everything looked good initially, it was too soon to tell if this would be a viable pregnancy. Previous miscarriages aside, my age alone put me in the high-risk category. When I had my first appointment with him the second week of June, he cautioned me to take it easy and gave me a list of vitamins to take and herbal supplements to help with the morning (noon and night) sickness. Graciously, he skipped the swag bag he'd given me so many times before. The last thing I needed was another set of business cards for massage therapists, baby photographers, and doulas. His strongest advice was to not count on anything until I headed into my second trimester, which was still several weeks away. Not that it was anything I hadn't already heard, he cautioned me in sharing the news with anyone until then.

No fucking problem.

The only reason Alejandro knew was because he was my best friend. And because he was on me like a jackal on a limp gazelle the minute I cracked my door that morning in Dallas. It would take an act of God before I'd divulge the news to anyone else (Josh included), though, which meant I would have to lie to them.

"I'm sorry, Josh. I'm under so much stress from work right now, I barely have enough time to sleep, much less socialize."

"Well, you better make time, girl. We'll be there next week and I expect to see you."

Shit. I forgot they were coming to Chicago.

"Josh, I can't. I've got . . ."

"I'll see you there, Carly," he instructed bluntly and hung up a moment later with a quick goodbye.

I set my phone on my desk and buried my head in my hands. I was so in over my head this time. It was one thing to deal with something like this when everything had a nice, tidy little explanation—you know, like a husband and a hearty "we were trying." This? Was a giant fucking mess.

"Carly?" Geoffrey's voice came over my intercom, interrupting my thoughts.

"Yeah?"

"You've got a meeting with Susan in ten minutes."

Great.

"Thanks, Geoffrey."

Painting on a smile and donning my work hat, I gathered what I needed for the meeting and headed off down the hall, compartmentalizing my life as I'd learned to do long ago.

I took the concert day off from work. The show was that night, but first I had to get through my appointment with a perinatologist at 9:00 a.m.—a suggestion my obstetrician made at my first appointment, just to "be on the safe side." Even though I wasn't technically having complications, the possibility was always there, so I made the appointment without an argument. Although, unless the guy had a magic wand and some Voodoo witchcraft going on, I didn't see the point.

Arriving early, as suggested, I spent a half-hour filling out paperwork and insurance forms. I cringed as I wrote down two numbers: the number of times I had been pregnant and the number of live births. If there was ever a way to make a woman feel like less of one, it would be with that combination of questions. As screwed up as this situation was with Dave, the thought of going through yet another miscarriage, especially alone, was something I dreaded even more.

The nurse called my name shortly after nine and I went through the usual rigmarole with weight, blood pressure, and urine tests. While I shivered in my thin cotton gown, waiting for Dr. Chang, I looked around at the framed pictures of babies I assumed he'd delivered over the years. So many of them looked *so* small—like smaller-than-a-can-of-soda small. I didn't understand how babies that tiny could survive. But, then again, I'd never grown anything larger than a wad of gum, so what did I know?

"Good morning, Carly!" Dr. Chang's cheerful voice pierced the silence of the exam room as he entered with his nurse, Jane. He extended his hand to shake mine and the nurse smiled in acknowledgement. "We're a pretty casual office around here, so I hope you don't mind me calling you by your first name. I'd let you call me Steve, but I'm pretty sure my attorneys and the State Medical Board would frown on the informality." He grinned with a wrinkle of his nose.

"That's fine, Dr. Chang," I replied. I liked this guy already. His smile was wide and seemingly genuine. He was tall with a muscular frame and seemed to be just a little older than I was—a far cry from the wrinkly, old Chinese man I was expecting. Dr. Reynolds was in his sixties with a long-receded hairline and a slight bend to his posture, so I guess I expected his referred colleagues to be the same.

Dr. Chang sat down on the stool next to the examining table and crossed his ankle over his knee. He took a moment to look over my chart then he closed the file folder and looked up at me.

"So, you've got a touch of tennis elbow, huh?" he teased with a smile.

I chuckled nervously, "I wish."

His demeanor became more serious and he scooted closer to me. "Okay, I've read through your records, but I want you to tell me a little bit about what we've got going on."

"Where do I start?"

"Well, I think we can skip the first twelve to fourteen years of your life, but let's start close to the beginning. What were the first complications you had where your lady parts are concerned?"

I had dreaded this part of the appointment since I first called the office to schedule it. Dr. Reynolds knew my history because he'd pored over my medical records with a fine-tooth comb and whatever he didn't see in the records, my ex-husband Trey had detailed for him on our first visit. I'd never had to say a word.

Now, not only was I alone, Dr. Chang seemed to be one of those "in your own words" kind of doctors. He already knew what was in my chart, but he wanted my take on things. Normally, I liked this because it meant they didn't make assumptions about my health. But this time, it meant I would have to recall that hideous night so long ago.

"About nine years ago, I was attacked in my home. He raped me and stabbed me in the abdomen and back." I was clinical in my response, trying to keep as much emotion out as possible. "The surgeon said he stitched me back together, but couldn't promise anything as far as my fertility was concerned."

If Dr. Chang was surprised, his face didn't reveal it. He nodded encouragingly. Jane stood behind him, a bit stone-faced.

"Since then, I've had several miscarriages."

"Sounds like you've had a hell of a go of it, Carly." The doctor's tone was soft, but matter-of-fact. I appreciate his casual candor and the lack of sugar-coating in his tone.

"To say the least."

He glanced at my chart again, "So, you've been pregnant at least five times?"

"That I know of." The number seemed much darker being spoken aloud.

"And the longest pregnancy lasted about two months?"

I nodded again.

"And the date of your last period?"

"I conceived May 14th," I stated confidently, ignoring his question.

"You're sure of that?"

"100%." When you'd had sex one time in the last six months, you tend to remember it.

He noted the conception date on my chart, pulled out a little plastic dial from his coat pocket and wrote down something else.

"So, we're looking at a due date of February 4th," he looked up from his notes and smiled at me. "Congratulations, Carly. You're eight weeks along."

Eight weeks.

The magic number.

Eight weeks was the longest I'd carried any of my babies. Two were gone in the first month, one had lasted into the middle of the trimester but only one had made it two months. I didn't hold out hope. I didn't have any to hold out, honestly.

"Let's get you checked out, and then scoot you down the hall for some baby pictures. How's that sound?"

I was used to Dr. Reynolds' lack of enthusiasm . . . his somber personality . . . his constant reality checks. Dr. Chang's positive attitude was a bit unnerving.

"Doctor, I have to be honest," I began. "I'm not getting my hopes up. I haven't told anyone about this pregnancy and, truthfully, I refuse to believe that I'll carry it full term. I just want you . . ." I paused to gather my emotions, twisting the sheet around my fingers nervously. "I just want you to know that. You don't have to pretend this baby is gonna be okay. I'm a realist."

His smile turned to a serious expression and he stood, putting his hand on mine. "Carly, I can certainly understand your hesitation in being excited. After five lost babies, it's completely natural to think 'why should this one be any different?' but I'm here to tell you—this one *can* be different."

I subtly shook my head with a twinge of stubbornness.

"You have to remember, high-risk pregnancies are my specialty. I've been working with troublesome uteruses my entire career and if you don't take anything else out of this appointment with me today, I want you to take this—we *will* figure out how to give you a baby. I can't guarantee anything; no doctor can. You know that. But, I do promise you that we'll figure out what's wrong and do everything we can to fix it. Do you trust me?"

I laughed nervously, "No."

He smirked and looked over at Jane, who hid a smile.

"Well, at least you're honest," he said. "Now tell me why you don't believe me."

"I'm too old. My body's too damaged. There's too much scar tissue. I'm too old."

"You said that one already," Dr. Chang winked. "First of all, you're not too old. Women are having babies well into their forties these days—all of them healthy and without even the slightest complication. As for your body? It's been through a tough time, no doubt, but it doesn't mean you can't have children. Don't buy into the BS, Carly. You're a survivor and you owe yourself that much faith."

When I wiped away a stray tear, he patted my leg and told me to lie back. Jane took the chart and began to write down what the doctor dictated as he examined me.

Twenty minutes later, when he inserted the ultrasound wand inside me, I was given the first bean-shaped glimpse of hope I'd felt in years.

Chapter 13

I DROVE TO THE CONCERT ARENA THAT AFTERNOON WITH A small pep in my step, thanks to Dr. Chang. I still couldn't believe I'd made it to eight weeks already. No cramping, no spotting, no danger signs of pending doom. Still though, I didn't want to get my hopes up too much.

With the Bean on the brain, I headed to the venue around three and wound up arguing with the guard at the gate.

"I'm sorry, ma'am. The gates aren't open until five p.m." Some teenage punk on steroids and a power trip was manning entry at this particular gate.

"I understand that. What I'm asking, apparently ineffectively, is if there's a place I can pull over to call into one of the artists to have him escort me in." While patience wasn't normally my strong suit, the extra rest had given me a small supply of it.

"Ma'am, you can't come in. You'll need to leave and come back at five o'clock."

I sighed, and with all the clarity I could muster, I slowly explained my question again. "I understand that you can't open the gates until five. I know that. You've made that *very* clear. Congratulations. You're great at your job." I blinked rapidly and flashed him a huge—albeit fake—smile. "Is there. A place. I can pull over. So I can call my friend. Who is *inside* the gate. So he. Can come get me?" I stopped after every other word, emphasizing my point as clearly as possible. There were hand gestures involved—most of them intending to be helpful. "I'm friends. With one of the guys. In the band performing. Tonight. At this arena."

Young Barney Fife apparently had enough of my condescension and pulled his radio off its base, calling into the main office somewhere within Fort Knox. My patience was running thin. I slammed the car into park and rested my elbow on my open window, planting my chin in my hand. I tapped my fingers on the steering wheel.

I listened to the conversation between the kid and his supervisor and waited for him to tell me for the eighth time that I needed to move. Sure enough, a minute later he leaned through the window along with his attitude.

"Ma'am, you have to leave. Now. I've called my supervisor and he's instructed me to . . ."

"Call the police. Yeah, I heard." I rolled my eyes. "Thaaaaaanks."

Asshole.

I popped the car into drive and veered to the right and whipped a U-ie, racing back down the long driveway. Crossing the street and turning into a strip mall, I called Josh and explained the situation.

"Just leave the car there at the mall. Jamie's gotta go over there to some music store to hand out freebies for tonight anyway. I'll have him pick you up and bring you back." Jamie was the hired gopher for this tour. I'd met him briefly when we were in Dallas.

"He should be there soon, but just in case, jot down his number," Josh said, relaying Jamie's number for me. "I've got Face to Face fan meets at four, but just wait for me in the bus. I'll text you the door code when I hang up." The fan meetings usually took a couple hours.

For having started out the evening feeling good, my frustration level grew quickly, and after almost an hour and a half of sitting in the parking lot with my thumb up my ass, I was ready to just go home. The heat was miserable and my stomach had started to gurgle.

Thankfully, that was when my phone decided to ring. It was Jamie asking my location. I described my car and where I was parked. A couple moments later, a white van pulled up and Jamie rolled down the window, offering an apologetic smile.

"Sorry it took so long. I ended up having to go back to the venue to get more tickets to give out and . . ." He sighed. "Anyway . . . giant mess. I'm sorry."

"It happens." I knew he was sincere in his apology, so I was sincere in my forgiveness.

"While I'm thinking about it, here's your pass," he said, handing me a shiny laminated card on a lanyard. I thanked him, slung it around my neck and tucked it inside my collar. No sense stirring up the natives if I didn't need to.

"Do you wanna follow me back to the arena or leave your car here?" he asked.

"If the security guys will let me in, I'll just follow you,

but they didn't seem too enthusiastic about the idea earlier." I relayed my story, to which Jamie just rolled his eyes and nodded.

"Yeah, they were told to keep fans out of the area today. I'm sorry they didn't let you through. You should've been on the list."

"List?"

"Yeah, the list of people with clearance to come in."

"Of course there's a list," I facepalmed and sighed. Damn Josh for not telling me. "Why wouldn't there be a list?"

Jamie looked confused, but I waved him off.

"It's totally fine. I'll follow you back."

Ten minutes later, I parked my car, locked the doors and followed Jamie to the gate by the buses. We flashed our lanyards and Barney Fife let us through. While I'm sure I only imagined his scowl, I didn't hesitate to shout a flippant "Booyah, motherfucker!" as I drove by the guard shack.

Jamie waved a polite goodbye after I assured him I knew where to go, and I headed toward Josh's bus while he took off jogging toward the arena doors.

When I reached the bus, I punched in the code and opened the door. Climbing on board, I pulled the door shut behind me and set my purse on the couch. The place was a mess. Newspapers laid across the table and a towel had been draped over the back of a chair. There was a bottle of Glenfiddich on the counter and a lowball glass with a dribble of amber colored liquid at the bottom sitting next to it. Shaking my head, I rinsed out the glass and put the bottle of scotch back on the shelf. I tried picking up some of the clutter and at least throw some trash away, but as I looked around, I realized it would be a losing battle. I did grab some of the clothes lying around, though, and headed to the back of the bus to put them in the hamper.

I opened the door to the bedroom and grinned nostalgically. Josh's sheets were strewn all over the bed and there were clothes tossed on the floor.

Some things never change.

Scanning the room, I took it all in. Pictures lined the ledge behind the bed and there was a small stack of books on the nightstand. His iPod and a set of ear buds rested on top of the books. Leaning over, I took a closer look at the pictures. There were children at various ages whom I assumed were nieces and nephews, one of him with his parents when he was younger, one of him and his brother Matt, and, tucked in the back corner, a snapshot I'd never seen before of him and me dancing at his parents' anniversary party in 1993. I chuckled out loud at how young we looked and how big our hair was then. Good times, indeed. I was curious to know how long that picture had had a place on the shelf. I replaced the photo and turned around.

A full-length mirror on the back of the door reflected light from the window and shone against the side of the closet next to the door. He'd left the closet partially open and I saw pants and shirts hanging haphazardly on the rack. Running my fingers along the sleeves, I smiled. I recognized the faint scent of his Carolina Herrera cologne drifting in the air. He'd worn it for years and regardless of wherever I smelled it, it always reminded me of him. On the other side of the door was a built-in dresser. On the top of it sat a brass coin dish with some loose change tossed in it. A watch and some receipts sat on top of the change. One of the drawers had a gray t-shirt sticking out of it, preventing it from closing all the way. I pulled the drawer open just enough to tuck the shirt in and closed it again.

That's my Josh.

I stopped and shook my head. *My* Josh?

Those days are long gone, Carly. Why the hell was I even thinking about it? Dave was the one I cared about. Dave was the one I had been building a relationship with. Dave was the one I'd made love to in Miam . . .

"Oh my God," I said out loud.

I spun around and pushed open the closet door with a hard shove. Burying my face in the clothes that hung there, I inhaled deeply.

Carolina Herrera.

That's what I smelled on my sheets that morning in Miami.

Reeling, I took several steps back and when I felt the mattress against the back of my knees, I sat down and leaned forward, trying to catch my breath.

What did I do?!

Question after question came to mind but the one that never left is how could I feel, with such certainty, it had been Dave in my bed that night if it wasn't? Surely, there was an explanation of some type. Why wouldn't Josh have said something afterward if it had been him?

I mean, it *had* to be Dave. *Didn't it?*

I thought back to the afternoon in Dallas and the conversation that seemed so confusing at the time.

"Look, I think you've got some stuff to work out on your own."

"On my own? Dave, what are you talking about?"

"You really don't know?"

"Don't know what!?" He was talking in circles and it was pissing me off.

"You know, Carly," he said, standing up quickly. "I dunno what's worse; you acting like you don't remember or the fact that it's not a big deal to you."

It started making sense: his words that afternoon, his angry words since, the cold shoulder I got whenever I was around him.

I glanced at my watch. Face to Face should be wrapping up soon, but before I could confront Josh, I had to talk to Dave. I had to find out for sure. If what I suspected was true, this changed everything. Absolutely fucking everything.

I yanked the door open and practically ran off the bus, barely remembering to grab my purse on the way out. When I was outside, I turned in circles, looking for the "Swagger Wagon"—the bus belonging to Dave and Bobby. I finally caught a glimpse of a fan-made bedazzled sign in the window and hurried over.

I tugged at the door handle, but it was locked and the bus windows were dark. Of course it would be locked. Everybody's busy inside, you know, getting ready to put on a fucking concert.

Jesus, Carly, pull yourself together! I wasn't thinking clearly and if I wasn't careful, I'd throw myself into an anxiety attack.

Just then, I heard my name and spun around to see Alejandro coming toward me.

"Oh hey," I said in greeting, hoping my skyrocketing blood pressure wouldn't tip him off. I didn't need to deal with one of Alex's tantrums on top of this. "I didn't expect to see you already."

"Eh, what can I say, Marc offered me a delicious dinner of baked chicken, lime Jell-O and potato salad if I got here early enough." Alex's dry tone gave away his sarcasm. "He knows the way to my heart is through arena catering."

"Because nothing says 'I love you' like indigestion and the taste of watered down Kool-Aid," I said with a playful inflection to my voice that I didn't particularly feel.

"Where are you headed?" he asked, as we began walking toward Marc's bus.

I didn't want to reveal to Alejandro what my mind had concocted yet. "I was gonna see if I could find Dave and talk to him before the show."

He stopped and put his hand on my arm, "Girl, don't get him all riled up before they go on stage. Please?"

"Alejandro, I have to talk to him," I shook my head sadly. "This has gone on too long and I have to get some answers." Not the answers I was originally searching for, of course, but answers nonetheless.

Alex looked at me suspiciously, but thankfully didn't argue. He gave me a hug and whispered a message of good luck in my ear before he punched in the code for Marc's bus and climbed on board. I returned to the Swagger Wagon and waited impatiently outside the door.

Fifteen minutes later, Bobby rounded the front of the bus, thumbs flying across the screen of his Blackberry. I cleared my throat gently and offered him a smile.

"Hey!" he said, lifting his head and looking at me. "How's my girl?" He hugged me with one of his familiar moan-in-your-ear hugs and unlocked the bus door. Following him, I climbed the stairs and flopped onto one of the couches.

"So," he began, pulling a Red Bull from the fridge. "To

what do I owe this honor?" He offered me one as well, but I declined.

Deciding I wasn't in the mood for small talk, I told him. "I need to talk to Dave."

Bobby's face dropped and even from where I was sitting, I could see him clench his teeth. "Right now?"

I nodded, feigning more courage than I actually possessed.

He sighed and looked at me over his Red Bull can as he took a sip. Though my heart was pounding in my chest, I didn't break the stare. I needed to do this.

"Carly," he said after a few moments of silence. "He's just starting to get over this thing. Can you please not stir the pot tonight?"

"So you know then?" I said more matter-of-factly than as a question.

"All I know is that you hurt him wicked bad," Bobby offered. I couldn't tell if he knew more than he was letting on or not. Either way, he knew enough and that sucked.

"Bobby, I realize it's not the best timing. I know it doesn't make touring with him any easier, but there are things you don't know about that I have to straighten out," I pleaded. "I have to . . ."

I was interrupted by the sound of the bus door opening. Dave took a couple of long leaps up the stairs and was standing in the doorway before I had to chance to take a breath. The smile he'd been wearing dropped from his face when he saw me.

"What the fuck are you doing here?"

Bobby took that as his cue to leave. He grabbed a second Red Bull from the fridge, leaned over and kissed the top of my head as he passed me. He patted his friend on the shoulder when he walked by him and left without a word.

"You didn't answer me," Dave persisted. His voice was acidic, and I suspected I would have a very small window to ask what I wanted to ask before he started in with name-calling and yelling.

I stood and prayed the butterflies in my stomach would just die down, at least until I got off this bus. It most definitely wouldn't help if I had to stop and take time to vomit.

"Dave, we need to talk about Miami."

"I don't think so." He stood like a bouncer; his feet were shoulder-width apart, his chest was puffed out and he crossed his arms over it.

I swallowed hard. If I did do what I thought I had in Miami, he certainly didn't owe me any kindness.

"I know I had a lot to drink at the club that night."

His jaw clenched and as he let out a breath, his nostrils flared.

"And we talked early in the night and you told me that you . . ." I hated even bringing it up. ". . . that you wanted me."

"You wanna rub a little *more* salt in my wounds, Carly?"

I let my eyes fall as my heart did. It was obvious this was hurting him. "Dave, I know this isn't easy, but I have to know what happened that night. Please just bear with me."

He tightened his jaw again and exhaled loudly. "Fine. Yes. That's what I said."

"And then what?"

"What do you mean, 'then what?'" he barked. "You got shitfaced and made an ass out of me. What more is there to know?"

I sighed and leaned back against the table.

"You broke my heart, Carly." Dave stepped toward me and I finally heard the pain in his voice instead of just the anger. "You slept with my band mate and you broke my fucking heart." His words were like a knife to the chest. It was true. I bit my lip to keep from crying.

"Dave," I said softly, "I didn't remember until today."

"What, is that supposed to make it better?" he fired back. "Is that supposed to erase what you did? Gee, sorry, Carly, but it doesn't work like that."

"No, that's not it," I answered. "God, Dave, I am *so* very, very sorry I hurt you. I'm sorry I did what I did. I didn't realize it happened. I was so stupid, so foolish, so careless, and I am so sorry for everything."

He stared at me, his jaw tight.

My heart ached for what I'd done to him . . . to myself.

"For what it's worth, I thought it was you. I *wanted* it to be you."

"Don't, Carly," he shook his head.

"I can't help it, Dave. It's the truth." I stood and reached for him, but he raised his hands and backed away.

"It isn't the truth, Carly!" he exploded in frustration. "If it was the truth, then you would've been alone when I came into your room that night instead of sprawled all over McCarthy like you were a second fucking skin!"

I recoiled at his words. *He saw us. Together.* Humiliated didn't begin to describe how I felt.

"Dave, I am *so* deeply sorry."

"Save it," he snapped. "You need to go. Go back to Josh. Go back home. Go to Hell, for all I care. Just go." He shoved his hands in his pockets, lowered his gaze to the floor and turned to the side, allowing me room to pass.

"Dave . . ."

He raised his head and I saw the muscles in his jaw harden. Without another word, I stepped past him and left.

Hot tears of embarrassment spilled down my cheeks as I walked toward Josh's bus. I didn't know why he hadn't said anything, but now that the truth was out there, I had to find out. Nausea churned in my stomach and a pounding headache had taken up residence behind my eyes.

Just as I reached for the door handle of the bus, Josh popped around the corner and opened it from the inside.

"Jesus, Coop," he said. "Where've you been? I was about to send out the fuckin' national *guahd*."

I dismissed him with a shake of my head and ran to the bathroom, voiding my stomach until I had nothing left but the empty heave of my shoulders. Josh knocked at the door impatiently.

"Carly? *Ah* you okay? What's wrong?"

I pulled myself up from the floor and flushed the toilet. I opened the door and, ignoring Josh, I went to the sink and rinsed my mouth out.

"Carly?" his voice was soft as he ran his hand across my upper back. "Talk to me."

I spun around.

"Why didn't you tell me?"

"Why didn't I tell you what?" He frowned, confusion forming a V above his nose.

"That we had sex in Miami!" My voice cracked and I bit back a sob.

"Tell you?" The crease got deeper between his eyes and he reached out, wiping my tears away with his thumbs. "Coop, you were there. Why would I . . .?" His voice trailed off as if he was trying to make sense of what I was asking.

"How could you have taken advantage of me like that?" My earlier embarrassment was replaced with betrayal.

A dark cloud of guilt crossed his face and he backed away, "Carly, I . . ."

"You knew how drunk I was, Josh!" I sobbed. "How could you?"

"Carly, you acted like you were sober. I thought you were!" Josh explained.

"You have to tell me everything, Josh." I needed to know everything I couldn't remember on my own.

"You don't remember anything?"

I shrugged.

He leaned against the counter and crossed his arms, "When we first left the bar, you were pretty tanked. You remember that, right?"

"Vaguely."

"Okay," he continued. "I came and checked on you about an hour or so later and you were asleep, but I got you some more water and kissed your forehead when I left. Sound familiar?"

I grunted. "Kinda."

"When I came back the third time, you were still asleep and I sat down on the bed and started talking to you." He sat down on the chair opposite the sink and took my hands in his. I was still angry with him, but I needed to know what else happened, so I let him. His thumbs drew lazy circles on the backs of my knuckles as he continued. "You were still acting silly and we played a game of charades, but then it was like you came-to instantly and you responded to my kisses. When I told you I loved you, you cried like you knew exactly what I said." His eyes searched mine for some sense of recollection. "You even said it back."

I remembered the charades. And I remembered the sex, but in my head it wasn't him. I most definitely didn't remember saying it back.

He squeezed my hands, "Carly, you *really* don't remember us making love?"

I gave a half-shrug and pulled my hands back, tucking them under my elbows as I hugged myself. I stared at my feet for a moment, then met Josh's gaze again. "I remember what happened, Josh. I just," I closed my eyes and sighed, "I just thought it was with Dave."

"Why would you think it was Dave?"

Slightly insulted, I straightened my posture and huffed. "Why not?"

"Well, no offense, Carly, but he doesn't seem like your type."

"Well, no offense, Josh, but my *type* seems to be really great at breaking my heart."

"Touché," he replied in defeat.

Retreating to proverbial corners, we were silent again for a few moments before Josh spoke.

"Carly, I told you I loved you. Does that mean anything to you?"

I inhaled and bit my bottom lip before nodding. "It always has." *That was the problem.*

"Then what do we need to do to get past this?"

I nearly choked on a snort. "Oh, Josh." He had no idea what had truly transpired that night in Miami and I had four more weeks before I could safely tell him—four more weeks until my first trimester was done.

"What? Why the snort?"

I shook my head, "Just . . . uh . . . I just need some time." Josh nodded in concession and his eyes dropped to his hands where he picked at his thumbnail as he often did when he was anxious.

We sat there for a few minutes and listened as the crowd noise around the arena grew louder as more people arrived. We didn't speak, didn't touch, didn't even look at one another. We just existed. I understood my faulty memory where Miami was concerned had hurt Josh and, knowing that Catholic guilt of his a little too well, I suspected he also felt really bad at the realization that he'd taken advantage of the situation. He'd be licking his wounds for a little while. I, too, had to swallow what this turn of events meant for me and for us, where it left our friendship or if it meant something more, but most importantly, how it would affect this baby.

The baby. I touched my stomach instinctively and swallowed hard. This changed everything. It was too much to think about right now.

I surmised that my presence at the show tonight would not only be uncomfortable (for all of us) but it would be selfish on my part. I wanted to see them perform, as my love extended to all four members of the group, but not at the detriment of the show. When everything calmed down a bit and tempers weren't so high, maybe I'd catch another concert, but I'd done enough damage in the small amount of time I'd been there already. It was time to go home.

I stood and walked toward the door. I reached out to squeeze Josh's shoulder in a farewell gesture, but he wrapped his fingers around my wrist and stopped me. He stood and turned me toward him.

"Carly, I'm sorry."

His bright eyes cut through the wall I'd put up earlier, and I couldn't speak. My resolve was teetering on the edge and I was afraid if I said anything, I'd confess to everything. That wasn't what either of us needed right now. The corners of my mouth turned upward just enough to soften my face and I reached up to his, cupping his cheek in my hand. I ran my thumb along his scruffy whiskers and pressed my lips against his in the slightest whisper of a kiss before I walked off the bus.

Chapter 14

FOR THE NEXT COUPLE OF WEEKS, I BECAME PRETTY wrapped up in watching for signs of miscarriage. It sounded bad, but when you've had as many as I have had, you tend to be pretty pessimistic, "the inevitable" always lurking in the shadows. As I eased into my tenth week of pregnancy, without a hint at disaster, I started to relax a bit. In talking to Alejandro, I started referring to the baby as the "Bean," so everything didn't seem so clinical and statistical. Cravings had kicked in full force and Alex constantly gave me grief about the amount of Ben and Jerry's that filled our freezer. I was just thankful I had any appetite whatsoever; what I ate was irrelevant.

Josh had waited almost a week before he picked up with his "Good morning" texts again. I had missed them, but I waited another week before I responded:

> I've eaten my weight in ice cream.
> Is the tour over yet?

He replied immediately. Apparently two weeks was long enough to go without talking to me.

> One more week. Save me a pint and some Rold Gold? -jm

I didn't respond. I didn't know what to say. I was so confused.

My brain was on overload as I tried to sort out my feelings. My heart ached over what I'd done to Dave. Though my memory made me think I had returned his words of love, I wasn't sure if I actually *did* love him, but we were certainly headed in that direction. He was such an attentive father to his children and, of course, it went without saying that I adored the kids, too. I didn't want to think about the confusion they must be feeling right now, considering I used to talk to them as much as I did their dad. I hoped Dave had spared their hearts and made up an excuse for my absence.

I enjoyed the easy flirtation between Dave and me—the teasing, the silliness. I missed having him worry about my health and ask me each night whether I'd eaten right or worked out that day. I missed his middle-of-the-night texts when he couldn't sleep. I missed his hyena laugh—one I was certain I wouldn't hear again for quite a while. Yet, I had no one to blame for this loss but myself. I couldn't accuse Josh even though I wanted to. The bottom line was, I had been the one to drink myself stupid and nobody was responsible for the choices I made that night except me.

Josh genuinely thought I had sobered up. He thought I wanted *him*. He thought it was his mind and body that had seduced me that night. He thought I'd come full circle and fallen back in love with him.

The real question was—had I ever fallen out?

I couldn't remember a time when I hadn't loved Josh McCarthy at least a little bit. Not even during my marriage, when I would Google his images, then sneakily delete my browser history to keep it from Trey. I was fourteen when Josh's blue eyes first caught my attention, eighteen when he stole the rest of me . . . not that I didn't give it up willingly. Just when I thought I'd gotten over him and settled into life as a single career woman of my twenties, Josh roared into my life again. Now, here we were again, another day. Another try?

I once told Josh that Trey never stood a chance because of him and, if I were being honest with myself that was still probably true. Then, along came Dave.

I loved Dave's strength and sense of humor, even as crass as it could be. I loved his sentimental nature, too. His children were just a bonus. How I loved them. But did I care about Dave because of how great he was or because he was the closest I'd get to Josh after all those years?

My life was so fucked up. I hadn't been this much of a mess since the rape, nine years before. I took pride in how in-control I was of my life up to that point. I had schedules and discipline, and I rarely let my hair down without absolute certainty I could do it without it affecting my life in the long run. Then, I went to Miami. In one drunken night, I'd thrown rules to the wind and wound up pregnant. While I'd dreamed about having children with Josh years ago, the timing of all of this was far from perfect. In fact, considering he was in the midst of finalizing his divorce, it was about as far from perfect as it could possibly get.

My nights were restless from all the stress, which made my morning sickness worse. With just a couple weeks left in my first trimester, I hoped the nausea would completely disappear soon and that my appetite for anything besides ice cream would return. I'd lost ten pounds and while the doctor wasn't too concerned, I was. I wasn't skinny by anyone's stretch of the imagination, but ten pounds was a lot of weight to lose in such a short amount of time, and I felt fatigued most of the time. I slept often, but rarely felt rested. I found myself falling asleep everywhere: at my desk, in meetings, in the shower, standing in the kitchen making dinner, everywhere . . . that was, except bed.

`I take that as a no? -jm`

Another text message brought me out of my thoughts. I read it and hoped I wasn't making a huge mistake in my response:

`I'll bring the pretzels. You buy the ice cream.`

Until that moment, I hadn't given a single thought to going to LA. Hell, I didn't even know if my doctors would give me the go-ahead to fly in the first place. But, I guess I'd deal with that when the time came. Spontaneity wasn't my strength, but I wasn't sure what strengths I had left, at that point.

My phone rang a moment later.

Before I could even get my "hello" out, Josh was exploding with questions on his end of the line. "Are you serious? You're not kidding around, are you? You're coming to LA for real? *For real*, for real? You hate LA! Why are you coming to LA? When? How? Carly?!"

"Jesus, Josh, breathe!" I chuckled. "I could use a vacation and I thought I'd come see you when tour's over. Can you spare a guest room for a few days?"

"Of course!" *Of coahse.* Damn him and his dropped R.

"When will you get there? How long are you staying?"

"Slow down, hon. I haven't even bought my tickets yet."

"Then get online and buy them!" I'd be lying if I said the excitement in his voice didn't make me smile at least a little bit. "What are you waiting for?"

"Well, given the fact that I literally *just* decided to make the trip, I'd say I'm waiting to make sure my boss gives me the time off."

"Ugh!" His melodramatic frustration amused me. "You make me crazy, woman. It's not nice to get me all riled up if you don't even know you can come yet!"

I wasn't worried about Susan giving me the time off. I was, however, concerned about my doctors letting me fly. The risk was concerning, but I *needed* to talk to Josh about the Bean, and since the trip coincided with the first week of my second trimester, the likelihood of something happening was much smaller. Surely, my doctors would see that.

Promising Josh I'd be in touch the minute I bought tickets, I hung up and tried to concentrate on the rest of my work day.

Monday morning, after I got the time off approved by my boss, I called Dr. Chang's office and told the nurse what my plans were. The doctor called me back that afternoon and other than cautioning me against sitting for too long in one spot to prevent blood clots in my legs, he gave me a thumbs-up. I sighed in relief, booked my trip and emailed Josh with my itinerary.

He responded with an exuberant "YESSSSSSSSSSS!"

I hoped his enthusiasm wouldn't fade once I told him the real reason for my visit.

"I'm sorry, I think I just hallucinated," Alejandro said, after sucking back his entire glass of pinot, "You said you slept with *Josh* in Miami?" His voice got a little pitchy at the end and I could do nothing but nod.

Up 'til then, I'd been able to keep this monstrous news to myself. Well, between Dave, Josh, and me, that is. But I knew that I had to tell Alex before I went to LA. My doctors seemed confident at my visit the day before that my pregnancy was out of the danger zone and therefore, it was time to get my shit figured out. That started with telling my roommate and best friend the truth about what happened that night in Florida.

"Last I knew, it was Dave! Now you're saying it was Josh? Do I wanna know how this happened?" He covered his face loosely with his hand and gave me that uncomfortable look as if I would break out with words like "vagina" or "orgasm" any minute. I spared him the details, but explained how I had become so mixed up.

"Carly," he shook his head sadly as he poured himself another glass of wine. "What are you gonna do?"

"Well," I said as I smoothed my hand over my belly, "it would appear that I'm gonna have a baby."

"I know that, smart ass." He swatted my knee. "I meant about this situation with Josh and Dave? Jesus, are you trying to break up the band, Yoko?"

I resented his implication and told him as much.

"I'm not a fucking Yoko, Alejandro. I just . . ."

"You just what, Carly?" He started speaking with his hands and I knew it was all downhill from here. I steeled myself for the verbal arsenal he was about to unleash. "You just decided to hint at one of the members of this little boy band you wanna shag him silly, then you take another one back to your room and screw him instead? I mean, c'mon, Carly! What were you thinking? What if Dave finds out?!" Exasperation filled his voice, his hands more animated now and wine sloshed over the rim of his glass.

"He knows," I said softly.

Alex nearly pushed the chair over when he jumped out of it, "WHAT?!"

"Jesus, Alejandro. Chill." I was really not in the mood for theatrics and melodrama tonight. "Dave knows. He's pissed. He hates me. He's not talking to Josh. But the band has *not* broken up, so please, just chill the fuck out."

"Oh my God, Carly. Why did you wait so long to tell me?" He took his seat again and crossed his legs, his foot bouncing a mile a minute. He always bounced his foot when he was worked up. "I mean, don't you think this is something I should've known about? My boyfriend is a part of this group, too. Shouldn't he be aware of what's going on?"

"Quite honestly, Alex? No." I sighed and stood up. "This really has nothing to do with you, with Marc, or anybody else for that matter. I didn't tell you because I've been a little busy trying not to lose this fucking baby! What's done is done. I can't change it. I can't fix it. All I can do is move on. But first, I need to tell Josh. So, if you don't mind keeping your mouth shut until I get back from LA, I'd be much obliged." I walked into the kitchen and put my glass in the sink before I started heading down the hall.

"Wait a minute," he said, following me. "Josh doesn't know it's his yet?"

"Josh doesn't even know I'm pregnant, Alejandro. Nobody does, except you."

Alex sighed and crossed his arms over his chest. "And how much longer are you keeping it a secret?"

"I leave for California in the morning. Once I tell Josh, then I can make it public. Until then . . ." My voice drifted off, but Alex knew what I meant and he nodded in agreement.

"This isn't your finest moment, Carly, and God knows you've had plenty of un-fine moments. Just . . ." he paused and pursed his lips in disapproval. "Stop with the fucking secrets, will you? I've asked you before, but this time, I'm serious. Stop."

"I promise."

He came over and pulled me into his arms for a hug. "If you need anything, you know I'm here for you and while I can't promise I won't flip out, I'll try harder not to be so judgmental."

"I appreciate it." I kissed his cheek and retreated to my bedroom where I finished packing my suitcase before going to bed. My flight left at 6 a.m. and if I didn't get enough sleep, I'd spend the majority of the flight in the lavatory.

"You sick, girl?" Josh's wrist rested on the steering wheel and his other hand rested on mine, his thumb grazing the tops of my knuckles. He looked good for just having come off a thirty-city tour a week earlier. His skin was tan and for the few brief moments in the airport, when he had his aviators off, I could see how bright his eyes were. He looked happy and healthy. I, however, must look like hell if Josh noticed.

I actually thought I was holding my own. Granted, I

hadn't been in the air thirty minutes before I got sick, but, thankfully, it had just been a passing bout of nausea. I spent the rest of the flight with my face pressed against the cool window sipping 7-Up and nibbling on crackers. When I landed, I bee-lined for a bathroom to fix my hair and breath. Apparently, my effort was for naught. Of all the times for Josh to actually pay attention to detail, of course it would be then. The time back in 2002, when I cut six inches off my hair and made the horrible choice of dying it platinum blonde, went virtually unnoticed, but today, when I'm just slightly travel-weary, he noticed. I chuckled to myself.

"Meh." I shrugged. "I got a little nauseous on the flight from the turbulence, but I'm okay now. Why? Do I look that bad?"

Josh looked over at me as we slowed to a stop at a traffic light. "Nah. You're beautiful as always. You're just quiet. It's not like you."

"Oh."

"It's no biggie." He squeezed my hand and we eased away from the intersection. "I just want you to enjoy this week. No stress, no work, no crazy. Just peace and quiet."

If only he knew.

We pulled into his driveway a little while later and he carried my bag inside. The minute I stepped in the mud room, Tango, his Shih Tzu was at my feet, his tail, along with the rest of his little body, wagging excitedly. Just as I'd done before, I gave in to his big, brown eyes and picked him up. He greeted me with a swipe of his tongue on my cheek. I scratched him behind the ears and promised to snuggle with him later. I put him back down, following Josh into the kitchen.

I'd been given the grand tour of the place when I was

here last time, but the feel of it was different without Abby's touch. The foyer had been repainted, as had the kitchen. New photographs and artwork hung on the hallway walls and an enormous La-Z-Boy had replaced an antique settee that sat in one corner of the family room. I suspected it was one of those recliners with a built-in fridge in the arm of the chair. It had "Josh" written all over it. I smirked in appreciation as I thought about my own hideous "post-divorce" chair with the leopard-print piping at home.

"Nice chair."

He smirked and motioned with a jerk of his chin. "C'mon, girl. Let's get you settled."

I followed him upstairs to a cozy room at the front of the house. I gasped slightly when he opened the door. This was my . . . *our* apartment in New York. Floor to ceiling bookshelves filled one wall, two walls were white wainscoting, and the last wall was detailed with exposed brick. A giant brushed-silver four-poster bed sat in the middle of the room. On the black dresser next to the closet was a silver figurine of the Empire State Building. Black picture frames on the opposite wall housed menu covers from some of our favorite restaurants in New York City. Above the bed was a giant black and white portrait of the Brooklyn Bridge. As I looked closer, I realized something familiar about the photo.

"Josh, is that . . .?"

He nodded, ". . . the one you took on that photo walk we did? Yeah."

"But where did you get it?" I was baffled. I had lost those negatives ages ago.

"I was going through my stuff when Abby moved out and found a box of yours that somehow got mixed in with my things. I had it blown up." He set my suitcase on a vintage trunk at the foot of the bed and went to the closet, pulling out an old shoebox I'd long since forgotten about. There were pictures, an old watch that didn't run anymore, my nameplate from my first job with the Village Voice, and my mother's rosary. I hadn't seen any of it in years and, other than my mom's prayer beads, I hadn't missed anything in particular. When I was done thumbing through the contents, I looked back up at the picture on the wall. A smile curled the corners of my mouth and my eyes began to tear up.

"Thank you, Josh."

"It's okay that I did that?"

I nodded and wiped my eyes with the back of my finger. I turned my attention back to the room. Almost every detail was exactly like my brownstone in New York. The same dresser, the same bedframe, even the same wispy curtains hanging in the windows. "I can't believe you did all this.

"It was always my favorite place." Josh shrugged. "Did I get everything right? I couldn't *remembah* some things, so I kinda guessed."

"It's perfect."

"Coop, you sure you're okay?" Josh tilted his head and I could see the concern in his eyes.

I smiled through tears, "I will be."

"You just need some California sunshine. C'mon. Get into your bathing suit and let's go for a swim."

Like my pregnant ass was getting into anything made of spandex. I dismissed his suggestion "Actually, I need to go buy a new suit. I ruined mine in the laundry last week."

Josh wiggled his wonky eyebrows flirtatiously, "We can always skinny dip."

I smirked and just shook my head. "With your neighbors ogling from their second-story windows? Not a chance, McCarthy."

"It was worth a try. At least put on some shorts and a tank top. You're so white, you're practically transparent." He winked at me, kissed my forehead, and backed outta the room, before turning and bounding down the stairs.

He was right. Other than a day at the beach on the Fourth of July, my pasty skin hadn't seen much sun. I decided to hop in the shower and wash the travel stench off me before I hit the patio for some UV rays.

Fifteen minutes later, I emerged from my room with my quandary of damp curls pulled up into a casual ponytail. I threw on a baggy tank top to camouflage my tummy and a pair of gym shorts. For good measure, I tied a denim shirt around my waist and trotted down the steps. As I rounded the landing halfway down the stairs, I paused at the window and caught a glimpse of Josh and Tango playing fetch in the backyard.

I watched Josh toss a tennis ball across the yard. Tango took off like a bullet, his black and white fur nothing but a blurred streak of gray in the grass. The dog was so eager to please. The minute Josh released the ball he ran after it and brought it back, dropping it obediently at Josh's feet, his tail wagging furiously. After the first few throws, I could tell Tango was growing tired, but he refused to stop. With his tongue hanging out and his body heaving in a heavy pant, he continued playing fetch. Even when Josh chucked the ball in the pool, Tango went after it. With a giant splash, a quick retrieve and a rapid paddle to the steps where he stopped only long enough to shake the water loose from his fur, the dog continued in his pursuit several more times. Finally, out of exhaustion, Tango retrieved the ball one last time and retreated to a spot under the table on the patio. Josh reached down to scratch his wet head and headed toward the pool, tossing in the automatic cleaner.

When he returned to the patio, I met him with a cold Stella Artois and a bottle of water for myself.

He took the green bottle, tapped the neck against my Fiji in salud and took a swig. Wiping his mouth with the back of his hand as he sat down in a chaise, he tilted his head at me. "No beer for you?"

A smile I couldn't hold back spread across my face as I shook my head and joined him on a matching chaise, leaning my head back against the pillow and crossing my ankles, one over the other. The warm LA sun beat down on me and I graciously soaked it in.

"Well, it's a good thing, really," Josh said as he took another sip. "I always thought you drank too much." Though I couldn't see his teasing eyes behind the mirrored lenses of his aviators, his smirk gave him away.

I slugged his arm, "Pot or kettle, Irishman?"

"Whaaaaaa? This is my first *beeah*!"

"Uh huh. I'm talkin' about all the times you woke up on your lawn, smartass."

He held his bottle just inches from his lips and grinned. "You knew about that?"

"A little birdie told me."

"Lies. Allllllllll lies."

"Oh, of course," I nodded conspiratorially, "Because *we* never drank to oblivion and woke up in . . . say, Hoboken wearing nothing but our underwear and cowboy hats . . .

wondering how the fuck we got there." Sarcasm dripped from my words and I laughed out loud when he lowered his sunglasses to the tip of his nose like David Caruso.

"Exactly," he said. "But anyway, why are you makin' me drink alone?? I got a six pack of Corona 'specially for you. There's limes and everything."

"You mean 'there *are* limes' and it's only noon, Josh. I'm not Irish, remember?" I winked at him.

"Fuckin' *grammah* police."

I shrugged and unscrewed the cap on my water, taking a big swig. "It's what I do."

He smirked and took another drink of his beer.

"So, tour . . . it was good? No more fighting?"

"I wouldn't say there's fighting, no." Josh shook his head then picked at the label on his bottle. "It's not unicorns and *glittah*, but there's no fighting."

"I call bullshit," I said, twisting my body around on the chaise, facing him and resting my elbows on my knees.

Josh's expression grew more neutral and he pursed his lips before taking another drink from his bottle. I knew behind those mirrored lenses, he was hiding the truth. I'd talked to Alejandro, after all, and Marc told him how miserable things had been those last few weeks of tour. Bobby had met some girl in Chicago and his amorous state had turned him all Rodney-King with everybody spouting "Can't we all just get alongs" every time he turned around, and Marc was steering clear of the situation altogether. Josh wasn't oblivious to anything, but he also knew there was nothing he could do to fix the situation, so he tended to pretend it didn't exist. Then, there was Dave who, in typical Roxbury style, brooded. There, of course, was nothing he could do to remedy the problem either, but it didn't stop him from moping about, or when tempers flared, thumping his chest a time or two. He was becoming more like Callahan every day, it seemed. Marc had left no detail out where the whole situation was concerned, and Alex made no effort to hide his frustration about the stress this whole thing was causing the group.

The guilt weighed heavily on my shoulders, but I knew I couldn't fix it. I could only move forward and mend fences where I could. It was a slow process, but at least the tour was over and everybody could go back to neutral corners to lick their wounds for a while.

"Look, Coop," Josh finally said. "We fucked up. We know that. But we can't go back. We can't undo what we did. And honestly, I wouldn't want to." I felt his stare until I finally looked up, acknowledging him.

A lot of things about Josh had changed since I met him, but those eyes would always melt my heart. They had always expressed his emotions when words would not suffice: excitement, fear, joy, sadness, seduction. They had been my weakness for over twenty years and while my resolve had been fairly strong for the majority of that time, today wasn't one of those times.

Reaching up, I cupped his face in my hand, pressing my lips against his. He reciprocated by pushing me backward against the cushion of the chair and running his hand along the side of my hip as our kiss deepened. Tongues teasing and bodies reacting physically to a force neither of us could deny any longer, I felt electrified. His fingers slid along my skin as they snaked beneath the hem of my shirt and I shivered at his touch.

How I could've mistaken his tenderness for Dave's in Miami was beyond me. I knew this man's caress as well as I knew how to breathe.

"Well, isn't this cozy?" a snippy voice interrupted from the patio door.

Josh jerked away from me and turned toward the house.

"Abby! What the hell are you doing here?"

"I came to get my grandmother's trunk from the attic," she sneered. "Didn't realize you'd have *company*." Her glare cut through me before her eyes snapped back to Josh.

I tugged at the bottom of my tank top and sat up. Guilt washed over me, though I knew I had no reason to feel bad. Josh was a free man and even back in May, he'd been separated from Abby.

"Let yourself in, why don't you," his reply dripped with sarcasm.

"Well, isn't it still technically *my* house too, Josh?"

"Actually, no," he replied. "It stopped being your house about a week ago."

Abby's eyes returned to me. I refused to back down. I didn't trust her. Like in the wild, the minute eye contact is broken, the stronger animal will attack the weaker one. This gazelle wasn't going down today.

"Relax. It's not like you two were going at it . . . yet," she sneered. If she'd been a cheetah, her tail would've been twitching, waiting for me to make a move.

"Don't be a bitch," Josh warned her. "I'll go get your trunk. Why don't you wait inside?" His tone was much less one of helpful and more one of refereeing. When she finally broke her stare and turned around, heading back into the house, Josh leaned down and kissed me softly. "I'll be right back."

I nodded and finally exhaled. I hadn't realized I'd been

holding my breath until then. I blew another deep breath through my nose and stood up. I didn't want to go inside, but I couldn't sit still until she was gone, either. I slowly climbed the concrete steps surrounding the patio, busying myself with the rose bushes as I went along, picking off dry leaves and wilted blooms.

I reached over the banister to pick a fresh blossom and didn't hear Abby come up behind me until it was too late.

"You must think I'm pretty stupid, don't you?"

I froze mid-reach and lifted my head, afraid to turn around. Even for as brazen as I could be and had been at times in my professional world, I despised confrontation and had no interest in dealing with Josh's estranged wife now—or ever—for that matter.

Knowing she had my attention, she continued, "I knew you'd come sniffing around, but I thought you'd at least have the decency to wait until the ink was dry on the divorce papers."

I tensed at her accusations, but tried to ignore her. I didn't have the energy to get into a fight with Abby and didn't feel like fishing for what she actually knew, so I deflected instead.

"How heavy is your grandmother's trunk? Maybe Josh needs help." I stood and faced her, brushing off my hands before stuffing them in my pockets.

"I'm sure he's fine." She clenched her teeth and I noticed her jaw jerk slightly.

I finally turned, walking into the house. The sooner Josh got the trunk from the attic, the sooner Abby would leave and I could get back to the difficult task of telling him about Bean. As I walked through the kitchen and down the hall toward the staircase, Abby didn't relent.

"You think you're so smart," she continued with her verbal assault as we climbed the stairs. "You think nobody knows."

I muffled my surprise, but refused to turn around, fearing the panic would show in my face. "Knows what, Abby?"

"That you've been fucking my husband for years and that's the reason *your* husband left you."

"Excuse me?!" I was done with her accusations. I spun around quickly, not realizing how close she was behind me. My knee knocked against her hip and I lost my footing. With a sharp gasp, I grappled for the railing, but missed and tumbled down the stairs. The last thing I remember before my world went dark was Abby screaming for Josh.

Chapter 15

My head pounded with a throbbing pain as I came to. A soft beep pulsed in an even cadence somewhere to my right. The smell of antiseptic permeated the air and a cool wisp of oxygen tickled my nose. I moved my head slightly and felt the tug of plastic tubing tucked behind my ears. When I tried to open my eyes, the bright overhead lights blinded me, causing me to pinch them shut again, but I mentally perked up as I heard Josh's voice.

"When can she go home, Doctor?"

Another voice caught my attention. "Perhaps in a day or two. We definitely want to keep her overnight for observation. The sprained wrist will take some time to heal and the swelling from where she hit her head will eventually go down. In the grand scheme, this fall wasn't as bad as it could've been, but Ms. Cooper's going to be more miserable than normal because we can't really give her much for the pain. It would be too much of a risk for the baby at this point."

"The baby?"

Oh God! I wanted to scream out, but couldn't do more than let out a weak whimper that went unnoticed. I tried opening my eyes, but the grogginess won the fight and I lay there helplessly listening to the disaster taking place at the foot of my bed.

Was the baby okay? Please let Bean be okay! Wait . . . the baby! Josh can't find out this way! Shit! Various emotions raced through me so fast I could barely keep up.

"The baby's just fine for right now, Mr. McCarthy. But with Ms. Cooper's age and her history, she's at an extremely high risk for miscarriage, so we want to keep a close eye on her." The doctor continued, "The ultrasound shows movement and the baby's heart rate is pretty strong, so I don't think she'll have any problems, but I'm recommending complete bed rest for the next two weeks. We'll reevaluate after that."

Relief flooded through me about the baby and my eyes fluttered open enough to see Josh nod in understanding. The doctor shook his hand and left the room. Josh ran his hand through his hair and let out a long sigh. I closed my eyes again before he noticed I was awake.

I didn't want him to find out about the baby this way. I wanted to tell him myself. I wanted to talk to him about us, first. I wanted to ease into it. All of those options were gone now.

And bed rest? Where? I had to get home. I had a job. I had people counting on me. People who didn't even know I was pregnant yet, much less why I needed to take time off because of doctor-ordered bed rest. *Beguile* just laid off thirty people in my office the year before, and I had barely made the cut. I was still trying to prove myself worthy of keeping. My head spun as I tried to process everything.

The monitor nearby began to beep more rapidly and a buzzer sounded. I heard Josh call my name in alarm as the door swung open and a woman's authoritative voice asked him to leave. I wanted to call out . . . beg him not to go . . . feared that if he left, he wouldn't come back. But before I could open my mouth, a cold sensation hit the vein inside of my elbow, zipped up my arm and my world went dark.

"Carly?"

I barely heard Bobby's whisper over the soft pulsing beep of the monitor next to my bed.

"Girl, you gotta wake up." His voice seemed so mournful.

As my mind became more alert, so did my body. The pain in my head seemed to have subsided a bit, but overall, I felt groggy and weak. I whimpered a little and opened my eyes. The room was mostly dark now, save a dimly lit lamp in the corner.

Bobby rested his hand on the top of my head and rubbed his thumb back and forth along my hairline, but when he heard me begin to stir, he stopped. His hazel eyes were bloodshot and I knew without asking that he'd been here for hours. What I didn't know was whether Josh was still here somewhere, too.

"Carly, babe . . ." He reached down and stroked my cheek. "Are you awake?"

I moaned a soft, "Mmm," and attempted to nod my head.

Bobby leaned over me and pushed a button on my bed, kissing my forehead as he sat back down and picked up my hand. He didn't let go until the nurse came in and bumped him out of the way.

"Carly?" She violated my dark sanctuary by shining a small flashlight in my eyes. I clamped my eyelids tight, but she pulled them open one at a time. "Carly, can you hear me?"

"Yeah." I almost didn't recognize my own voice.

"Welcome back, kiddo," her voice was kind. "Do you know where you are?"

I managed a slight nod in affirmation.

"Good girl. And do you know why?" She asked, as she pushed buttons on the machines that beeped nearby and made notes in my chart.

"I fell."

"150/85. A little high, but that's to be expected right now." She flipped pages back and forth as she scribbled. Her kind face looked down at me again. "Yes, dear. You fell. Hit your head pretty hard, too. Can you tell me what hurts?"

I let out a sound somewhat resembling a snort. "E'rything."

She smirked at me and patted my arm again. "It's going to for a little while. That dose of Phenergan was just enough to last a couple hours and Dr. Miller won't authorize any more at this point. It's too risky."

I winced at her silent reference to the baby and couldn't even bring myself to look at Bobby, who was pacing in my periphery. Closing my eyes, I nodded dismissively.

The nurse swapped out the ice bag under my bad wrist and wrapped it gently in a towel. "Don't move this too much, okay?"

I nodded again.

"I'll let the doctor know she's awake, Mr. Callahan," the nurse lowered her voice to a whisper. "Is there anything I can get you?"

I assumed Bobby shook his head.

"All right then. Just buzz me if you need anything. I'll be back in a little while with some dinner for her." I heard the door close behind her.

Bobby sat back down and leaned toward me, picking up my hand again.

"You know, girl. If you wanted to see me, you could've just called. You didn't have to throw yourself down the fucking stairs to get my attention." His lip curled up in that familiar smirk.

I barked in laughter, which quickly turned to tears.

"Aww, c'mere." He wrapped his arms around me and let me cry. I lay there afterward and the emotions came whirring back.

"He called you," I said as more of a statement than a question.

He nodded.

"So you know?"

He nodded again, lowering his eyes to our hands.

"How much of it?"

"Everything, I think."

"Where is he now?"

"He's at home, Carly." He bit his bottom lip and exhaled loudly. "I can't believe he had to find out this way. Were you planning on telling him at all?"

"Of course," I said. "I just didn't get the chance."

He pushed himself up off the chair and crossed over to the window by the foot of my bed. Leaning against the window frame, he moved the blinds and peered out. The sun spotlighted his face and I could read the disappointment all over it. Bobby was the type of person who didn't hold back when it came to sharing what was on his mind. He didn't believe in keeping secrets, either—at least not of this magnitude. This was one of those times. It wasn't like I hadn't intended to tell Josh about the baby.

"You're disappointed with me for something I had no control over," I reasoned.

"You were on tour with us, Carly! How many cities? Jesus!" He turned toward me again and stood with his hands on his hips, looking like every cop he'd ever portrayed. "Why didn't you tell him?"

"I was trying to!" I jerked up to a sitting position and my monitor beeped in warning. I sighed and flopped back against the pillow in defeat. I took a couple of deep breaths before I continued. "I wasn't there more than an hour, and I didn't want to just show up at his door step and say 'Hi Josh! I know I haven't seen you in a month, but I'm pregnant with your baby. Can you get my luggage from the car?'"

Bobby's silence was rare, so I took it as encouragement to continue.

"This isn't something I share openly because frankly, it isn't anyone's business, but my uterus is a black hole. It's where good things go to die. I've lost count of how many miscarriages I've had through the years."

Fortunately, Bobby spared me the expression of the pity most people gave me upon hearing about my fertility issues.

"When I found out I was pregnant, I assumed I would lose it like I had all the others and there was no point in telling anybody anything. The first time I got pregnant, it was shortly after Trey and I got married. And I learned the hard way by telling him the minute I took the test. We called our families and friends, registered at every baby store in the city and not even a month later, we had to call everyone back and cancel our registries. It was devastating. I couldn't go through that again and I wasn't about to put Josh through any more stress on top of tour, his divorce, or this stuff with Dave."

"Okay, but you were in town for what, five or six hours and you didn't think of a time to tell him?"

"If you found out you were going to be a dad, wouldn't you want that moment to be as special as could be?" I asked.

"Carly, I get your point. You wanted Josh to always remember that moment. I just don't understand why you didn't tell him before now. Even with the problems you had, he deserved to know."

"And I had a right to keep it quiet."

"Why?"

"Because *I* have been through this a hundred times. Me. *My* broken body. *My* issues. *My* decision. I'm not rehashing it, B." We played stare-down until I finally looked away. "So, how bad is it? Think he'll talk to me again?"

Bobby nodded as he sat down on the edge of my bed. "He'll talk to you again. He's just really hurt right now. And totally fucking overwhelmed. You've had like three months to get used to this. He's had like three minutes."

I hoped he was right.

Bobby leaned over, kissed my forehead again and stood up.

"I'm gonna go grab something to eat. You need anything?"

I shook my head, "No thanks. I'm not hungry."

"It ain't just you I'm worried about, girl," he cautioned before gingerly touching my belly and giving me a quick kiss before he left.

I watched him leave before I turned toward the window and saw a helicopter hover over the trauma center across the street before landing on its roof. My mind drifted to Josh and a helicopter ride we took once. I'd never been in one before and he wanted to show me a different view of New York. We flew over every borough of the city and out to the Hamptons where he surprised me with a small gathering of our friends for my birthday. It was one of my favorite memories.

Would I get to make more memories with him? God knows I fucked this one up.

I had it planned out so perfectly in my head. We would make dinner and while he finished up last minute details in the kitchen, I would put his present on his plate. He'd sit down and see the gift. With that playful look in his eyes, he'd pick it up and look at me in amusement while he unwrapped it. He'd pull the ribbons and paper off and for a moment, it wouldn't register with him what photo was in the frame, but the minute it hit him, it would hit him hard. His eyes would fill with tears as he ran his fingers down the glass covering the baby's sonogram. He'd sweep me in his arms, carry me upstairs and we'd make love in celebration of the life we'd created that night in Florida.

But none of that happened, and I wondered if it ever would. Even in the best circumstance, it wouldn't happen like *that.*

Right now, for all I knew, Josh was repacking my suitcase and either taking it over to Bobby's or bringing it here to leave at the nurse's station for me. The thought of it made me sick. I rolled on my side, wrapped myself into a ball and let the tears come.

The grief overcame me and I succumbed to its suffocation. Deep, wracking sobs echoed in the room and I lost track of time as I recalled the times Josh and I had shared over the years.

Our first kiss.

"You know," he began, a smirk forming on his lips. "I still don't know your name."

I covered my mouth and giggled behind my hand. "It's Carly Cooper."

He nodded and said, "Carly. I like it."

Cahlee. Kryptonite, indeed. He reached down with his free hand and brushed my hair away from my face, his thumb trailing my cheek as he looked at my lips. "Can I kiss you, Carly?"

I managed a smile and whispered a meek "okay," as he leaned down and pressed his mouth to mine. His lips were soft and tender, as was his touch. He pulled away and looked at me again, a smile lighting up his face. He stroked my cheek with his thumb again.

"That was nice."

"Mmm hmm." My heart was at a standstill.

"I better get goin'," he sighed. "But I'll see you tomorrow."

The thought of his kisses still left me breathless.

I thought about Prom night, a few months after that kiss. The after-Prom party was being held at a fire station in town and we'd snuck upstairs to the only empty bunk room in the whole building.

"Shh," Josh warned playfully as he squeezed into the bunk beside me, pressing me firmly against the wall. I'd given a painful groan when his knee hit my thigh. "People are gonna heah you!"

"Are you kidding?" I said in a slight whisper, just in case. "Nobody can hear us. They can't hear shit over the Beastie Boys

blaring over the speakers downstairs."

"Still! We gotta be careful!"

We hadn't been intimate together since Spring Break two months earlier and our libidos had gotten far too carried away at the dance for our own good.

The recessed lamp next to my head provided very little light and with as tight of a space as the bunk was, we couldn't see much beyond our faces, but that was enough for me. The berth filled with the scent of Josh's cologne and I inhaled deeply. The musky scent was intoxicating to me. He was shirtless and while he didn't have bulky muscles, his upper body was solid and his arms were welcoming as he pulled me into them. He'd changed into a t-shirt and basketball shorts after the dance and there was very little separating our bodies.

Thankfully, I'd kept my wardrobe basic, too. A baby doll dress and panties were easy to change into for the party and, as it turned out, would give Josh easy access to my naked skin.

Josh's long eyelashes fluttered closed as he leaned down and covered my mouth with his. While I'd become familiar with his stolen kisses here and there all night, we'd been very careful not to show public displays of affection. The chaperones had kicked out several couples when they caught them making out. But now, his teeth nipped at my bottom lip and I opened my mouth in a soft sigh. Not wasting an opportunity, Josh's kiss deepened as he slipped his tongue between my lips and lingered there, exploring and probing.

I slid my hand along his head and snaked my fingers into his hair. I loved his curls, especially when he didn't weigh them down with gel and mousse. When I gripped a handful of hair and raked my fingers up his back, Josh let out a low moan and broke the kiss.

"Fuck, Carly!" he hissed as he pressed his forehead to mine. "If you ain't careful . . ." He punctuated his statement with a growl and I couldn't help smiling.

"If I'm not careful, what?"

He lifted his head and looked at me. Words were pointless once I saw his expression. His eyes were almost black with lust and I knew there was no going back.

My voice deepened a bit and I repeated my question as I silently tugged my dress over my head and tossed it behind me. My nipples puckered at the exposure and I began to shiver. "If I'm not careful . . .?"

"Coopah . . . we're gonna get busted," he warned, his accent making even my name sound erotic. He broke his stare as his eyes wandered downward. "You dunno what you're getting yourself into."

I reached down between us and let the back of my hand graze his hardening arousal before reaching around to grip a handful of his ass.

"I think I've got a pretty good idea, McCarthy."

Instinctually, he grinded against me and I wrapped one leg around his hips, pulling him closer. He shifted his hips and I felt the rock-hard heat of his body against mine.

"Goddamn, girl!" he growled in my ear then grinned before kissing me again. His hands slid down my body and sliding his fingers inside the thin elastic band of my panties, he touched me in ways that still amazed me.

He kissed me as he slowly pulled the thin layer of silky material from my legs, leaving me naked beneath him. When he sensed my apprehension, he took my hands and placed them on his body, urging me to touch him.

Fueled by my curiosity and libido, I kissed him as I passed my hands over his chest . . . his ribcage . . . across to his back and finally settled them at his hips. My nails tickled him there until Josh wiggled with a slight whimper. Courageously, I reached around, slipping my fingers inside his shorts and cupped his ass. It changed his whimper to a deep groan in my ear. I parted my knees, allowing him to crawl between them. His weight against me seemed to feed my fervor and I tugged at his waistband. With a couple of shimmies and some creative footwork, he was soon naked and pressed against me.

Josh lined my collarbone with kisses and he worked his way down my chest. He paused to draw my nipples into his mouth, sucking gently, carefully gauging my response before moving further. Each touch of his lips brought a murmur from mine.

"Ooh!"

"Right there."

"I like that."

Each word I muttered urged him further and just when I thought my body would explode with one more kiss, he pressed his engorged head against me and gently pushed himself inside. We immediately found our rhythm and I had to bury my face in his chest to keep from crying out. Our bodies were a perfect fit and moved together like music, each thrust part of a rising crescendo.

"Josh! I'm . . . oh my God!" My mind went blank and I clenched my eyes shut. My body twitched and I couldn't make a noise, except to gasp for air.

A minute later, Josh's body stiffened above me, his face contorted into a pained expression and with a grunt, he buried his face in my neck. Finally, his knees buckled and he collapsed on top of me. Sweat-slicked and breathless, we lay there, relishing in the moment.

Our chemistry had always been good. *Always.*

I thought about the night we ran into each other on the street in New York in 2001. There was definite chemistry at play then, too. And the following morning. And subsequent mornings thereafter. But our relationship, as hot as it was, was so much more than just great sex.

I remembered the time, a few months after we'd reunited in New York, when I found a lump in my breast. He didn't leave my side for four days until I heard back from my doctor that it wasn't cancer. He'd actually been the one to notice the lump, so he was with me from the very beginning of the ordeal. I couldn't have asked for a better person to get me through the doctors' appointments and mammograms. He intercepted phone calls and indulged me in all the ice cream I could eat. When the radiologist called with the good news, we celebrated together.

It's not to say we didn't fight. I remembered the day I found out he'd gotten a DUI. Alex had accidentally spilled the beans one night on the phone and while it happened before we got back together, I was upset at the fact that he'd hidden it from me. Alex tried to swear me to secrecy, but I was too mad. I let Josh have it with both barrels when he came home from his show that night. It was petty and childish at the time, but that fight fueled a nasty tantrum that I held on to for over a week. But the make-up sex was so worth it.

It wasn't long after that when we went to his parents' house for Christmas. We'd gone to Newbury Street for last minute shopping and as the sun set on the Common, he proposed to me with a Cartier ring he'd picked out just a few months after we met. Of course, I said yes, but just weeks before our wedding day, I sent him to LA to chase an opportunity I didn't think he should pass up. The following year, he broke the news that he'd met someone else. When I got his wedding invitation, I finally gathered the courage to put closure on us. That's not to say I got over him quickly. It took me ages to get over us.

I had the same empty feeling in the pit of my stomach now. I had cried all there was to cry and all that remained was one hell of a headache.

And, the glimmer of hope growing cell-by-cell inside me.

Chapter 16

DR. MILLER CAME THE NEXT MORNING AND TOLD ME everything looked good with my CT scan and the baby's ultrasound and that I was free to go, provided someone could drive me home. He confirmed my eavesdropping from the day before, regarding two weeks of bed rest and probably two weeks after that before I could travel.

"Doctor," I began explaining, "I know the importance of watching my P's and Q's, but I live in Chicago and I need to get back home."

"Carly, I'm not bending on this," his stance was firm. "You are obviously free to do what you want to do, but I highly recommend listening to me. I've spoken with your doctors back home and they're in agreement that you stay put for the time being."

I flopped my head back on the pillow and winced as it throbbed.

The doctor's mouth curled up into the slightest smirk.

"Fine," I surrendered. "Can I at least work remotely?"

"As long as it doesn't require strenuous activity, you can—"

"Thank—"

". . . in two weeks."

I closed my eyes, gritted my teeth and sighed like a petulant child.

"Carly, bed rest means bed rest. You need to be in bed. Lying flat is ideal, but at the very most propped up on pillows for the next two weeks. You can get up to use the bathroom and that's it. No baths and your showers must be no longer than ten minutes."

"Christ, am I on house arrest?"

"If it meant you staying in bed, I'd make it happen, but no. You're not on house arrest. But I would like your word that you'll follow my orders."

"I'll make sure she stays in bed, Dr. Miller."

Millah. Josh. I blinked a couple times to make sure I wasn't imagining him there.

"Ahh, Mr. McCarthy," he said, greeting Josh with a handshake. "I'm glad to see you back and willing to take on responsibility for our patient here."

"I'll do what I can," he said as his eyes finally met mine. I saw the disappointment in his face and my heart sank. I didn't know how I could make this right, but I knew I had to.

The doctor exited a moment later, leaving Josh and me by ourselves. He stood with his shoulder leaned against the corner of the wall and he stared at the floor by the foot of my bed.

"So . . ." I tried to ease the tension, waiting for his usual reciprocal, "So . . ." but it never came. "Josh, I'm sorry."

He continued staring at the floor.

"Can we please talk about this?" His silence was killing me.

He exhaled sharply and looked up at me.

"Let's get you home," he said, acting as though I hadn't said a word. He went to the closet and got out the plastic bag containing the clothes I wore in here the day before.

"Josh . . ."

"I said," he repeated, "Let's get you home. We've got a whole month to talk."

He pulled my shorts, t-shirt, and shoes from the bag and laid them on the bed. Wordlessly, he held his hand out, pulled me up to a sitting position on the side of the bed and helped me change into my street clothes. The irony that the last time he'd done this I'd gotten pregnant wasn't lost on me.

An hour later, he guided me into the house and when we went upstairs, he led me past my room and into the master bedroom.

"Um, why are you putting me in here?"

"To keep an eye on you."

"Josh," I said, resignedly, "I won't get out of bed except to pee. I promise. I'm perfectly okay with being down the hall."

"Yeah?" He said, as he finally turned to face me. "Well, I'm not."

"What?"

"I'm not okay with you being down the hall."

"Josh, you're being ridiculous," I argued as I started to walk toward the door. "I'm fine in my room."

"This," he said, grabbing my hand to stop me, "is your room."

If the doctor wanted me to keep my blood pressure

down, he sent me home with the wrong person. This man was maddening.

"I put your clothes in that dresser over there," he said, pointing to a tall chest of drawers in the corner on the far side of the room. "Your make-up and hair stuff is in the bathroom. Your phone is there on the nightstand. The battery was low, so I plugged it in for you. I left your other things in the suitcase and put it in the closet."

I knew the "other things" he was talking about. It was the wrapped picture of our child's ultrasound. I was curious whether he'd opened it or not, but knew better than to start digging around in my luggage now.

"I'm gonna go get you a cup of tea. Do you want anything else? A sandwich, maybe?" he asked, a bit too formally for my taste, but I wasn't going to argue. I wanted to make things right and if that was going to happen, it would have to be on Josh's terms.

"I'm not hungry, but the tea sounds good. Thank you."

"Why don't you get in bed and I'll be back in a minute."

I nodded and waited for him to leave before I changed my clothes and crawled into bed.

His bed.

I had only glanced over this room on my tour of his house last spring, but it was completely different from what I remembered. It had been painted a butter yellow, and black-and-white wedding photographs had lined the walls in thick black frames. Now, it was painted tone-on-tone white with wide glossy vertical stripes. Color photographs of New England landmarks now hung where the wedding pictures had been and the large abstract painting which had hung above the white brick fireplace across from the bed had been replaced with a flat screen television. Abby's presence had been obliterated from the room.

The thought of Abby brought a tightening to my chest as I suddenly remembered she was here when I fell. I knew she hadn't pushed me or done anything else sinister, but my dislike for her was much stronger now. She'd been so condemning and downright slanderous with what she said to me before the fall. While I rarely made it a habit of wishing bad things to happen to people, it crossed my mind, if only for a moment.

My thoughts of molasses-covered Abby staked to an anthill were interrupted by the sound of my phone alerting me to appointments next week at work. I scrolled through the notes attached to three different notifications and sighed, knowing I wouldn't make any of these meetings.

I needed to call Susan and let her know what was going on. Nothing like asking for a leave of absence when you just took on the responsibilities of half the department.

I hit the speed dial for Susan and waited to be patched through.

"Susan Reed speaking."

"Hey, Susan, it's Carly."

"Carly?" she sounded surprised. "I didn't expect to hear from you this week. Aren't you supposed to be on vacation?"

"Something like that."

"You do realize when you take vacation, you don't have to work, right? We're not paying you overtime," she joked. "What's on your mind, kid?"

I smiled. She was only five years older than I was, but she referred to everybody in the office as "kid," including some of her higher-ups. I enjoyed working for Susan and hated that my situation was going to put her in a bind.

"Well, I've hit kind of a snafu," I began. "I'm going to need some more time off and see what I can do about working remotely through most of August."

"Hold on a sec, Carly." I heard her cover the phone and holler for her assistant to shut her door. "Okay, sorry about that. Now, what's going on? You need more time off?"

I drew a breath and covered my face with my hand.

"Yeah, I'm afraid I do." I hated that this conversation couldn't take place in person. "Um, I've had a small accident and I'm gonna be fine, but the doctor won't let me leave Los Angeles for about a month. In fact, I'm kind of on bed rest for two weeks."

"Carly, what the hell happened? Are you okay?" Susan's voice became worried and I could picture her sitting back in her chair, forehead wrinkled in concern.

"God, I hate having this conversation over the phone. Do you want the *Reader's Digest* version or the whole book?"

"Give it to me straight, kid," she replied. "I gotta know what we're workin' with here."

"Long story short, I'm pregnant," I blurted out. "I was going to tell you as soon as I got back to Chicago, but I managed to fall down a flight of stairs and whacked my head pretty good, so the doctors won't let me travel until they know the baby's okay."

"A baby, Carly? I didn't even know you were seeing anyone."

"Yeah," I bit back a snort and quickly came up with a cover story. "I try and keep the personal life personal and the professional life professional. But I swear I was gonna tell you the minute I got back from California."

"I'm not worried about that part. Women get pregnant all the time; we'll work with you," she reassured me. "It's you I'm worried about. Do you have a concussion? Any broken bones? Is the baby okay?"

"I've got a sprained wrist, but everything else is fine," I told her. "I'm just worried about my job."

"You've got nothing to worry about, Carly. Your job will be here when you get back," she said. "We'll get some FMLA forms for you to fill out and submit them to human resources but that's not a big deal. You just concentrate on getting better and when you're ready to come back, we'll be here."

"What about working remotely for the next few weeks?"

"Blah! Forget it. You just take care of you and that baby right now. I'll email you those forms, have your doctor fill them out and fax them back, okay?"

"Okay."

"We'll talk soon, Carly," she said. "Oh . . . congratulations, Mommy."

I couldn't help but smile at the word "mommy." It was the first time anyone had really said the word and it sunk in that I was going to have a baby.

I promised to keep in touch and hung up the phone.

I was relieved that she'd taken the news so well, but quite honestly, I didn't know what I would do for the next month while I waited for travel clearance from my doctors. The only people I knew out here besides Josh and Bobby were work colleagues. Not that I could leave to socialize with them anyway.

"One cup of tea and some cookies for the patient," Josh announced, breaking my train of thought as he set a tray in front of me. He put my tea on the nightstand next to me and spread out a linen napkin across my lap.

"Josh, I think I can manage a napkin by myself."

He clenched his jaw and nodded, and I wished I hadn't said anything at all.

"I'm sorry, Josh. I didn't mean anything by it. I just," I sighed. "I just don't want to be any more of a burden than I already am. I know this is a hell of a lot more than you bargained for and I . . ."

"Stop."

"Wha . . .?"

"Just stop. Stop with the apologizing and stop with the I'm-such-an-inconvenience crap. Just stop it."

I closed my mouth and bit my lip, looking down at my tray.

"Before we go any further," he began as he sat down on the edge of the bed next to me, pushing the tray to the side. "I have to ask. And I know it's probably gonna piss you off, but I have to know for sure . . ."

He waited until I looked up at him before continuing.

"Is it mine?"

"Without a doubt."

"There's nobody else?"

I shook my head and swallowed hard.

"Because I know you had somethin' going with Dave," he said. I just wanna make sure there's—"

"Things with Dave are done," I said, more calmly than I felt. "And they never went that far anyway."

I wanted to be angry with Josh for asking, but I knew his reasons were justified.

"One more thing," he added.

I nodded and waited for him to speak.

"Why didn't you tell me, Carly?" The circles under his eyes and the redness in them gave away how hard these last couple days had been and my heart felt heavy in my chest.

I thought about all the explaining I'd done to Bobby and Alejandro both and those excuses seemed lame now. They'd been right; Josh deserved to know.

"I was going to," I began and drew a deep breath of courage. "I had it all planned out, actually. There's a present for you. It's . . . it's in my suitcase. Will you go get it?"

He paused for a moment as if debating with himself then retreated to the closet and returned a moment later with the white box, wrapped in cheerful yellow ribbons.

He tried handing it to me, but I motioned for him to open it.

"I know it's a bit anti-climactic now, but under the circumstances, it's the best I can do," I said.

Silently, he pulled off the shiny bow and loosened the ribbon. Opening the box, he pulled out a silver picture frame. It was encircled with Celtic knots and a Claddagh at the bottom. The sonogram printout inside showed Bean's head with a little fist raised like it was sucking its thumb.

Josh's red eyes welled up and he dragged his fingertips down the glass and I saw him swallow hard. His eyes met mine.

"It's really happening," he said, without the slightest tone of question in his voice. His lips spread in a wide smile as he looked back down at the photo and sat down beside me on the bed.

"Yeah, it's really happening," I said, as my eyes began to sting with the threat of tears, "I'm so sorry I didn't tell you. I didn't want you to find out like that. I wanted it to be special and unforgettable and amazing . . . I blew it."

"Shh," he silenced me with a kiss to my temple before he pulled my head into his shoulder. I clutched him tightly and let the tears fall. I was angry with myself for not having told him sooner, frustrated at my body for being so fragile, confused over my relationship with him, fearful for our future, remorseful for what we'd done to Dave, sadness for the babies I'd lost, and relief for the one I carried now.

Josh held me as I cried, his lips pressed to the top of my head and gently stroking my back as I emptied out the emotions I'd spent so long keeping to myself. I finally pulled away, sinking back into the pillows.

"No more secrets?"

"No more secrets." I shook my head vehemently. "I swear."

"Then can we finally quit dancing around the subject of us?"

"There's an 'us?'" I asked, softly.

Josh picked up my hand and brushed his lips against the back of it. "There's always been an 'us,' Coop. Always."

He reached up with the edge of the sheet and dabbed my eyes dry . . . the same way he'd done when he visited us in Chicago the year before. I'd fought so hard to be strong then. To resist him. To do the right thing by Abby. And none of it mattered, because it still came down to Josh and me.

"God, I'm such a mess." I sniffled and tugged a tissue from the box on the nightstand, wiping my nose.

"Preggo hormones are a bitch, huh?" Josh's eyes sparkled with playfulness and he winked at me.

"You don't even know the half of it. Hormones, morning sickness." I shook my head in frustration. "Oh and the falling asleep like a narcoleptic is fun, too."

He smiled at me and brushed my hair from my eyes, running his thumb over my eyebrow.

"You do look tired."

"Not quite the compliment I was hoping for, Joshua." I smirked.

"Those will come later, after you've gotten some sleep," he said. "Drink some tea, and then try and take a nap."

I didn't want to sleep but knew I couldn't fight the exhaustion any longer. Even my body defied me by choosing that moment to betray me with a huge yawn.

"See?" Josh grinned. "Sleep."

"Yes, Dad." I mocked his nurturing, not even realizing what I'd said until Josh stopped mid-step and turned back to look at me.

"Dad." A giant smile spread across his face. "Holy shit! I'm gonna be a dad!" He jumped onto the bed again and pulled me into a hug. "Thank you, Carly."

"Don't thank me yet, Josh," I deflected. "Chickens and hatching eggs and all that." I didn't want to think about anything happening to Bean, but it was an ever-present worry.

"I don't care about any of that." He looked down at my stomach and raised his eyebrows. "Can I?"

I gave a slight smile and nodded, pulling the sheets away. He pressed his hand against my stomach and while it was firmer and a bit rounder than the last time he'd touched it a few months ago, he, of course, couldn't feel anything move just yet. His eyes lit up just the same, though.

"When will we be able to feel it move?" he asked, his tone reflecting this new fascination.

"Not for several weeks yet," I answered. "But I'll be able to feel it before you will. You can hear the heartbeat, though."

"Like if I press my ear to it or something?" he asked naively and before I could correct him, he pushed my t-shirt up and wrapped his arms around my waist, his ear flattened against my bare belly. For a man who had so many nieces and nephews, his ignorance to all things pregnancy made me snicker.

"Stop laughing! I can't hear!" He chastised me with a frown.

"Honey, you won't hear anything like that." I chuckled and tousled his hair. "It takes a special stethoscope and a little amplifier. A doctor has to do it."

He sat up, indignant. "Then, I'll call one to come over."

I took his hand and laced my fingers in his. "You can hear it soon enough."

Josh's face dropped in disappointment, but he nodded. "How are you feeling? Do you need anything? Ice for your wrist? Tylenol for your head?"

I shook my head and squeezed his hand. "Just you," I replied with conviction. "All I need is you."

Chapter 17

I SPENT THE NEXT FEW DAYS WITH JOSH WAITING ON MY every need. I appreciated his efforts, but I was starting to go stir crazy. I missed home. I missed my job. I missed my routine. I missed feeling useful. I felt like an utter sloth, lying in bed all day and night.

Josh had shit to do and he was pushing it off. Not that he'd ever admit to it, of course, but I did have the good sense (if not the good morals not) to eavesdrop on his phone conversations when he thought I was asleep.

Alex called several times, as did Bobby. Marc called once, too. No word from Dave, of course, but that was expected—and deserved. Josh and I decided together to wait until my appointment, at the beginning of August, before we announced the pregnancy. With my history, I didn't want to get anyone's hopes up until we knew the baby was okay. I knew he was itching to call our families, but he agreed to wait.

After wasting away yet another afternoon during the second week of my prison sentence, I threw the covers back and went to the closet to look for my suitcase. I'd been wearing the same two sets of clothes since I got home from the hospital. My hair was a rat's nest and I hadn't put on make-up since the day I arrived in LA, ten days earlier. Eleven? I didn't even know. I'd watched every episode of *Friends,* at least, twice, knew the ins and outs of *The Price is Right* and could therapize the guests on *Dr. Phil* within five minutes of the start of each show. I was bored to death and needed some distraction.

Digging through my carry-on bag, I looked for my Kindle or a crossword puzzle or the back of a shampoo bottle . . . anything that would take my mind off of the fact that I could pinpoint down to the minute which commercials would air on which channels around the clock.

The noise drew my warden from the living room and I could hear him coming upstairs, bounding up the steps two at a time.

"Heyyyyyy," he said, leaning against the doorframe of the closet. "Uhh, whatcha' doin'?"

"I've got to do something with myself, Josh. I'm going crazy," I answered, pausing only for a moment to look at him. I immediately noticed the stern look that crossed his face. Ignoring it, I returned my attention to my bags, unzipping pocket after pocket. "What'd you do with my laptop? It isn't here."

He sighed and stepped into the closet, putting his hand under my elbow and lifting me to a standing position. "It's downstairs and you're not using it," his voice was kind, but firm.

"Josh, I can't sit still any longer. I'm losing my fucking mind," I argued. When I saw him draw a deep breath and sensed the lecture he was about to deliver, I changed my approach. "I feel fine. I haven't had a headache in almost a week. I'm not sore. I can even do this," I said as I swiveled my wrist, "without it even tingling. I need to do something!"

"Then work on baking that bun in your oven. You've got three more days before your doctor appointment and you're not doing anything until you get clearance."

I huffed about it, but knew he was right.

"Beautiful, I know you're bored, but just hold out a few more days." He lifted my hand to his lips and kissed my knuckles. "Besides, a few days in bed now is better than the next . . ." he squinted his eyes and began counting on his fingers, ". . . well, however many months."

"Six?" I offered.

"Something like that." He smiled. "I know it's not fun and I know you want to be working, but technically, this *is* your vacation, so can you try to enjoy it?"

"If this is vacation, where's the sun? And sangria? And junk food?" I whined shamelessly. When Josh pursed his lips in a frown, I countered, "Okay, no sangria, but sunshine and potato chips couldn't hurt. C'mon. Throw me a bone, McCarthy."

He smirked and wiggled his eyebrows.

I blushed at the thought and, for a moment, would've loved nothing more than to drag this man to bed and have my way with him, but I didn't figure that was any more of an option than the sangria was.

"You're not helping, Josh."

His smile faded and he pulled me in for a hug, his hands rubbing my back. He pulled back and looked down at me with a skeptical expression.

"Can you behave?"

I tilted my head, "What are you talking about?"

"If I let you sit out by the pool, do you promise not to try and go swimming or play with the dog or weed the flowers or some other stupid shit I haven't thought to mention?"

I nearly squeed at the thought of being outside the bedroom.

"I promise, I promise, I promise!"

Josh pursed his lips in thought. "All right. This goes against my better judgment, but I can't have you up here spelunking in the closet the minute I turn my back, so you win. Poolside with virgin daiquiris, it is."

I grinned wide and jumped into his arms.

"Cooooop!" he scolded as he put me back down gently. "This is the kind of stupid shit I'm talking about! Settle down, before you shake that baby loose!"

"Bean."

"Been what?"

"Bean," I corrected him. "It's what I'm calling the baby. Until I know what it is, I'm calling it Bean."

"Bean, Pod, Bun, Alien . . . whatever you're calling it, stop trying to shake it loose!" his tone was teasing, but I knew he meant it.

"Okay. I'll do better," I promised. "One thing before we go downstairs?"

"Okaaaaaaaay?" His suspicion was obvious.

"While I'm getting changed, will you please bring my laptop outside?"

"Why?"

"Because I want to catch up on Facebook and send Alex an email," I explained.

"Nope," he declined with a kiss to my nose and a swat to my behind. "Bed rest is bed rest. You wanna talk to somebody, call 'em on the phone."

"It was worth a shot," I grumbled behind him as I grabbed clothes from the dresser before retreating to the bathroom to shower and change.

The blazing California sun would normally cook my pale, Midwestern skin in no time at all, but Josh made me put on at least three layers of 400 SPF before he left to pick up dinner. Slathered in a coconut-scented armored suit, I lay back in the chaise, soaking in every glorious ray of sunshine I could get. A slight breeze kept both the heat and the noise of the nearby traffic at bay.

Josh came out a little while later, carrying a small box filled with white bags. A drink carrier dangled from his hand.

"All right, woman," he said as he set everything down on the patio table. "I think I bought all the junk food Hollywood has to offer, so if it's not enough, you're shit outta luck."

I laughed out loud as he started opening bags.

"I've got three orders of wings—mild, hot, and barbecue—because I know you like all three, two orders of chili cheese fries, and a family-sized onion rings. Oh, and a Coke. Although, it's caffeine-free, so don't get too excited."

"You're the best, Josh." I smiled as I ripped the wrapper off my straw and shoved it through the opening in my drink lid. "Thank you."

"You're welcome," he replied with a kiss to the top of my head.

When we'd worked our way through half the wings, he

looked over at me with sauce spread from one side of his face to the other and I broke out into hearty laughter.

"Whaaa?" he asked, as he flicked his tongue against the corner of his mouth and got approximately 1/100th of the sauce off his face.

"You're a hot mess," I chuckled. Holding up a napkin wrapped around my forefinger, "C'mere."

He leaned forward and when I got the rest of his face clean, he grinned from ear to ear.

It was my turn to question him.

"What's that look for?"

"I'm just glad you're here," he replied, though he didn't stop looking at me with a schmoopy expression on his face.

"I'm glad I'm here, too."

"I was hoping you'd say that," he said, popping a cheese fry in his mouth. "I want you to stay."

I stopped mid-chew. I suspected this suggestion would come at some point during my vacation, especially after I told him about Bean, but was hoping I was just being paranoid. I didn't want to move to LA. I hadn't wanted to in 2003 and didn't want to now.

I had a life in Chicago.

And a great job.

And . . . well, absolutely nothing else. Ugh! My argument would never stick. And with a baby on the way, did I really want to be there alone? I mean, sure I had Alejandro, but I suspected at the first mention of moving east with Marc, Alex would be all over it. Neither of us talked to our families except at Christmas and even then, it was to offer excuses as to why we couldn't come home for the holidays. I knew Josh would never move to the Midwest. He had no reason to except Bean and I didn't figure that would be enough to make him leave California.

Still. Me in Los Angeles . . . permanently? I couldn't picture it.

"Did you hear me?" he asked.

I nodded and swallowed my bite of food.

"And?" Josh had stopped eating and was looking at me.

When I met his eyes, I saw the kid I'd fallen in love all those years ago. I saw the curly mop top always hanging over one eyebrow. I saw the slightly upturned nose and the teeth that had always seemed a bit too big for his mouth. I saw the St. Christopher's medallion he wore around his neck the night we met. I saw the hurt in his giant blue eyes when Bobby would make fun of something he'd done or said. I saw the familiar lips that had given me my first kiss and so many kisses since then. I saw the cockiness he could never quite hide from the world but could never seem to keep when he'd been around me. I saw the boy who'd stolen my heart in a music video in 1988 and had never given it back.

I remember the anger and frustration I felt when we lost contact my freshman year of college. It wasn't just losing Josh that hurt. It was losing the dreams he and I had spent every minute of our lives talking about—our careers, our future together. It took me a long time to feel comfortable opening up to men again after that breakup—just in time for Josh to sweep back in and knock me off my feet for a second time. I'd thought that the maturing we'd done in those ten years would be enough, that we could build on the foundation we'd constructed years earlier. So did he. We dared to dream again about careers and futures and—after that walk through the Common that chilly December evening—marriage and children. Once again, however, we walked away. And the devastation I felt after that break-up was one I don't think I ever fully recovered from. So much had happened since then. My tender heart couldn't take another break-up. Neither could my sanity.

"Carly?" He laid his hand on mine, thumb stroking my knuckles.

"Yes."

No! What the fuck? Oh my God, where had that come from?

Josh jumped off the chair, knocking chicken wings everywhere and spilling his beer in the process. Tango took off running out of fear of the foamy spray. Josh let out a whoop and flung himself across me, straddling my lap and the chaise I lounged in. He was a bit more careful in taking my clamshell of chili fries and setting it on the table. Even so, napkins got caught on the breeze and blew into the pool and over the fence into the neighbors' yard.

I started to protest, but before I could even speak a single word, he covered my mouth with his and promptly swept me off my feet as only he could do.

So much for protesting.

He pulled away just before my body spontaneously combusted and his eyes, bright with excitement, gazed into mine.

"You're seriously staying in LA?"

I inhaled deeply. "Well, I can't *stay* here this trip—I've got way too much to wrap up in Chicago, but yes, I will move to Los Angeles."

He grinned, pulled me in for another quick kiss and hug before he sat back on the chair. He brought my legs out from under his and draped them over his thighs.

"When?"

I laughed. "Well, I've got to give notice at work and, of course, tell Alejandro and I've got to find a good team of doctors and get medical records transferred and—"

"So, what . . . a couple weeks?"

"More like a couple months, Josh."

"Two months?" he said as his shoulders dropped.

"Honey, it's not like I can just drop everything and jet off to a new city," I tried to explain. "I've got responsibilities, and people are counting on me. I fought hard to keep my job at *Beguile* when everybody else was getting canned. It won't look good on my résumé if I leave Susan without notice."

He stood up and stepped away, picking up what he'd knocked over earlier. As he snatched napkins and chicken bones off the grass and shoved them in the empty bag, I could tell he was upset.

"Josh, I'm sorry, but isn't it enough that I'm moving all the way out here?"

He spun around with a hurt look on his face. "Of course, it is, Coop! I just . . ." he let out a huff as he sat down on his chair, facing me. "I just feel like I've missed out on so much already, and it kills me to think that you and the baby are going to be gone from me another two months."

He raised a valid point.

"And honestly, Carly, if you move here, what resumé do you really need? You're the mother of my child . . . *our* child. That's your job."

And there's where his valid points stopped. My independent and somewhat-feminist nerves flared.

"Josh, I hate to break the news to you, but women have juggled careers and motherhood for several decades now.

There's no reason why I can't do both."

He stopped and looked at me as if I'd grown a second head.

"Why would you want to?" he asked.

"Are you kidding?"

"No, I'm not kidding," he replied. "What's more important than raising our child?"

Well, when he put it like that.

He crouched down next to me and covered my hands with one hand and with the other, brushed hair out of my face. "Beautiful, you've worked hard your whole life. You're successful, you're talented, and you've proven your worth in every way possible."

Every way except motherhood.

"This baby changes everything, Coop. Can't you see that?"

"Of course I can. I just don't want—"

"To be a burden. I know. I get it," he said with a sigh.

He didn't let me finish my thought. And that thought had nothing to do with being a burden. It had to do with the possibility of another broken heart six months from now when he decided to pursue a different career path. Or when I decided I couldn't hack the west coast. I didn't even know how to put it into words without sounding like a skeptic. Or completely paranoid. Or both.

Josh stood, kissed that special spot on my forehead and ran his thumb along my cheekbone.

"I won't push it anymore today, but we're not done talking about this." His voice was gentle, but his stubborn Irish determination showed through. I was too tired to fight him more on it at that point.

Chapter 18

"C'mon, Coop! We're gonna be late for your appointment!"

I buttoned my shirt as I made my way downstairs.

"Josh, the appointment isn't until two o'clock. It's not even one yet," I said, looking at my watch. "What's the rush?"

"You've got *papahwork* to fill out," he said. "Besides, traffic will be a bitch this time of day."

"At one in the afternoon?"

Josh nodded emphatically.

"On Melrose?" I blinked as my forehead creased in disbelief.

Josh nodded again and shoved my purse toward me.

"Please tell me you're not gonna be like this for the next six months?" I grumbled, but knew Josh had never been early for anything in his life. It was unlikely I had anything to worry about.

"I don't like being late. That's all," he said in defense as he chirped the car alarm and opened my door.

"Josh, you're late for everything."

"And I don't like it."

"You're going to drive me to drink."

"No. I'm going to drive you to your *doctah's* appointment, if you'll get in the damn car." He looked so adorable all huffy and puffy, motioning in irritation at the passenger seat.

"Somebody's a little anxious," I teased him as I sat down and buckled my seat belt.

He barely offered me a grin as he came around the front of the car and settled into the driver's seat, firing the car to life. Twenty minutes and a little bit of small talk later, he whipped into an underground parking garage in Beverly Hills.

"What are you doing?" I asked, with a slight squeak to my voice.

"Um, *pahkin'* the *cah*?"

"*Under* the building?"

"Yes. That's typically where underground garages *ah* built."

"What if there's an earthquake?"

The panic was evident in my tone, but apparently not the least bit obvious to him because he shook his head with a smirk and I could've sworn he rolled his eyes as he pulled around a pillar and headed toward the valet desk.

"Joshua! Answer me! What if there's an earthquake while we're getting out of the car?"

"Christ, will you relax, Carly?" He chuckled and patted my hand patronizingly. "There's not gonna be an earthquake."

In the grand scheme of things, I didn't have many phobias. I didn't like spiders, but didn't fear them. Wasn't afraid of heights or flying. Wasn't really a germophobe, either. (Although, c'mon. It's just the polite thing to do to wash your hands and cough into your elbow.) And while I didn't consider myself claustrophobic, I was, in fact, deathly afraid of getting trapped underground during an earthquake.

Having come from Minnesota and living on the east coast much of my life, earthquakes weren't something I had ever experienced, so it didn't really make sense that of all the natural disasters that could happen, my warped brain chose this one. But, there it was. Having lived in California for several years and probably having experienced a dozen or more fair-sized quakes in that time, Josh was quite unsympathetic about my fears.

"There was an earthquake last Monday!"

Josh raised an eyebrow at me and flattened his lips in a look of skepticism.

"Remember? I woke you up, screaming?" I could feel my blood pressure rise just thinking about it.

Josh exploded in laughter.

"Why are you laughing? It's not funny!"

"Coop, that wasn't an earthquake."

"It was, too! The whole house shook!"

His eyes glistened from laughing so hard. "Coop, it was the fuckin' *gahbage* truck!"

I clamped my mouth shut and glared at him as he got out of the car. The valet captain opened my door and I got out, ignoring Josh's extended hand and walked to the elevator with my arms crossed.

"So what, you're not gonna hold my hand now?" he teased.

Fortunately for me, the elevator opened and I stepped inside, punching the button for the doctor's office. I crossed my arms again and snuffed at him as he stepped up beside me and offered his hand again.

I snubbed him again.

"C'mon Carly, it was funny! You'd have laughed your ass off if it was me."

I was nearly in tears with anger at him for laughing at me.

"You're a prick, McCarthy."

He stepped in front of me and pinned me against the elevator wall, his hands firmly planted on my hips. *Damn him.*

"That may be the case, but you forgot all about the underground garage – earthquake thing, didn't you?" He tilted his head and looked at me until I returned his gaze.

"I hatechu."

He wrapped me in his arms and when I reluctantly put my arms around him in return, he kissed my temple.

"Nah, you don't."

I blinked away the threatening tears before he could see them and lightly punched him in the stomach as he pulled away. "Jerk," I muttered as the elevator dinged and the doors opened. I wasn't about to admit he was right, and I knew if the tables had been turned, I'd have probably laughed myself into labor at the garbage truck thing. These hormones had my emotions all over the place and had left my sense of humor almost non-existent. And really, it wasn't nice of him to make fun of me, especially in my current state.

Fifteen minutes later, I only had a portion of my paperwork filled out when the nurse called my name. Josh nearly flew out of his chair and dragged me with him. His enthusiasm was sweet, but annoying. I didn't do "perky."

After a weigh-in, baseline blood-pressure check, and the

typical "how are you feeling today" line of questioning, they took us to the exam room. I was used to paper robes and sterile environments lacking in personality. I forgot we'd entered the 90210 zip code. The robes were pale pink silk and the rooms were twice the size of Dr. Chang's offices back home. Decorated in a contemporary design trend I was sure I'd seen in one of *Beguile's* recent centerfold layouts, I was taken aback. I prayed silently to myself that my insurance would cover the cost of this visit. Many more of these and I'd have to start selling my organs on eBay. This led me to think about what I would do to handle the medical bills if I left my job while I was still pregnant. There was no way I could afford the expense of prenatal visits, labor, delivery, and pediatrician visits without insurance. Josh clearly wasn't thinking about this part when he suggested I move to California.

"I'll step out so you can change," he said, breaking my train of thought. He was gone before I could reply that he didn't have to leave.

I hadn't really thought about what was going on—well, rather *not* going on—between us since I'd been here. Obviously, we weren't having sex. The man would barely let me take a shower without harping about the time I was spending in an upright position, much less would he let me engage in something that guaranteed to raise my blood pressure. We'd shared the same bed since the first night I got home from the hospital and there were many nights when I'd wake up with him wrapped around me, but there hadn't been anything more.

Things just felt a bit weird between us. We'd been together in Miami but had barely kissed since that night. We had created a life, yet hadn't gone out on a date in almost ten years. We were living in the same house, but Josh still felt like a stranger to me. If this was "happily ever after," Mother Goose had some serious explaining to do.

When I stopped my self-therapizing and changed into my robe, I opened the door and told Josh he could come back in. I climbed onto the table and pulled the sheet across my lap, covering my bare legs.

There was awkwardness in the room as Josh pretended to occupy himself with studying the posters on the wall and then the model on the shelf of the lower portion of a woman's body. I bit back a snort when he knocked it over and the baby inside the plastic uterus shot across the floor, skidding to a stop under the chair. He was still trying to put it back together when the doctor knocked on the door and came into the room.

"Good afternoon," she said, greeting us both with a firm handshake and a warm smile. "I'm Dr. Murphy, the perinatologist here. Dr. Miller asked that I meet with you today. I hope that's okay?" She spoke to both of us and waited for an affirmative answer.

"Of course, Dr. Murphy," I was the first to speak.

"Absolutely," Josh confirmed.

"Good, then. Let's get started." She flashed another smile at us then looked down at my chart. "Weight looks good, blood pressure's a little high, but I try not to be too mean about that on the first visit. Anything can set it off—stress, traffic, a sale at Jimmy Choo," she said as she looked up at me and winked. She took another studying gaze at my chart, flipping through the pages. She sat down on the stool at the foot of the exam table and crossed her legs. A minute later, she set my chart on her knee and turned her attention to me.

"Last week when Dr. Chang sent over your records, I spent almost the entire day looking through your medical history. I have to say, you're a lucky woman to be here, Ms. Cooper. It looks like you've had quite a few challenges over the years."

I nodded. "To say the least."

"But look at where you are today," she said, glancing over at Josh, who was nibbling away ferociously at his thumbnail then back at me. "You're feeling well?"

"Yeah, absolutely. My morning sickness has pretty much subsided, my headaches from the fall are gone and, other than the inconvenience of this wrap on my wrist, I'd say I'm doing pretty damn well, actually."

"Fantastic!" she said. "Any cravings? Aversions?"

"Nope."

Josh coughed. "*Liah.*"

I looked over at him with a furrowed brow.

"She's craving ice cream like crazy. Spicy foods, too. And the smell of my shampoo makes her nauseous," he answered, looking at Dr. Murphy. "Oh, and she gets heartburn *whenevah* she eats Chinese food."

I blinked several times. I had no idea Josh was even aware of these things. Again, I thought back to me chopping all my hair off that time several years ago.

Dr. Murphy jotted notes on my chart as he rattled them off.

"I do?"

Josh looked at me. "I think I'd know. I'm with you twenty-four-seven, Coop."

Dr. Murphy chuckled quietly as she finished up her notes. "What about sleep schedule? Is she getting up a lot at night?"

Josh answered her as if I wasn't even in the room. She continued to note my chart. When the questions were done, she stood up and set the chart on the desk beside her.

"Let's get the medical stuff out of the way, shall we?" Dr. Murphy asked as she pulled the stirrups out of the table and gently placed my feet in them.

Josh came over and stood by my side as I lay back on the table. He picked up my hand and rubbed it gently as the doctor examined me. She felt my abdomen and I tried hard not to wince as she pushed and prodded. I always hated this part of the exam. When she was finished, she pulled a measuring tape out of her pocket and measured my belly.

"Everything looks good, Carly." Her voice was chipper and I felt relieved.

"So," she said, clasping her hands in front of her, "feel like hearing the heartbeat?"

I perked up and before I could respond, Josh answered for us both with a resounding, "Yes!" He gave my forehead a quick peck and squeezed my hand, running his thumb over the back of it in his familiar, comforting way.

Dr. Murphy pulled the digital stethoscope from another pocket of her coat and placed the diaphragm against my abdomen. She adjusted the volume switch and after a moment we heard a slow, even whooshing sound. "Okay, Carly," she said, moving the wand around a bit. "That's your heartbeat. Notice how slow and steady it is?"

I nodded as Josh got closer, straining to hear more.

Just a few seconds later, a quicker swishing noise caught his attention. It was faint at first, then louder as Dr. Murphy centered in on it. Just like that, the petty earthquake argument from earlier and my concerns about my relationship with Josh disappeared. I looked up at Josh and held my breath as I listened to the miracle inside me. "There it is, kids. Meet your baby."

"Oh, my God," Josh murmured.

Fat tears spilled down my cheeks and I let out the breath I'd been holding. Josh leaned over and wrapped his arms around me, his own tears falling and splashing against my face.

"That's our Bean, Josh" I whispered. "That's our Bean!"

I felt like we'd just won the lottery. We had a long way yet to go and anything could happen, but in all the pregnancies I'd had, never once had I gotten to this point. Never had I gotten to hear the heartbeat. Everything felt so real now.

"We have to get one of these stethoscopes. I want to hear this every day," Josh said as his eyes met mine, tears still brimming over. "Where can we get one?"

Dr. Murphy grinned, "I'll give you the name of the medical supply store our office uses, Mr. McCarthy." She let us have one last minute of listening before she put the machine back in her pocket.

"The baby's heart rate is really good. It might seem fast, but that's because of its age of gestation. It'll slow down a little as you progress in your pregnancy," she explained as she looked at my chart again. "I see that you've already had an ultrasound and everything looked normal, but I think we'll do another one at your next visit in September, just to be on the safe side." She proceeded to ask Josh some questions about his health and family history, noting everything in my file.

"I don't think we need to do an amniocentesis, but we'll keep our options open if there is anything out of the ordinary in the ultrasound. I'm also recommending a Caesarean rather than natural child birth," she said.

I'd expected this. It hurt to hear nonetheless, but I had expected it.

"What? Why?" Josh replied. "Why can't she do natural child birth?

I squeezed his hand. "It's because of the attack, Josh. It's okay."

"She's right, Mr. McCarthy," the doctor said. "With having previous scar tissue, she's got a higher risk for uterine rupture than most women. That's not a chance we're willing to take, no matter how small it might be."

"We can't even try it?" Josh asked. "I mean she'll be at the hospital if something happens. Can't she just—"

"Josh," I interrupted. "It's okay. I'll have a C-section."

"Nothing is guaranteed," Dr. Murphy explained. "There's always that possibility that something could happen away from the hospital. If we schedule the C-section a couple weeks before the due date, there's a less-likely chance of something happening that's out of our control. We want mom and baby both to be healthy and safe."

Josh nodded, but I could tell he was disappointed that there would be no Lamaze classes or coaching me in the delivery room.

"Let's not borrow worries." The doctor patted my leg and helped me sit up. "Everything looks wonderful. The heartbeat is strong, you're feeling well. I think it's safe to say you're out of the woods, Carly."

"So we can tell family and friends about the baby now?" Josh asked with an excited voice.

"You mean you haven't already?"

"No, we wanted to wait until we heard everything was

okay with this visit today," I explained.

"Then get outta here and start calling everybody!" Dr. Murphy ordered with a wide smile on her face. "This baby's as close to perfect as you can get."

Chapter 19

Dr. Murphy gave me the okay to travel at my appointment, but since I really hadn't had a chance to enjoy my vacation, Josh asked me to stay longer so we could spend time together outside the house. He even invited me on an honest-to-goodness date.

I hadn't been on a date since the disastrous basketball game early last year with Keith, my downstairs neighbor, and honestly, that didn't really count. I was going with him simply to get out of the house and prove to myself I was over Trey. Besides, a basketball game wasn't really an occasion to get dolled up for. If I remembered right, I wore jeans, a borrowed Bulls jersey and a pair of sneakers. Keith was lucky I did my hair and put on make-up.

Tonight felt different. Josh and I knew each other inside out, so there were no surprises left with us, but that didn't mean I shouldn't make an effort to woo him. A couple days earlier, when Josh had a business meeting, I popped over to

Nordstrom's. I'd seen the orthopedic surgeon that morning who gave me a clean bill of health for my wrist and I wanted to celebrate with some retail therapy.

I found a great sale on summer clothes, which by the time I got back to Chicago would be out of season, but perfect for another month or two out here. I bought a couple of maxi dresses, a breezy blouse, and a cute pair of capris. While I had put on a few pounds, it wasn't blatantly obvious that I was pregnant yet, so the clothes would fit for a little while longer. With a final stop in the shoe department, I reluctantly bypassed a pair of killer stilettos for a more sensible cork wedge sandal. The heel was still high, but I justified my purchase by telling myself it was a platform and it technically wasn't as high as the stiletto would've been.

I took my time getting ready for our date. Warning Josh ahead of time not to rush me, he left me alone to get showered and changed. When I was in the bathroom putting on my make-up, he took the liberty of showering in the guest bathroom. At least Abby had trained him well in that respect. At the thought of her, I sneered and when I saw my unpleasant reflection in the mirror, I shook it off. No thoughts of the ex-wife. No more. She was gone.

Thanks to the prenatal vitamins I'd been choking down for the last three months, my hair had been growing at hypersonic speed, so I had pinned it up off my neck using a couple of styling sticks. This was also a tactical move on my part to win the war against humidity and the havoc it wreaked on my curls. While a few stubborn tendrils beat me at every turn, overall, my wild mane had been tamed. With a final dab of lip gloss, I stepped back and looked in the mirror.

Not bad.

A moment later, I shimmied into one of the maxi dresses I bought at Nordie's. It had a black strapless bodice and hugged my cleavage perfectly. My breasts had gotten bigger in the last month, but I was still able to pull off a strapless without a problem. The skirt was made of several layers of white gauzy fabric. Just like I'd suspected, the Bean was almost completely undetectable. I slipped my feet into the new wedges, laced them around my ankles and lower calves. With a final touch, I spritzed perfume on my wrists and added one final touch: the butterfly necklace Josh had given to me two decades earlier.

"Holy shit, Carly," Josh said when I walked into the kitchen to get a bottle of water from the fridge.

"What?" I asked, a bit alarmed that I was running late or had my dress tucked in my underwear. Both were typical behaviors for me at this stage of the game. Neither would surprise me.

"You look incredible!" He took my hand and pulled me against him, covering my mouth with his in a hungry kiss. As always, I went weak in the knees and gasped for breath when he finally pulled away.

"If that's what I get when I put on some makeup and do my hair, I'll be sure to do it more often," I teased. "Thank you."

"I mean it, beautiful. That dress is . . ." his voice trailed off as he focused on my necklace. "You still have this?"

"Of course," I said. "It was the first gift you ever gave me. I treasure it."

He cleared his throat and I could tell he was a little choked up. "Well, I treasure you. You're more beautiful than some old butterfly any day."

I blushed at his compliments, which seemed to come

more frequently since my doctor appointment the other day. His affection was also more recurrent. There hadn't been a night yet when he didn't kiss me goodnight. There also had been more random touching when doing the most menial things around the house, like making dinner or folding laundry. I supposed having the constant fear of miscarriage off my shoulders helped me become more open to returning his affection, as well. The less stress I felt about life, the better I was about not shutting out the world.

Josh kissed me once more before he went over to the counter and grabbed his wallet, tucking it into his pants pockets. *He* was the one who looked incredible—as if he needed help in that department. He had been sleeping better and relaxing more so the dark circles that usually plagued him at the end of a tour were gone. The stress load had also lightened for him, as well, so he was more generous with smiles now, too. He wore a light blue oxford shirt, rolled up at the cuffs and a pair of white pants. They framed his butt perfectly. Donning his signature aviators, he picked up his keys.

"Ready?"

"Always."

When he asked me to keep Friday open, he'd refused to tell me where we were going, just that I should dress comfortably, but not too casually. I hoped I wasn't over or underdressed, but I took Josh's reaction to mean I was okay for whatever he had planned.

We drove through Beverly Hills, Santa Monica, and up the PCH to Malibu. After a few winding turns, he pulled up to the most adorable restaurant right on the water. The place, while on the outside looked quite unassuming with white paint and limited signage, was decorated elegantly on the inside. On the western wall, windows stretched from one end to the other, allowing the most remarkable views of the ocean.

As we waited for our dinner, Josh took my hands in his and offered me one of his smirky smiles. This usually meant he was up to no good, but given his request earlier in the week that I not ask questions about our date tonight, I let him smirk and swallowed my curiosity.

"Carly," he said, drawing a deep breath, his smile fading a little. "I know things have been a little off between us since . . ." he paused and then gave a little chuckle. "Well . . . forever, really."

I grinned widely and nodded. He was right.

"Anyway, I know things haven't flowed well for us in quite a while, but I want to put it all behind us. I need you to know how much I care about you. I love Bean, of course, but I'm not even thinking about the baby right now. When I mentioned last week that I wanted you to move out here, I didn't want you to have any doubts that it's everything to do with you and how I feel."

I had to be honest; I did leap to the conclusion—at first, anyway—that the pregnancy is what made him jump so readily into cohabitation again. I admitted as much to him.

"I knew you'd probably think that, but you're wrong, beautiful," he said. "You having my baby is an incredible bonus to what we share, but it's so much more than that. Please tell me I'm not wrong in thinking that we've got something special here?"

"No, Josh. You're not wrong." He wasn't. I had just been too fucking afraid to admit it. "I want to be here. I want to live with you. I want to raise our baby together." With every ounce of courage I could scrape together, I put my feelings on the table. I was so sick of being afraid . . . so sick of fearing the worst all the time. "I just have to figure out how to work it all out. The move, the job thing and, above all else, I want to make sure you don't miss out on anything with this baby. I fucked up so big by not telling you right away. I can't fix it, but I want to do everything I can now to make that up to you. I just have to try to figure out how to do it."

"Let me help you," he offered.

I knew he wanted to take some of the burden off of me, but I also knew I needed to do this at my own pace. The move itself wasn't the issue. I could sell almost everything I owned and bring my remaining belongings in just a few boxes. Hell, for that matter, it was something Alex could do for me. But it was more than just packing and moving; it was shutting the door on my job, leaving my best friend, and saying goodbye to a world I'd known for the majority of my adult life. Dining at seaside restaurants in Malibu wasn't part of my normal Friday night. Even when Josh and I had been together in New York, it had been during more meager times when ordering pizza and renting a movie from Blockbuster on date night meant the rest of the week, we were eating sandwiches from home for lunch and Kraft macaroni and cheese for dinner. All of this would take some adjusting.

"I know you want to, honey, but I'll get it figured out. It's something I have to do myself." When I noticed his expression change, I added, "Soon. I promise. One trip back home to get things squared away and then I'll be back. I swear."

Before he could argue, the waiter brought our meals and our discussion of the move was shelved—permanently, I hoped.

After dinner, we carried our shoes and, hand-in-hand,

walked almost a half-mile up the coast and back. There was something comforting about the surf crashing against the sand and echoing off the cliffs behind us. It was soothing to the soul. Chicago had the lake and New York had Long Island, but half the year both of those places were covered with snow and ice. California had a definite advantage when it came to weather.

We returned to the car shortly before the sun set, despite my protests. I wanted to see a California sunset on the beach, but Josh was having none of it, saying we had one more stop and we were on a time crunch.

We hurried back to the highway, but instead of turning right to head back toward Los Angeles, Josh turned left and we headed further north.

"Honey, aren't we supposed to go that way?"

"Not yet."

"Umm, okay?"

He looked over at me, picked up my hand and kissed my knuckles. "Trust me."

Not like I had a choice. I hated not being in control, but I'd promised him a while back that I would try to do better about giving up the reins more. So, I sat back in the seat and tried to relax as I watched the sun sink further toward the horizon.

A few minutes later, we pulled into a large parking lot just off the highway. Josh got out of the car and came around to my side, taking my hand and helping me out.

Without a word, we walked through a tunnel that went under the highway and down a worn dirt path, the sun casting deep shadows across the walkway. Several minutes passed and curiosity finally got the best of me.

"At the risk of sounding like a six-year-old, how much

farther?"

He glanced over at me and smiled.

"Almost there," he answered. "Watch your step. There *ah* rocks all *ovah*. I don't want you to trip." We walked a bit farther and Josh led me down a wide set of wooden steps. By the time we got to the bottom, I had become winded and my back was killing me.

"I didn't realize we were going off-roading or I'd have worn different shoes," I complained.

"Cop a squat," he said. "I'll take them off."

I obliged and he tied the laces together and strung them over his shoulder as we rounded a giant rock, allowing me my first glimpse at the view before us.

I stood awestruck as water crashed against rocks a few feet to my left, splashing droplets of salt-water across the bottom of my skirt. I didn't care.

Vivid tones of orange and purple stained the sky like a hand-woven tapestry. The sun was what seemed like inches from the water and the bright golden glow reflected off the water, sending ripples of blue, gold, and purple into my periphery. It was the most beautiful thing I'd ever seen.

"Pretty amazing, huh?" Josh's voice in my ear brought me back to earth. He nestled up behind me, wrapping his arms around my waist, his hands embracing Bean in the process.

"Breathtaking."

A moment later, as the bottom arc of the sun met the water, I held my breath and watched as it slowly melted into the ocean. I couldn't take my eyes off it. Josh let go of me and picked up my hand.

"Come with me for a minute," he said.

"But, we'll miss it," I whined.

"No we won't. C'mon."

Reluctantly, I took his hand and we rounded another set of rocks. On the other side, he let go of my hand and jogged a little to the right. My eyes followed him and, at first, I was confused by the glow coming from inside a small cavernous opening. Josh's smile widened and he held out his hand for mine.

Stepping inside the cave, I was taken aback by the sheer volume of candles that lined the limited space. A blanket had been spread out in the center of the cave, and there was an upturned crate toward the far side that held a bouquet of roses and more candles. A small, wide log sat next to the crate and faced the front of the cavern.

"What's this?" I asked, a smile giving away my joy over his romantic gesture.

"Come sit down," he said, the corners of his mouth curled into the biggest smile I'd seen since I arrived in LA almost three weeks before. He tossed my shoes onto the blanket and held my hand as I lowered myself onto the log. "See? You can still see the sun."

I was overcome by emotion—the gorgeous sunset, the affection Josh'd been showing me all night, and now this enchanting surprise he'd somehow managed to pull off—and tears trickled down my cheeks.

"Aww, Coop," he cooed. "Don't cry." Sitting down beside me, he put his arm around my shoulders and pulled me against him.

I sniffled and closed my eyes as I soaked in every ounce of this perfect moment. For as much as we had screwed up over the years, things still felt so right when we were together. Our bodies fit like puzzle pieces. We'd both tried fitting together with other pieces in the box, but nothing ever felt as right as it did with Josh.

"Open your eyes, Carly," Josh whispered in my ear. "You don't want to miss this."

I took a deep, cleansing breath and my eyes fluttered open. The glow of the candles was overshadowed only by the sunset.

Until I looked down.

In Josh's hand was a familiar red box.

My breath caught in my chest and I choked back tears.

"Twice now, I let you slip away," he said, as he lowered himself to a crouch in front of me. The sun silhouetted him perfectly and the flicker of the candles lit up his face. "*Nevah* again. Every day for the rest of my life, I want to give you my attention, my affection, my love, and my last name. It's something I should've given you the first time I put this ring on your *fingah*.

"I want us to share a home . . . a life . . . grow old and raise our children *togethah*. I want to wake up next to you every morning and go to sleep next to you every night. I wanna give you the world, Carly, to make up for everything we've missed out on together over these lost years.

"All the choices I made in my life led to heartache and hurt because they took me away from you—away from where I'm meant to be. I can't imagine living apart from you for even one more day.

"Carly," he said, as he took the ring from the box and picked up my trembling hand. "Will you marry me?"

I looked at the man kneeling in front of me and I no longer saw the boy I'd fallen in love with at eighteen. I saw the man he'd become—the man I wanted to spend the rest of my life with.

"Yes," I whispered.

With shaking hands, he slipped the ring on my finger and brought it to his lips, sealing our commitment with a kiss. I threw my arms around him and through tears of joy, I watched as the top of the sun disappeared beneath the horizon.

Flames flickered from the candles placed around the bedroom that night. Like at the beach, I wasn't sure how Josh had pulled it off, but our room had turned into a fantasy suite straight out of the *Bachelor* and once again, he'd taken me by surprise with his romanticism. Right down to a bottle of sparkling apple cider, in place of champagne, his attention to detail was commendable. White rose petals covered every surface of the bed, the floor, and the hallway outside the door. Soft music played through the speakers throughout the house and we wasted no time in making use of the amorous setting.

With Josh's lips pressed to mine, he slowly undressed me with painstaking deliberation. My dress floated to the ground. His fingers, lips, and mouth caressed every inch of my shoulders, neck and breasts as he undressed me. When he knelt to take my panties off, he nuzzled his unshaven cheek against my leg and his exhaled breath gave me chills as it passed across the wetness at the crest of my thighs. Desire flooded through me and pooled between my legs. I'd never believed it was possible to ache from pure want . . . until then. He stood up and cupped the back of my neck, pulling my face to his until we shared the same breath.

There were no drunken games of charades, no mistaken

identities, no confusion or regrets this time. As his lips traveled across my jaw and down my neck, I unbuttoned his shirt and slipped it from his shoulders. His warm skin glowed in the candlelight and I yearned to touch it . . . kiss it . . . run my tongue along every sweet spot I could find. When our mouths locked again, he unfastened his belt as I tugged at the button and the zipper. With a slight rush of air hitting my ankles, his pants fell to our feet and I was thankful Josh had decided against wearing underwear.

His impressive length stood at attention and its heat brushed the soft skin of my inner thighs as Josh gently led me backward toward the bed. Our bodies landed in a soft *thwump*, as rose petals scattered like confetti around us. Josh rolled to the side, pulling me on top of him.

With my knees straddling his hips, I leaned over and grazed my lips across his and peppered baiting kisses along his jaw until I reached the bottom of his ear. I exhaled and felt him shiver, then gasp as I seized his earlobe between my teeth and flicked it with my tongue.

He ran his wide-spread fingers along my thighs and up to my waist. With a feather-like stroke, he touched my back and cupped my shoulders as he pulled us both to a sitting position.

Looking into my eyes, he slipped his fingers into my hair and pulled out the pins holding it up off my neck. I shook the curls loose and they fell in soft ringlets, framing my face. Josh brushed his fingers across my forehead pushing my hair aside and caressed my temple and cheek with the back of his fingers.

"I love you, Carly."

"I love you back," I replied. And I meant it.

Reaching between us, he guided his arousal into my swollen core and I moaned in response. Allowing me a moment to adjust to his size, he held me and scattered kisses across my neck and breasts. Josh's tongue snaked out, circling my left nipple, teasing me playfully. He grinned up at me before sucking the other one into his eager mouth, licking it gently before letting it pop back out. With a cool breath, he blew across my nipples until each was achingly taut, and my body quivered on full alert.

Wet and ready, my muscles welcomed what he offered and I began grinding against him. Lacing my fingers behind his neck, I slowly moved in rhythm with the motion of his hips. My bottom rested against the tops of his thighs and he held me close as we rocked back and forth, setting a slow and steady pace.

Like the cogwheel we'd always been, our bodies synced perfectly. When my hips came down, they met his, and when I rose again, they followed me. When I arched my back in pleasure, his hands slid upward and gently tugged at the hair at the base of my neck. This had always pulled me closer to the summit and I let out a kittenish whimper.

Josh's thrusts became more commanding and our sparsely-worded moans more vulgar. The friction raised our body temperatures, causing our skin to flush. The smell of sweat and sex saturated the air in the room and we grew hungrier for relief. When he bit down on the skin of my shoulder with a carnal need, the first wave of orgasm percolated from deep within me. His mouth moved quickly to my nipples again, sucking and nibbling them as well and I gripped his arms as the frenzied current crashed through me. Each crescendo of climax took me higher and higher until tears of release streamed down my face, and I collapsed against Josh's chest.

His hands slid from my hair to the backs of my shoulders and with a feral cry, he gripped my shoulders and pushed up with one last thrust, spilling himself inside me. The force of it milked one last tremor of climax from me and we clung to one another as the tide of pleasure receded.

We made love one more time before falling asleep, again sometime after midnight and once more when the sun came up the next morning. Each time was more beautiful than the last and I knew in my heart what I had to do.

Chapter 20

"WHY AREN'T YOU PACKED?"

I looked up from my magazine to see Josh standing in the kitchen doorway.

"Oh, hey!" I greeted him, kissing him when he came over to me.

"Yeah, hey," he said. "Why aren't you packed? You leave tomorrow morning."

"You tryin' to get rid of me already, McCarthy?" I teased.

Josh gave me a look of annoyance.

"God, you really *are* gonna be like this the whole pregnancy, aren't you?" I scowled at his expression. "Sit down," I said, patting the ottoman in front of me."

"Coop, your shit is strung from stem to stern of this house," he said, arm waving in typical dramatic-Josh form. "If you're going back to Chicago tomorrow, we gotta get you packed."

"Sit."

He huffed and put his hands on his hips, staring me down.

"Please?"

He took a quick glance of his watch and apparently decided it would take less time to indulge me than to argue with me because he sat down on the footstool, elbows on his knees.

I dog-eared my spot in the magazine and set it on the end table, then faced him again, tucking my legs beneath me.

"What would you say if I told you I don't have to go back to Chicago?" I nibbled my bottom lip as I examined his face for a reaction.

He didn't disappoint.

"I'd say that'd be fuckin' incredible, but how?"

"So," I began, "the other day, I called Susan and talked to her about working remotely. She said she thought it was a great way for me to ease back into a full workload."

He nodded. "Right. You told me that already."

"Well," I continued, "today, I got a phone call from Seth Eldridge. He's *Beguile's* senior editor out here on the west coast."

"You're killin' me, Coop."

"Well," I said with a smirk. God, I loved teasing him. "This morning, while you were at the studio with Bobby, I took a drive over to Santa Monica and met with Seth."

Josh's forehead was wrinkled in his signature scowl of curiosity, "And?"

"And they want to bring me on. Between you and me, they're looking at eventually moving all their offices to the West Coast and since I want to be here anyway, it's the perfect time to transition. Best of all? They want to make me West Coast Managing Editor," I told him, a smile spreading across my face. "I will be able to keep my job and move to Los Angeles. We both win."

"So you'll be working full-time?" The look on his face wasn't the one I'd anticipated when I went through this scenario in my head.

"Yes and no," I said, further explaining that I'd only be full-time until December and then I'd drop back to half-time. It would allow me to keep my benefits but still give me something to occupy my time when Josh was busy with the new album and small stint the band had discussed doing in Las Vegas. They'd talked about doing it all after the first of the year and since that fell into my third trimester, I knew travel would be out of the question for me. I would need something to keep my mind busy.

"And that's what you want to do?" His expression was still stoic and I felt a little disheartened.

"Josh, I know you think this ring on my finger alleviates my need to work outside the house, but unless something happens to prevent me from working, I plan on doing so—at least—until Bean is born."

"But you'll quit after the baby comes?"

"I'll *consider* it."

He sighed heavily and I had the feeling this was an argument we'd have for months to come, but for now, he backed off and gave me the smile I'd been hoping for.

"This means you can move to LA *soonah*, right?" And just like that, the sparkle in his eyes was back.

I flew back to Chicago that weekend with Josh in tow and we told Alejandro the news—both of our engagement and of my relocation to California.

Alex was surprised by neither bit of news and after a celebratory dinner, we spent all day Sunday and Monday packing up my belongings. It wouldn't have taken long if I'd just done it myself, but Josh refused to let me do any lifting whatsoever—not even laundry baskets—so I played supervisor from the chair as he and Alex did the packing for me. I tried not to feel bittersweet as I suspected this was the last time the three of us would be together like this. Things were changing so fast and, while I didn't want to stop them, I did feel strange not clinging to our past roles at least a little bit.

Josh crashed hard after all the packing and since Alejandro and I had always been night owls, we stayed up late, sitting out on our little patio overlooking the city.

When I moved in here last year, I hadn't ever considered that it would just be a transitional place for me until I found my way back to Josh. I'd always assumed my destiny laid elsewhere, so I hadn't given it a second thought. There was always a chance that Alex would meet someone, but even that wasn't something we'd talked much about. Alex and I had been so close for so long that the thought of us being apart again left me a little choked up.

"I'm gonna miss your crazy ass, you know," he said as he pulled a long draw off the Corona in his hand.

"Meh, you've got Marc," I joked. "That's enough neurosis to outlast anything I could give you."

But I knew what he meant: our relationship was changing. The years of single life were behind us now. Though they hadn't announced anything official, I figured it wouldn't be long before Marc asked Alejandro to move out east, if he hadn't already.

After one last salute to friendship, I downed the last gulp

of my one permitted glass of wine for the month and I bid Alejandro goodnight.

Tuesday, while Josh took care of last minute moving details, I drove to work by myself to pack up my office and get things arranged for my transfer, which would begin September 1st. For as excited as I was about the new responsibilities I'd be taking on, I did like the idea of not having to rush back to California right away. I'd never admit to Josh that I liked the time off, of course, or I'd never hear the end of it, but the truth was, I did enjoy the stress-free lifestyle.

With my things boxed up and inside the trailer of a Mayflower truck on its way to Los Angeles, Josh and I headed the opposite direction to Boston. Though the primary reason was to see his family and make our announcements, we also told Bobby we'd help him celebrate his fortieth birthday at the old club the guys played before they got famous and all still lived in Boston. Alejandro, of course, went with us—using the party as an excuse to see Marc, something he'd gotten very little ability to do lately.

Marc met us at the airport and the four of us went to lunch, after Josh and I picked up our rental car. He, too, wasn't surprised by our news, but was excited for us. As usual, he wasn't a man of many words. I suspected lingering exhaustion from tour combined with his hours at the law firm were responsible for the exhaustion I saw in his face. I didn't know how he managed two full-time careers, but he seemed happy, so I couldn't begrudge him.

After lunch, we bid Marc and Alejandro a quick goodbye as they headed north to Marc's house in the country and Josh and I got in the car and drove to West Roxbury to see his family. Josh said he'd spoken with Margaret briefly earlier in the week to let her know our time in Boston would be short, asking if she could arrange to have everybody over for dinner, so we could see as many siblings as possible while we were in town.

The McCarthys didn't disappoint. By the time we pulled up in front of the house, relatives of all ages swarmed the car and welcomed us with hugs, food, and dropped R's. The closeness and camaraderie the McCarthys had always shown me through the years was welcoming and warmed my heart. Seeing them together again made me wish my parents were still alive so they could be as much a part of Bean's life as the McCarthys would be.

I blinked away unshed tears and followed Josh into the house. Margaret came out of the kitchen, a dish towel tossed over one shoulder. She wrapped Josh in a matronly hug before holding his face firmly between her hands and kissing each of his cheeks. Colin's absence was noticeable and although Josh and I hadn't discussed his father's death since that day at the funeral, I knew it was on his mind, too. I could practically see Colin sitting in his Barcalounger, feet up with a beer in his hand. His boisterous personality is what I would always remember most about him.

Josh made re-introductions, as if I hadn't met anyone before. Of course, there were more family members than the last time I'd hung out with the McCarthy brood, but it wasn't hard to figure out which children belonged to whom. During the weeks I spent on bed rest, we'd gone through dozens of photo albums and he regaled story after story about what each sibling and their spouse had been up to since the last time I'd seen them.

When it seemed as though all the relatives had finally

arrived, we headed to the backyard where picnic tables had been set up. Matt was taking the last of the burgers off the grill while he chatted with his brothers-in-law. Matt's wife, Michele, along with Laura, Rebecca, and Maggie, Josh's sisters, helped settle in the younger kids at their own table. Margaret made her way outside and when everyone was finally settled, Josh took my hand and we stood up.

I drew a deep breath. We'd decided to wait to send out the pregnancy announcements until we got back from Boston, so our friends and family could be told in person. I was nervous about how well our news would be received. I knew how staunch Margaret was about Catholic protocol and I hoped she wouldn't be upset.

"Everybody," Josh began as he squeezed my hand, "we've got a couple of announcements to make."

"Joshua!" Margaret burst out as she pointed to my left hand. "You're gettin' married!" Damn! She was good! I chuckled and looked over at Josh, who just gave a grin and a shrug.

"What am I gonna do with her?" Josh asked in a low whisper before winking at me.

I held up my hand, fanning my fingers, showing the family my engagement ring. The family erupted in shrieks of excitement and I found myself nearly squeezed to death with hugs before everybody settled back down. It was reminiscent of the scene at Christmas a few years ago and I smiled at the recollection.

Margaret gave me an especially long hug and then pulled back, holding me by the shoulders. "It's about damn time, kid."

I wasn't sure if she was talking to me or Josh, but before I could respond, she continued. "Now," she asked me, "when are you two gonna give me a grandchild?"

"Not to pick on ya, sis," Matt said, "but you look like you're about halfway done." He pressed his hand to my stomach and I realized, in horror, that with all the hugging, the oxford shirt I'd been wearing had come loose and the form-fitting tank top I was wearing under it had become exposed.

Margaret looked down at my swollen belly and then back up at my face.

I froze.

She glanced over at Josh, whose cheeks had turned a bit pink.

"Well," Josh's mother began. "I'd say you kids are getting a head start on things. I like a girl who doesn't waste time." She embraced me again, pulling Josh into our hug.

Relief was an understatement.

There were more hugs, questions about the wedding, the baby, and everything in between filled the conversation at dinner and, for the first time in many years, I felt at home.

Later, when I was helping Michele and Rebecca with dishes, Margaret came into the kitchen and took me by the hand. She led me upstairs to her bedroom. Pointing to a bench at the foot of her bed, she told me to sit. She opened her closet door and pulled something out of the back of the rack. Before I could see what it was, she put it on the bed and took a seat in the chair across from me.

"*Cahly*," she said. "I'm not going to blow smoke up your ass. I'm not thrilled about this baby-before-bridal-bouquet thing, but it's too late and I'm too old to make a big fuss about it."

I started to speak, but she shook her head abruptly and put her finger to my lips. "Don't *bothah*, kid. I don't need an explanation. Don't want one. I just wanted to pull you aside and tell you how happy I am that you're back in our lives. Josh spent so much time doing the wrong things and being with the wrong woman—frigid bitch, if I may be so bold," she said, making a sign of the cross before looking to the ceiling and muttering what I assumed was an abbreviated "Hail Mary."

"Abigail never fit in *heah*. When he told me they were engaged, I congratulated them, of course—what kind of *mothah* would I be if I didn't—but I *nevah* liked her. And that whole business about not having kids? Don't get me *stahted*. Anyways, *bettah* things. *Bettah* things.

"He found you again *aftah* all this time and now a baby? Oh, *Cahlene*," she cooed. Margaret McCarthy was the only person on the planet I allowed to call me by my full name. "You've made this old fool very happy today." Her eyes welled up with tears. She tugged a Kleenex from the stretchy wristband of her watch and wiped them away. She patted my knee, then used it to brace herself as she rose from her seated position and went back to the garment bag she'd put on the bed a moment earlier.

"Now," Margaret said, "I don't expect you to *weah* my gown—God knows none of my *daughtahs* did and you'd swim in it, anyway—but I'd love for you to be able to use a *paht* of it—the lace, the buttons, the veil, something—on your wedding day. When is the wedding, anyway?"

"We haven't really decided yet," I answered, as I lightly fingered the lace and taffeta of the old dress. "God, Margaret, this is beautiful."

"When did we get formal again? Call me 'Ma,'" she scolded. "And don't be silly. This thing's old and yellowed and nothing like what you'd probably *weah*. But, you should be able to snip the buttons off and use them without too much hassle if you'd like to. I think you'll need to send it to the dry cleaner if you want to use the fabric, though."

I wasn't placating her in the least. My first wedding dress had been an expensive piece of designer formal wear that didn't at all feel like me. I'd sent it back to Josh when I returned my engagement ring. When Trey and I got married, I wore a second-hand Chanel suit I'd found at a thrift shop.

Traditional designs of wedding gowns had always drawn my attention and this dress was nothing, if not traditional. It was a perfect combination of taffeta and lace, and the veil was made from a fine, silk tulle that was popular during the fifties, when Margaret and Colin got married.

I'd only seen snapshots of my mom and dad's wedding and, by the time I came along, her dress had already been donated to Goodwill. My mother had never been one for tradition or family heirlooms. It made more sense to her to give things away than let them take up space in the attic or pass them along to us kids. The only reason I ended up with her rosary was because she had it with her when she died and my stepdad hadn't gotten the chance to get rid of it before I got there.

Margaret was so different from my mom. While my mother had been a bit wishy-washy, Margaret never had a problem telling people what she thought. Where my mother was a size six until the day she died, Margaret, well . . . wasn't. It had always endeared me to her. Hugging her always felt comfortable. She was a kind woman with a big heart. My mother, who had her kind moments, wasn't overly affectionate.

Even their taste in wedding attire was different. Mom's

dress had been cocktail-length, a common alternative to floor-length gowns at the time. It had a Peter Pan collar and, while it was covered with lace like Margaret's dress was, it only went to her knees, exposing her slender legs.

Holding up Margaret's dress, I turned to face the full-length mirror in the corner of the room. I tilted my head and analyzed everything about the gown from neckline to hem. While it was a couple sizes too big, the hourglass waist and form-fitted bodice would emphasize all of my best features, provided I had it tailored a little—but of course, only if we waited until after Bean was born. There was no way my rapidly-spreading waistline would pull off an hourglass shape right now.

"Nobody else has worn it?" I asked.

"Nobody."

"It's a shame," I said. "A gown like this should be enjoyed and passed down from generation to generation. It's gorgeous."

Margaret smiled and for a brief instance, I caught a glimpse of the young bride in her reflection over my shoulder. Her face shone with happy memories of her special day, and I knew I wanted to do what none of her daughters had done.

"Ma," I said, my eyes meeting hers in the mirror. "I want to wear the dress."

She looked at me with shock and then tried to dismiss my words with a wave of her hand.

"No, Ma. I mean it. I want to wear it, just how it was intended to be worn. I'll have to get it cleaned and altered a little, but," I said, turning to face her. "I want to wear your wedding dress when I marry Josh."

"I'd like that," she said, before crushing layers of taffeta and lace between us in a strong embrace. As she enveloped me in her arms, I knew I'd made the right decision.

Chapter 21

"Hey, girl." Bobby greeted me with a kiss and a slow-dance hug. He had texted me the night before with an invitation to coffee at a local hot spot in Boston's north end.

"Hey," I replied as I sat down with a cup of apple tea and a turnover. "How was Atlantic City?" He, his brother, and some of their old friends had spent the weekend gambling to celebrate a buddy's bachelor party.

He was mid-sip on a cup of tea, but he raised his eyebrow and gave me that infamous Callahan smirk.

"That good, huh?"

"It's always a good time," he smiled again then looked down at my plate. "You didn't get a cannoli?"

"Nah, not much of a fan."

He stared at me like I'd grown horns.

"Stop lookin' at me like that, Callahan," I warned as I took the first bite of my pastry.

"All right. I won't push you. I don't want wasabi in my tea," he said with a wink, referring to the sushi incident in LA.

"Smart choice," I replied with a grin.

"So," he said, after a couple minutes of silence. "Engaged, huh?"

"You helped him do all that, didn't you?"

"I don't know what you're talking about." His smile gave him away.

"Thank you," I said, pulling him in for a quick peck and a hug. "It was amazing."

"You deserve the best, Carly," he said, squeezing my hand.

He was quiet for a couple more minutes.

"I have a confession," he said, after swallowing the last bite of his cannoli and wiping his mouth.

"Oh, honey," I grinned. "If you're here to profess your undying lust for me, it's okay. I already know. Josh's okay with it, as long as we keep our flings to just once a month."

He grinned briefly before he became stoic again.

I didn't like this.

"B, what is it?" I said. "You're kinda freakin' me out."

He took a deep breath and pushed his tea aside.

"I talked to Dave last week."

Almost instantly, my chest got tight, and I felt my heart beating in my ears.

"Oh?" I asked, gulping hard. "How is he?"

"He's doin' a'ight," he said, giving me a side-eyed glance, which I didn't acknowledge. "Your name came up."

For lack of a better response, I nodded with a raise of my eyebrows.

"It probably wasn't my place to say anything, but umm," he hesitated until I looked over at him. "Well, I told him about the baby and your engagement to Josh."

I didn't know whether to be grateful or upset.

"Oh?" I repeated.

"I knew you guys would be here for my birthday party, and he'd talked about coming up and I just," he drew a deep breath and exhaled, "I just didn't want him blindsided by anything. I hope you're not mad."

Relief washed over me as I thought about it more. "No," I finally said. "It's okay. I'm glad you told him."

"You sure?"

"Yeah," I reassured him. "I mean, I'm sure the proper thing would've been for Josh or me to tell him, but I doubt he would've wanted to hear from us. At least it came from you and not because of an article in *People* or some 'Save the Date' postcard that somehow reached his mailbox."

Bobby nodded and watched me as I picked at my turnover.

"How'd he take the news?" I asked quietly.

"You know Dave," he said. "He never shows too much emotion, but he seemed okay. He didn't offer congratulations or anything, of course, but he didn't slam the phone down in my ear, either."

"Well, isn't he seeing someone anyway?" I asked. "Marc mentioned something at lunch yesterday."

"Yeah, but you and I both know it doesn't matter. It all hurts the same when you find out an ex is with someone else."

I thought back to the breakdown I had when I found out Josh and Abby were engaged. Bobby was right. "I just want him to be happy," I replied. "I don't need his blessing or even his forgiveness at this point. I just want him to be happy."

"I think he is."

"What about you," I changed the subject. "Tell me more about this Olivia person."

Bobby's face lit up and he hid a grin behind his cup of tea.

I urged him further, "C'mon, B. Spill it."

"How do you know about her?"

"A little birdie told me."

"Uh huh," he said. He gave me a suspicious gaze. When I didn't back down, he gave in. "She's good. You'll get to meet her tonight. She flies in this afternoon."

"So? Tell me about her. Scale of one-to-hottie?"

He grinned again, "She's beautiful."

"Lemme guess—leggy brunette with a nice rack? Oh, I forget, you're an ass man." I loved seeing Bobby blush. "Okay, okay, I'll stop. Where'd you meet her again?"

"She was at the Chicago show. Her and her sister came for a Face to Face."

I waited for him to continue. When he didn't, I prodded further. "Don't make me drag every detail out of you, Bobby. Tell me!"

He laughed and shrugged. "I dunno what you wanna know. She's a voice coach and just moved to Los Angeles to work for one of those *American Idol*-type shows."

"And?"

"And what?"

"Are you totally smitten or what?"

"She'll do," he grinned again.

Getting details out of Bobby was like pulling teeth on a chicken. I gave up and asked him about the party plans for that night instead, which killed the better part of an hour. We parted ways a short time after that and I spent the rest of the morning in the Back Bay, browsing in shops on Newbury and Boylston. I picked up a cute dress to wear to the party that camouflaged my quickly-growing girth. I'd brought a dress with me, but it was a bit tighter than this one and the last thing I wanted to do was flaunt my condition in front of Dave. He seemed to be moving on, but there was no point in parading about and antagonizing him.

As it turned out, my worry was needless; Dave didn't show up. Apparently, Max got food poisoning and he didn't want to be a thousand miles away when little man needed his dad. The party was crazy and the VIP area was super small. My nerves were on end for much of the party, though it did afford me the opportunity to talk to Olivia a bit.

She had short dark hair, long legs and was incredibly beautiful, just like Bobby had told me earlier. She had a personality to match. She was full of smiles despite the sneers and upturned noses some of the more passionate Bobby girls gave her most of the night.

"So what do you think of all this?" I asked her as Bobby was flirting up the fans and taking pictures over near the bar.

She chuckled softly. "I'd be lying if I said I loved it, but I know he lives for this stuff. This fish bowl VIP thing doesn't do much for me. Besides, I knew what I signed on for before I came on board."

Her eyes crossed the room and, like in a scene from a movie, Bobby lifted his sunglasses and glanced her way, giving her a wink just as another fan saddled up next to him for a photo. To the amateur eye, he could've been looking at anyone, but being just to the side of his direct line of sight, I knew who it was meant for and so did she.

She winked back and his face lit up.

I recalled the few times I hung out with Josh at public

events, like this one, and remembered fondly the same luminescent looks he'd give me from across the room. I sincerely hoped Bobby and Olivia experienced the same happiness Josh and I had come to find. God knew he deserved it, and from everything I could tell, she did, too.

"Don't break his heart," I said, not taking my eyes off Bobby.

"You don't have to worry about that, Carly." Olivia seemed to understand my protective nature and didn't hold my abrasive approach against me. "I'm more worried about him breaking mine."

I covered her hand with mine and gave it a squeeze. "I haven't seen him light up like this in all the years I've known him. I think you guys will be just fine." I smiled at her and turned back to the guys.

After firing up the crowd with an impromptu, albeit off-tune, sing-along, Josh finally returned by my side shortly before midnight. I'd stifled at least a dozen yawns and told him I was ready to go.

Just as he started to pull Lamar aside to let him know we were getting ready to leave, Bobby's voice came over the microphone. He shushed the crowd and asked the DJ to turn down the music. I glanced over at Olivia, sensing this was about the time Bobby was going to blow up her world by making an introduction.

I was wrong.

"Now that I've got your attention," he said with a glance over toward us. "I just want to make an announcement to the Josh girls out there in the crowd."

Oh, shit.

"Ahh, *faawk*!" Josh muttered as he sighed and turned

around, painting on a stage smile I'd have recognized a thousand feet away as being fake.

"It seems your boy Josh is off the market, ladies!" Bobby proclaimed as he started walking toward us.

I'm gonna kill him. I'm gonna kill him. I'm gonna . . .

"Go," Josh whisper-screamed into my ear as he shoved me into Lamar's arms. The bodyguard had me to the back of VIP and out the door before I could hear the next words out of Bobby's mouth. I waited in the car for Josh, sitting on my hands to keep from screaming at Callahan via text.

A few moments later, the driver's door opened and Josh slid behind the wheel, mumbling curse words under his breath. Lamar stood at the front of the car watching for traffic and when it was clear, he motioned for us to go. I waited until we were halfway back to West Roxbury before I said anything.

"You okay?"

"Huh?" Josh glanced over at me distractedly. "Yeah, yeah, I'm fine. I just dunno what he was thinking. He knows how shit like this fires up the crazies." He shook his head in frustration.

"Well, I guess it's not like we could keep it quiet anymore. Things are changing." I ran my hand over my stomach and reached out for Josh's hand. He picked it up, ran his thumb over my knuckles, and then brought them to his lips.

"I love you, Coop."

"I love you, back."

"I wanna feel it again!"

I laughed as Josh ran his hand all over the side of my belly, trying to find Bean's wiggly feet.

"Honey, I can't make it happen on cue," I replied. "Bean kicks when he wants to."

"He?" Josh smiled as he looked up at me. "You found out what we're having?"

"No," I answered. "We agreed we didn't want to know, remember?"

"Of course I remember. That's why I asked." His hand still searched my stomach for movement.

"The masculine reference is typically the default when more than one gender is involved or if a gender is unkno—""

Josh silenced me with a kiss and I giggled beneath his lips.

"You hate it when I get all Lit-major, don't you?"

"Yes," he said between kisses. "Doh! Did you feel that?" His excitement showed on his face as he pulled back and looked from my belly to my face and back to my belly again.

"Feel what?" I nearly bit a hole through my lip to keep from laughing.

"Woman!" Josh scolded as he tickled me until I almost peed my pants.

The doorbell interrupted the tickle fest and Josh got up to pay the delivery guy for our pizza.

As we worked our way through a large sausage and mushroom, Josh talked about the trip he was getting ready to take to surprise a venue full of Trainwreckz in Toronto. They finished filming the video for their new single last week and the fans were chomping at the bit for its release. So Bobby put together a small video release party to show off their hard work. It was supposed to just be Bobby because Marc and Dave were both busy, and Josh had been on the fence because of the baby. Since my last doctor's appointment went well though, Josh decided to fly up there to surprise the fans.

Social media was on fire with excitement, both at the anticipation of new music and the talk about us that Bobby got started at his birthday party. Thankfully, he'd left out the part about me being pregnant. We both hoped the new album would cool the coals in the hearts of the fans, but at this point, it was anybody's guess.

My job was going well and, for as much as I resisted the thought of moving to LA in the beginning, I settled into the Angelino life fairly quickly. I knew which times of the day to avoid the 405. I learned which coffee shops to hit on my way to work and which grocery stores to avoid on my way home. I even figured out the secret to parking in Beverly Hills so I didn't have to use the underground garage at my obstetrician's office.

When Josh wasn't tying up loose ends with the new album and the Vegas shows in January, we spent our time together planning the wedding. We decided to get married at Josh's childhood church in Boston. Between Margaret's distaste for flying and the majority of Josh's family living in Massachusetts, it made the most sense to get married close to home. Only a church as large as St. Thomas Aquinas was big enough to hold all of our friends and relatives. The list of invitees was already close to four hundred. At this rate, we'd have to put people in the rectory and televise it via closed-circuit TV.

Josh wanted to get married sooner rather than later, but between needing to give the church at least six months' notice, working around the prospective summer tour, and giving our guests enough time to plan for travel, the soonest we could get married was the end of June. I figured if Bean came in February it would still give me over four months to get back to my pre-pregnancy weight so I could fit into Margaret's dress. I prayed I stayed on the same weight gain course I'd been on thus far. So far, I'd only put on about ten pounds, but I still had my last trimester to go.

"Everything looks fantastic, Carly," Dr. Murphy said at my last appointment. "Heart rate is strong, your weight is good. Your BP is still a little high, so try to spend a little less time on the 405." She winked at me.

"I keep tellin' her she needs to take a leave of absence from work, Doc." Josh offered. It was true. There wasn't a week that passed when Josh didn't pressure me to leave my job.

"Well, that call should be hers to make," Dr. Murphy replied, glancing at me with a smile that reminded me she'd witnessed this chivalrous argument before. "It would help your blood pressure, Carly, but the decision is yours. We can find other ways to deal with your stress."

"I'll think about it," I said, giving her the same textbook response I'd been giving Josh for weeks. He confirmed it with an eye roll.

"So, shall we get this little movie star on film?"

"Absolutely!" Josh agreed, all but yanking me off the table to head to the ultrasound room down the hall.

A few minutes later, we were looking at a three-dimensional view of our baby—ten little fingers, ten little toes, and one ginormous head. Josh and I gripped each other's hands like a lifeline as we watched the facial expressions our child gave us. We again opted out of finding out the baby's sex, though Josh did pout about it a little when Dr. Murphy told us it was in prime position to tell.

We left the doctor's office and Josh drove straight to La

Bambina, one of LA's best baby boutiques. Josh was known for his frugality—even teased for it a lot of the time—but people would have stopped their teasing if they'd seen him with our personal shopper and the registry the two of them put together. At first, he was willing to buy everything himself, but when she mentioned setting up a baby shower registry, he was all over the idea. We bought the crib and a rocking chair, but Josh and I registered for almost all the baby's everyday needs and wants.

As we lay in bed that night, I thought back on the length of our relationship—all fifteen-plus years of it. We'd come so far during that time. Josh and I had dealt with our breakups, as well as the loss of our first child. We'd overcome the demons of our twenties that had led us both down a path of partying and promiscuity. We'd also both made it through the trenches of divorce. We were so blessed to have overcome all the obstacles and be where we were now.

"Whatcha thinkin' about?" Josh whispered, as he cuddled up behind me and covered my belly with his hand. I linked my fingers with his and snuggled closer to him.

"You."

"My wicked good looks and irresistible charm?"

"Nah. More like your enormous schlong."

Josh growled playfully in my ear and nuzzled my neck with his scruffy face. I squealed and wiggled out of his reach, rolling over to face him.

He cupped my face and drew my lips to his. He pulled back and looked at me, the corner of his mouth turning up in a smile. His thumb grazed my cheek bone and he kissed each of my eye lids. His voice was breathy and smelled faintly of his mint toothpaste when he spoke. "She was never you."

I swallowed hard and looked at him.

"From the time I met Abby, I compared her to you, Coop. And I was so damn dead-set on acting like I didn't need you, I convinced myself she measured up." He brushed an unruly curl from my forehead and kissed the skin beneath it. "She called me last week."

I felt my chest get tight with anger and, if I was being truly honest, insecurity, too. Regardless of his reasoning, he had chosen her over me at one point, after all. I cleared my throat. "Abby called you?

Josh nodded and sighed. "She told me what she said to you the day of your accident. Carly, I can't even begin to tell you how sorry I am for the horrible shit she said."

"It's over, Josh. It doesn't matter now. We know the truth."

"The truth is she knew I never got over you," he said quietly.

"Josh, if I had known—"

"I did okay for a long time," he interrupted. "I mean, you were married. I was married. I convinced myself it was all for the *bettah*. Then I came to Chicago to see you and Alex. And the minute I saw you again, it was like it used to be." He smiled at the memory.

"My marriage to Trey wasn't a bad one, really," I confessed. "It just wasn't really great, either."

"Same with mine," he replied. "Abby had her moments, of course, but overall, she was a good wife. We just weren't a good fit."

"Exactly."

"But you and me? We're a good fit."

"So much better than we were back then," I said, with a content smile.

"Definitely *bettah*," Josh breathed into my ear as he reached over me to turn out the light.

Chapter 22

"BEAUTIFUL, YOU'VE GOTTA CHEER UP."

I ignored Josh's request and tried to focus on my book. I'd been reading the same paragraph for ten minutes, unable to concentrate. I was too upset.

"Coop," he said, as he squatted down in front of me and took the book out of my hands. "You know this is what's best for you and the baby. Dr. Murphy told you that high blood pressure could be a sign of pre-eclampsia. She just wants you to err on the side of caution."

I huffed and scowled at Josh. "I could've kept working from home, at least."

"Nobody's arguing that fact, Coop." He surprised me by keeping his tone calm despite my insolence. "But we decided before Thanksgiving that you would leave your job *aftah* the baby came anyway. What's it *mattah* whether it's now or in a month?"

"Because—" I paused. What *did* it matter?

Josh raised his eyebrows and the corner of his mouth turned up in a smirk.

"Beeeeeecaaaaause?"

I sighed. I hated it when he was right. Thankfully, he saved me the pain of admitting it.

Josh ran his hands up my hips and gently untied the belt to my sweater, letting it fall open. He placed a path of kisses across the swell of my waist and laid his head down so his cheek rested near my belly button. His fingers stroked random patterns against my stomach as he bonded with the baby. Bing Crosby played quietly through the house's sound system.

Christmas lights twinkled on the tree in the corner and a fire crackled in the hearth. We'd flown both of our families to California to celebrate the holidays since I was in my third trimester and couldn't travel. Everybody had left a couple of days ago and the silence finally returned to our home.

Closing my eyes, I listened as Josh began to sing "O' Holy Night" to Bean. The baby squirmed at the sound of its daddy's voice, and I grew misty-eyed. The song had always been my favorite Christmas carol to begin with, but with Josh's sweet tenor and the wriggling in my belly, it was a little overwhelming. I gently twirled Josh's hair around my index finger as I ran my hands absentmindedly through his curls. The scent of pine and bayberry drifted in the air as I relished in the peace I felt.

Josh stopped mid-verse and his head jerked up. "What was that?"

My eyebrows creased with confusion. "What was what?"

He pressed both hands against my stomach and watched my face intently.

"Quick *fawkin'* with me, *Coopah*! What *is* that?"

"What are you talking about?"

"Your stomach got really *hahd*. Felt like you went all Rob-Pattison-Twilight-belly on me."

I laughed, "Okay, we'll discuss your *Twilight* reference later, but first, you need to relax. It does that from time to time."

"Why? Doesn't it hurt? Will it hurt Bean? Why does it do that?" If I hadn't seen him studying *What to Expect When You're Expecting* like it was some sort of maternity bible, I'd think he was completely clueless about pregnancy the way he threw out questions.

"It's fine, honey. They're called Braxton Hicks contractions and they're just getting my body ready for labor," I explained. "Remember, you asked me about these when you read about them in the book?"

"But you're not going through labor," he said, ignoring my question.

"My uterus didn't get the memo," I said with a chuckle.

"Don't they hurt?" he repeated.

"Sometimes, but I didn't even feel that one."

"Your stomach just turned to stone and you didn't feel it?" His disbelief was apparent. "You're gonna breeze through the birth of this baby!"

I snorted, "Yeaaaaah, 'cause it's all that easy."

"Do we need to be timing this shit?" He kept rubbing my stomach and eventually the contraction ended.

I smiled and ran my hand over Josh's, "Nope. It's just a practice run, babe. It's fine. I get them all the time."

He shook his head, "You amaze me."

"Yeah, well, I haven't had the baby yet."

Josh slid his hand up my jawbone and settled his finger

into the hair behind my ear. Drawing my mouth to his, he kissed me softly. "You're amazing, no *mattah* what."

"Okay, so you've got shows every night this week and Monday, Tuesday, and Wednesday of next week, right?" I asked Josh, as I went through the calendar on my phone.

"Right," he responded as he scrolled through his own calendar. "And we've got an appointment with *Doctah* Murphy next . . . what, Thursday?"

"Yes. Will you be able to make it?"

"Yeah. It's in the afternoon, so I should be okay," he said.

"Don't forget next Saturday we've got dinner plans at Olivia's."

His upper lip quivered a little bit as he fought back a scowl.

"What's with the look?"

"It's our last weekend without parental responsibilities. Do we *have* to spend it with *othah* people?"

"Honey, every day is like a weekend with us and the C-section isn't scheduled until the end of the month, anyway," I reasoned. "Bobby and Olivia have wanted to spend some time with us. The baby shower was too chaotic to really enjoy the time with them."

"The *showah* wasn't *that* chaotic," he argued.

"Maybe not for you, but Olivia ran herself ragged all day making sure everything was perfect." And she had. That poor girl was wired up before it started and totally strung out by the time it ended two hours later. "You and Bobby had it easy, hiding out in the man cave most of the time. We should've hauled your asses out of there and put you in charge of presents or something. What's done is done," I sighed, "besides, Marc and Alejandro arrive late Friday night so they can be here for Bean's birth the following week. So, suck it up, princess, we're having dinner with our friends Saturday night."

"Fine," he mumbled, knowing better than to argue with me at this point. He clicked a couple more buttons on the screen then shoved his phone back in his pocket as he got up from the chair. He put our plates in the sink and grabbed me another bottle of water from the fridge. I frowned.

"Do I have to?"

Josh gave me a look.

"Seriously, this is like the tenth bottle of water today. I'm not a camel," I whined.

"And you've got two more to go before you're done for the day," he said as he kissed the top of my head. "Drink."

The appointment with Dr. Murphy didn't go as well as I'd hoped the day before. My blood pressure was still high and she was concerned about the swelling I'd developed in my ankles and feet. She said if I didn't stay at home with my feet up and drink more water she'd put me on bed rest. I had no interest in doing that again, so I promised I'd lounge on the couch for the next week and drink at least twice the recommended amount of water. I wanted nothing more than a giant Coke and an order of fries, but I also promised to ease up on my salt intake, too.

I sighed and unscrewed the cap on my water, slugging back almost half of it before I set the bottle down. "Happy, warden?"

"You'll think '*wahden*' when I hire a nurse to take care of you while I'm gone," Josh said as he took out chicken out of the fridge for dinner.

"You wouldn't dare."

He raised one eyebrow and looked at me.

"Ugh," I groaned as I took another sip of water. "I'll be good." When he was satisfied with my answer, he returned to the task of making dinner, and I watched him as he grilled chicken breasts on the Foreman.

"I'm gonna miss you while you're gone," I said at the dinner table that night. "This is the first time you've been away for more than a day or two."

He smiled at me and picked up my hand, kissing the back of it. "I'll miss you, too." Josh paused for a minute and looked up at me. "*Ah* you sure you don't want me to have somebody come stay with you? I'm sure Olivia wouldn't mind."

"I'll be fine, honey." Olivia and I got along wonderfully and had developed a quick friendship, but I didn't want to impose on her, especially when there was no reason to.

He ran his thumb over my knuckles and after a moment, acquiesced. As he dished up our dinner, I looked at him and could sense the anxiety in his body language. He put our plates on the table and sat down, digging in silently.

"You're worried about me, aren't you?" I said, after taking a bite. It was more of a statement than a question.

"You said it yourself," he said. "We haven't spent more than a day or two *apaht* since August. And I don't like the idea of my pregnant fiancée being here alone. We can cancel these shows, you know."

"You'll do no such thing," I said. "Josh, I will be fine. Olivia's fifteen minutes away. I'm not due for another month anyway."

"Three weeks and you're delivering in two."

I pursed my lips and raised an eyebrow at him.

“Fine,” he said, letting go of my hand and patting the back of it. “But, I’m calling you every day.”

“I wouldn’t expect anything less.”

“And every night.”

“I wouldn’t want it any other way.”

“And I’ll text you, too.”

“I’ll have my phone with me at all times.”

“You’re patronizing me, aren’t you?” He sat back in the chair and crossed his arms over his chest.

“Yes, dear.”

“You’re a pain in my ass.”

“I do my best,” I said with a smirk, as I continued eating my dinner.

“I should be home sometime *aftah* midnight Saturday,” he said a few minutes later, “but then I fly out again first thing Monday morning.”

“No, you don’t.” I replied from behind my napkin as I finished chewing a bite of chicken. “Your manager called and they scheduled a bunch of TV and radio interviews, so you guys will be in Vegas all weekend.”

“He what?” Josh nearly choked on his salad. “Why didn’t he tell me?”

“Because he told me, and I’m telling you.”

“I leave tomorrow, Carly. Don’t you think this information would’ve helpful to know before now?”

“Absolutely,” I agreed. “But he just called this afternoon while you were out, so I’m telling you now.”

Josh growled under his breath and stabbed a piece of chicken so hard he hit the plate with the prongs of his fork. “I hate when he does this.”

“I know, but it’s not like we were gonna have much time

anyway," I reasoned. "You'll be tired from the show and go straight to bed Saturday night and spend all day Sunday gearing up to leave Monday morning. Take some time and enjoy the calm before the storm, honey."

"All right," Josh said with a sigh. "Nothing I can do about it now, anyway."

"If it'll make you feel better, I'll see if Olivia's free this weekend. Maybe she can take me for a mani-pedi or something."

Josh gave me another one of those looks.

"I told Dr. Murphy I'd stay off my feet and I will," I said, raising my hands in surrender, "I won't drive. And I won't be walking, except to the car and back. And honestly, with as much fucking water as she's got me drinking, I'm putting in that many miles from here to the bathroom eleventy times a day, anyway."

"Fine, but so help me God, woman . . ." his voice trailed off, as did his nonverbalized threat.

The car came early the next morning and picked Josh up for his flight to Las Vegas. I spent the next few days playing games on Facebook, taking bubble baths, reading, and running up our satellite bill watching movies-on-demand.

As promised, I heard from Josh every day, every night and had, at least, a dozen texts a day, asking me some variation of the same three questions: "Are you resting?" "Are you drinking enough water?" and "Have you gone into labor?" I answered each question appropriately, meaning whatever it took to keep him on their little mini-tour and off my back.

Olivia came over Saturday and surprised me with a trip

to a spa for a day of pampering. She booked us for a whole gamut of indulgences including massages, manicures, and haircuts. Between the two hours on the massage table and the hour I spent in the aesthetician's chair getting a facial, I was a ball of putty by the time we were finished.

We meandered back home after several hours in Burbank, but only after stopping to eat at DeMucci's for dinner. Between the two of us—well, three—if you counted Bean (I did), we devoured an appetizer of calamari, two Caesar salads, and a giant spread of pasta dishes the chef prepared family-style. We opted to take dessert home for later.

While I still considered Alejandro my best friend, Olivia and I had gotten close over the last few months. She was an even mix of spunk and sass but knew when to be quiet and reserved, too. As far as I was concerned, she was a perfect match for Bobby. From what I'd seen, she balanced out his chaotic nature well and, no doubt, held him accountable when he acted a little too, well, Callahan-ish, for lack of a better term.

She dropped me off and made sure I was settled before she left, ensuring I had both her house number and her cell programmed in my phone in case of an emergency. I assured her I would call if anything happened and waved goodnight as she drove away. I let the dog out, changed into my pajamas and, with Tango curled up on what was left of my lap, I fell asleep watching *Pride and Prejudice*.

By the time Thursday rolled around, I had exhausted every new movie on pay-per-view as well as a good share of options on Netflix. I spent a small fortune on Amazon buying books, and I'd lost count of the number of Farmville crops I was raising on Facebook. To say I was bored would be a vast understatement.

Josh's flight was delayed and landed just in time for my appointment with Dr. Murphy that Thursday. I picked him up at the airport, for which I was chastised, of course, and we headed straight to the doctor's office.

After the usual weigh-in, blood pressure check, and pee-in-the-cup, I donned a gown and crawled up on the examining table. As long as everything went smoothly today, this would be my last prenatal visit before my C-section the following Tuesday.

"You look nervous, beautiful. You okay?"

I nodded. How could I tell him I was suddenly scared shitless? This time next week, we'd have a newborn baby in the house—a child who was fully and totally dependent on us to feed it, clothe it, raise it, and teach it right from wrong. I practically hyperventilated at the thought of it all. Thank God the nurse took my blood pressure before the weight of the situation landed on my shoulders. Dr. Murphy would have had me hospitalized before the hour was out.

"You've always been a shitty *liah*, Coop." He grinned at me as he picked up my hand and brought it to his lips. His thumb caressed my knuckles in his soothing way and he leaned down to kiss my temple.

"It's just overwhelming all of a sudden, Josh. I was the youngest in my family. I never babysat neighborhood kids. I don't know anything about babies and I'm nervous as hell that I don't have that mothering instinct." Words rolled off my tongue and merged with one another as I rattled off my thoughts.

"Hey, hey, hey," Josh murmured. "You're gonna be just fine, Carly. You were great with Max and Tori and my nieces and nephews in Boston, too. Every time I've seen you with a child, you just get this glow like you were born to do this." He stroked my cheek soothingly and kissed my temple again. "Please don't worry."

A moment later, the doctor knocked on the door and came in. "Hey there," Dr. Murphy said enthusiastically as she greeted us both with a handshake. "By the looks of these numbers, I'd say you're doing well, am I right?"

I nodded, "I've been doing everything by the book, Doc, and the puffiness in my feet seems to have gone down a little bit."

She gripped my foot between her thumb and fist and seemed satisfied by the lack of indent when she let go. "It does seem better, doesn't it? I'm glad to see that. You had me scared there for a minute, Carly. Thought I was going to have to slap you on bed rest." She smiled before looking down at my chart. "Your blood pressure is still borderline, but it's lower than it has been, so I'll let it slide. Have you been taking it easy with your sodium intake?"

"Josh hid the salt shaker and has emptied the house of potato chips and ramen noodles," I shot a glare at my fiancé. "Trust me, there's been no extra salt in my diet." Josh smiled smugly at the doctor who gave him a conspiratorial wink.

She took measurements, palpated my enormous belly, and did a pelvic exam. These appointments had become banal over the last several months and even with as scared I was to have a newborn, I was plenty done with my obstetrician's diving expeditions of my hoo-hah.

"Things look and feel good, Carly," she confirmed as she tossed the latex gloves in the trash and picked up my chart. She jotted some things down as Josh helped me sit up again.

"We still seem to be good to go for Tuesday's appointment." She smiled as she went over the details of what to expect the day of the surgery. She answered our questions and after giving us a check-list of things to do for pre-op, she reminded us about the importance of watching for signs of labor.

"The minute you start having contractions or if there's a change in vaginal discharge, you need to call the office," she said. "And if, God forbid, your water breaks, just call me on the way to the hospital. Don't waste time waiting for a call-back from me, okay?"

"Got it," I said. "I'm worried about false alarms, though. I've had a lot of Braxton Hicks the last couple weeks. I don't want to call you every time one of those stupid things hit."

"If you're worried about being able to tell real from false labor, time it," she suggested. "False labor will be sporadic and unpredictable. Real labor will be steady and consistent."

Josh nodded and rubbed my back as he listened to the doctor.

"Keep your cell phones close by at all times. Call my service, night or day, as often as you need to. I don't care about that," she reassured me. "My only concern is you delivering a healthy baby while keeping yourself safe. You still need to watch your water consumption and salt intake. And," she added, "your uterine wall is stretched pretty thin right now, too. We don't want it to rupture when those contractions get stronger."

Well, *that* did wonders for my anxiety.

"I'm scaring you," said Dr. Murphy. "I don't mean to. Women with previous uterine scarring give birth to healthy babies all the time, so don't dwell on it, Carly. We're going to do everything we can to ensure you and the baby are fine."

I drew a deep breath and nodded, trying to focus on the positive so I didn't send myself into a panic attack.

"Now, Mr. McCarthy," she said, patting his shoulder. "Get this girl some ice cream and take her home to rest."

"Yes, ma'am."

This was really happening. I felt like pinching myself. I had a full-sized, wiggly baby, ready to be born any day, and it still hadn't fully sunk in yet. My dreams the next two nights were filled with different scenarios from the mildly amusing to the downright terrifying. Things like having a water birth in our backyard pool with Bobby as my doula and Dr. Murphy pulling out a litter of puppies when she cut me open during the C-section. Needless to say, I didn't get much sleep.

I lay awake Saturday morning and watched as the sun began peeking through the slit in the blinds. If I'd have been more mobile, I would say I tossed and turned all night, but the truth was, I could barely manage to shift my arms, much less my whole blimp-sized body. My mind was restless, and I couldn't shake the uneasiness I felt from the other day.

"You're doing that thing again," Josh whispered as he curled up behind me and rested his hand on what was probably Bean's butt. His palm stretched out over my stomach and he stroked it comfortingly.

"What thing?" I asked, closing my eyes and nestling back into him.

He wadded up his pillow and rested his head on it as he brushed my hair away from my ear and kissed it softly.

"You're breathing shallow and your foot is twitching," he noted. "Which tells me you're either in pain or you're worried. So which is it?"

"Just a little bit of anxiety, honey," I reassured him. "I'll be okay."

"The Braxton Hicks getting to you?" he asked as he gently rubbed the side of my now-tightened stomach. "They seem to be pretty constant this week."

"Little bit, but nothing a warm shower can't fix, I'm sure." It was comforting to know Josh was so in-tune with my body and the cues it was sending out. He noticed my engagement ring was a little snug on my finger before we'd gone to bed the previous night, so he rubbed my hands and feet to relieve some of the edema. When I made the mistake of trying to stretch my legs in my sleep, he woke up immediately upon hearing my cries and kneaded the Charlie horse out of my calf muscle. And at the moment, he was massaging the faux contractions that had plagued me steadily for the last several days.

"I'll go get one *stahted*," he said, kissing me quickly before getting out of bed. I heard the water go on in the bathroom and a minute later, he came back and helped me to my feet.

While earlier in our relationship, a shared shower meant hot, slippery sex, recent ones were more functional than fun. I sat on the built-in tiled bench while Josh crouched down and washed my legs and feet. He even managed to help me shave the parts of my legs I couldn't reach—which were plentiful. Next, he loofahed my neck and back, paying special attention to my elbows and hips, which even seemed to be out of reach at this late stage of my pregnancy. Finally, he took his time washing my curls that had grown considerably since I'd had them trimmed at the spa just a week before.

While I sat on the bench with conditioner in my hair, he gave himself a quick scour. I had to hand it to him he had the rushed shower thing down to an art. When he was satisfactorily clean, he pulled me to my feet again and rinsed out the conditioner.

A few minutes later, I was wrapped in a warm robe and sitting at the bedroom vanity while he squatted down in front of me, applying lotion to my legs. After we were dried off and dressed, we spent the rest of the morning curled up on the couch, eating breakfast and watching TV. Thankfully, the false contractions had eased up after the shower, and we headed to Olivia's mid-afternoon.

"Oh, my God!" Olivia exclaimed as her body shook with laughter as she looked at Bobby. "You did *not*!"

"Oh, he certainly did!" I replied, tears forming in the corner of my eyes from laughing so hard. "And then he got all pissed off when I didn't get all schmoopy over his porn voice."

Olivia fanned her hands in front of her red face. "Ugh, I hate that voice!

"Right?" Marc agreed. "I overheard it once at a Face to Face and wanted to scrub my ears with acid-covered Q-Tips. Nasty."

"You know I'm sitting right here, *ladies*," Bobby said without a tone of humor in his voice, which got me to cracking up all over again, especially when I saw the look Marc shot him over the feminine reference. "And, I'll have you know, thousands of women have lost their shit over that voice!" He jutted his chin in stubborn defiance and I stifled a snort. I knew that bullheadedness well.

Olivia smirked at him and petted his face. "Of course they did, handsome."

Callahan's hazing continued for at least another half-hour before my contractions returned. They weren't as bad as the ones I woke up with, but these went all the way around my waist, spread up into my chest and settled into my back. Between the contractions and the rich food I had with dinner, my heartburn had flared up and I was half-nauseous.

"You feelin' all right, Coop?" Josh's brow furrowed and he rubbed my arm. "You don't look so hot."

"Yeah, I'm fine. Just some heartburn. Dinner doesn't seem to be setting well with me," I replied as I started to get up. Just then, the contraction that had held my uterus hostage ended abruptly, pain shot across my belly, and my legs went a bit weak. I gasped hard as if somebody sucked the air from my lungs.

"Carly?" Alex said, quickly standing up beside me and gripping my elbow. "You okay?"

I blew out the breath I'd been holding in a quick rush. "Whew! Yeah, just one hell of a contraction."

"Um," Marc piped up. "I realize I'm not the most qualified to question the goings-on of the female anatomy, but aren't contractions a sign of labor?" The worried look on his face would've been comical if I wasn't a little concerned about this very thing myself.

"They're not real ones, Marc," Josh replied. "She's been having these false labor pains for a while. They've just been getting *strongah*. The *doctah* says it's normal."

"I don't want to alarm you, honey," Olivia interrupted. "But I've been watching you for the last couple hours, and your face keeps tensing up about every twenty minutes or so. Are you *sure* it's not real labor?"

Josh looked at me and his facial expression quickly changed. "I think we should go," he decided, cupping my other elbow in his hand to help me stand up.

"Probably not a bad idea," I confirmed with a nod. I sounded much calmer than I felt. The heartburn was getting considerably worse and while the contractions had stopped, I still hurt from my breasts down to the tops of my legs and all the way across my lower back. I was light-headed and just didn't feel *right.*

"Let me just go to the bathroom before we leave. I swear, I peed my pants laughing at you assholes," I said, trying to make light of things. As it was, they were gawking at me like I was about to spew a child from my loins right there on Olivia's dining room table.

"B, can you go *staht* my car?" Josh asked Bobby as he tossed him the keys. Catching them, Bobby hurried to the front door. "C'mon, beautiful, let's walk," he said to me as we made our way to the bathroom.

I refused to let Josh come in with me, so it took me a minute to pull my pants down and get situated. When I looked down at my underwear, I shrieked in fear and hollered for Josh. The door flew open half a second later and panic covered Josh's face when he saw the pool of blood. Another half-second passed before Josh pulled out his phone and dialed 911.

When the others heard me yell, they barreled down the hall to see what was wrong. Josh's face was twisted in fear as he waited on hold for the operator and Olivia, thinking a little more clearly, asked Alex to help me stand up so she could pull my pants up and wrap me in a robe.

Bobby came back inside a moment later and his eyes went wide at the sight of me in the bathroom doorway, ensconced by Marc, Alex, and Olivia. Josh paced up and down the hall trying to answer the operator's questions. When Bobby finally realized what was happening, he rushed to me and, as gently as he could, he picked me up.

"Fuck the ambulance! Let's go!" Bobby shouted as he carried me down the hall, through the living room and out the front door. Josh was hot on our heels, still relaying the situation to the emergency dispatch. Olivia grabbed our purses along with a blanket she snagged from the back of the couch, while Marc and Alex locked the house and ran to their car.

The winter air was brisk enough, but combined with my lower-half being wet with blood, I shivered so hard my head jerked rhythmically. Pain throbbed from my ribs to my knees and I was so light-headed I could hardly focus my eyes on Josh as he repeated questions to me the operator asked him. I didn't have the time for tears; everything happened so quickly.

Bobby got Josh and I settled in the back seat with the blanket, then he hopped in the front with Olivia and we peeled out of the driveway, Marc and Alex right on our bumper. When Josh got put on hold again, he clicked the "end" button and tossed his phone so hard it ricocheted off the back window and landed in pieces somewhere on the floor.

"Fuck, fuck, fuck!" Frustrated, he rummaged through my purse for my phone and handed it to Olivia. "Scroll down to 'Dr. Murphy – Emergency!'" he ordered in a panic as he raked his fingers through his hair. "Call that *numbah* and tell them Carly's in labor and something's wrong. Tell 'em we're on our way to Cedars-Sinai."

I knew something was wrong, of course. I would have to be blind and dumb not to assume the worst with all the blood I saw, but, to have him verbalize it scared me. I clutched his hand in one hand, held my seizing belly with the other, and let the tears fall.

Olivia immediately obeyed Josh's instructions and by the time she got off the phone with Dr. Murphy's answering service, we were on the west end of Beverly Boulevard, just a couple minutes from the hospital.

Hang on, Bean. Just a little bit longer. I whispered under my breath.

We squealed into the emergency room driveway and before Bobby even had the car in, park attendants wheeled out a gurney and helped me out of the car.

"It's gonna be okay, beautiful," Josh coaxed. "We're at the hospital and everything's gonna be fine."

His voice was shaky, but I wanted to believe him. I wanted to think Bean and I were going to be all right. I wanted to think about anything other than the excruciating pain, blinding dizziness, and the shivering convulsions that rendered my limbs useless.

He ran alongside the gurney, squeezing my hand as we blew through door after door, finally reaching a private room somewhere in the bowels of the emergency department.

Josh stroked his thumb over my knuckles in his comforting way as the nurses cut open my clothes and placed sticky discs on my chest and abdomen. I shook in fear and prayed to God that, above anything else, the baby was still alive.

"Sir, I'm going to have to ask you to step out," I heard someone say as I felt Josh pull on my hand before he released it completely.

"No!" I squeaked out in a raspy cry grasping for his fingers. "Josh! Don't leave me!"

"I'll be right outside, beautiful. Stay strong," he called out. "I'll be back as soon as I can. I prom—" Josh's voice was cut off by the strong, swift closing of a door.

The nurse placed an oxygen mask over my face and I sobbed beneath the small plastic dome, sucking in ragged, desperate breaths.

"Ms. Cooper, you need to slow down your breathing," a voice cautioned.

Monitors beeped all around me but even as the room faded in and out of focus, my ears picked up the slow, steady swooshing of Bean's heartbeat. I closed my eyes and focused on that sound. I knew it would get me through whatever came next.

"We've got a fetal heartbeat!"

Swoosh.

"We gotta get that baby out of there before it bradies!"

Whoosh.

"I need two bags of O-neg, stat!"

Swoosh.

The random acronyms and medical terms tossed out by hospital staff made no sense to me and I stopped listening.

Whoosh.

"Carly? It's Dr. Murphy."

Swoosh.

My eyes fluttered open enough to see my doctor standing over me.

Whoosh.

"You ready to deliver this baby?"

Swoosh.

I nodded weakly just before I felt a pinch on my hand as the nurse stuck me for an IV and my eyes rolled back in my head.

Whoosh.

Epilogue

I dabbed on the last bit of lipstick and looked in the mirror, gently smacking my lips. Using the tip of my pinky, I whisked away a smudge of gloss in the corner of my mouth and wiped it on a tissue.

Over my shoulder, I saw my best friend peek his head in the door.

"Almost show time, honey! You about ready?"

He had argued with me about being my Man of Honor, claiming wedding coordinators around the world would be kvetching if they knew there wasn't a woman standing next to the bride on her wedding day. I told him I didn't give a damn what the coordinators of the world thought . . . that I wanted no one but him standing next to me today.

"Almost," I said with a smile.

He gave me a wink and popped back out, closing the door with a soft click behind him.

I had spent what seemed like half my life planning my

wedding. I'd known since I was a little girl what flowers I would carry, which flavor cake would be served and what my ring would look like. Over the course of the last few months, everything had been worked out in painstaking detail and, fortunately for me, my fiancé was gracious enough to let me have my way.

On the night he proposed, the solitaire he pulled out was exactly what I'd wanted. He slipped it on my finger and whispered his promises to me as his shaky voice drew emotion from my sentimental heart. My tearful acceptance was just as wavering and full of promises. It was a moment I would never forget.

I closed my eyes and whispered a quick prayer, running my thumb back and forth over my mother's rosary, one of the few things I have that belonged to her. I wore another heirloom around my neck: her dainty butterfly pendant with wings so lifelike, you'd have thought a real butterfly had been preserved in liquid gold.

When the prayer was done, I loosely wrapped the rosary around the sturdier flowers in my bouquet and drew a deep breath. When I looked up, I saw a familiar pair of crystal blue eyes staring back at me from the doorway. The corners of his eyes had crinkled with age, but he would always be the most handsome man I'd ever known.

I stood and turned to face my father.

"You *ah* beautiful," he said, his voice cracking ever so slightly as he looked me over from head to toe. He reached out and took my hand, lifting it up in encouragement to spin around. Once I completed the circle, he shook his head and tears came to his eyes.

"Dad, you promised you weren't going to cry!" I teased,

hoping my own tears wouldn't spill over and wreck my makeup.

"I'm sorry, Hope. I didn't think it would get to me like this. You just . . ." he paused and swallowed hard. "You just look so much like your *mothah* and every day I see it more and more. I wish she was here."

"She is," I smiled, stroking the butterfly pendant lightly with my fingertips.

"You wore it."

"Of course!"

Dad had pulled me aside the night before at the rehearsal dinner and slipped the necklace into my hand. He'd told me the story of how he'd given it to my mother when she was just a young girl and she'd kept it until she died, despite their many separations. I knew the memory was fresh in my father's mind, too. I gently wiped away his tear with my thumb before I stood on my tip-toes, wrapped my arms around his neck, and kissed his cheek.

When we finally broke our embrace, he reached up and flipped the silk tulle veil over my face. The rustle of my grandmother's vintage taffeta was the only noise in the hallway as we walked toward the sanctuary of the church. Hearing "Canon in D" begin, I knew it was the start of my "happily ever after."

I'd spent my life listening to my father tell me over and over again of the love story between him and my mother, who'd died giving birth to me. Despite how their story ended, it made me believe in fairy tales, and I wanted what they had.

Some people pined away for years over lost loved ones, but my dad wasn't one of those people. Sure, he missed her, but he never let it detract from his happiness. He always said he was lucky to have had her for the time he did. He knew he could never love anyone like he had loved her, so he never tried. Instead, he focused his energy on raising me. As a single father, since the day I was born, it was a task that, I was sure, was full of struggles, but he managed to do it.

He read me bedtime stories every night, went to every dance recital, learned how to French braid my hair, and regaled the memories of the times when he and my mom were together, ensuring that I never felt like I was motherless. I knew her favorite color, the perfume she wore the day they met, her nicknames, her quirks, her phobias, and her insecurities. He told me of her strengths and her talents, her dreams, her beauty, her desire to have a baby, and the fact that I was her last hope at motherhood, hence—my namesake.

When Christopher came to him last year to ask permission to marry me, he gave it happily, but cautioned him to make sure, without a doubt that he knew he was making a lifetime commitment to me. Dad made him promise not to make the mistakes he'd made at our age by walking away, no matter what the reason, whether it is for his career or another woman. After Chris promised him there would be no walking away, Dad asked him if he would consider giving me my mother's engagement ring. From what I was told, he didn't even blink before he agreed.

We paused at the door of the sanctuary as the music changed and my guests rose to their feet. Down the long aisle, my eyes met those of my fiancé and I squeezed my dad's arm.

When we reached the altar where Chris and the priest stood, Dad lifted my hand and kissed the back of it, running his worn hands over my knuckles.

With a weathered voice, he whispered, "I love you, Bean."

. . . the end.

Author's Note

I know. I KNOW! I'm sorry. You're sobbing right now and it's all my fault. I accept that and take the blame for breaking your heart. Please know, though, that I am hurting just as much as you are. This story has brought me more grief with its fictional characters than I have experienced when losing real people in my life. Writing the epilogue of this book sent me spiraling into a deep depression, and I considered for a very long time rewriting the ending. But that wouldn't have done their story justice.

The first thing many readers want to know before opening a book is if there's a "happily ever after." The next thing they want to know is whether the ending is predictable. Well, this book was not predictable, but I do believe every story is a happily ever after, even if they don't end the way I want them to.

I also think that happy endings aren't actually in the end; they're the little hoorays you get with everyday life: a first date gone well, a promotion at work, the birth of a child, buying a new home, the licks of love from a new puppy, finding that missing earring. They're of thousands of little things that make you smile.

Carly had those little things too. She wanted to see her favorite band. She wanted to go to college and make a name for herself in journalism. She wanted to be married. She wanted to have a baby. She wanted to spend the rest of her life with Josh. She wanted to be happy.

Sometimes things got a little out of order and they didn't always happen when we wanted them to, but they happened.

And I know it's hard to accept her death, Josh's loss, and the fact that Hope never knew her mother. Believe me, I know. But this was Carly's journey, and I just feel blessed to have been a part of it. I hope you do, too.

Acknowledgements

I have some of the most incredible readers in the world. Thank you for your love, feedback, suggestions, comments, and constant word-of-mouth promotion. You've come to love these characters as much as I have and that means so much to me!

To my betas, Ann Marie, Allison, Laura, Trenda, and Jennifer: I'm keeping you forever! You're never afraid to tell me when something doesn't work and never reluctant to tell me when they do. You give me honesty and truth with every correspondence and I thank you!

As an independent author, the best tool we have for success is a great group of bloggers and reviewers. I couldn't possibly name them all, but to those who have featured my books and put up with my readers shoving my books in your face, thank you! You're priceless!

My dearest Jacquelyn: I'm sorry I broke you. Okay, actually, I'm not, but I hope you're able to find a good therapist to get through what I did to you with this book. Also, I hope you know, you're going to be my editor forever. Your encouragement, cussing, and crying restored the faith I lost in myself and I am eternally grateful!

Kim, my darling. This cover is the best of them all and is as perfect as I knew it would be. I could never have found anyone else to give a face to my stories the way that you have with these three books. Your talent is limitless and your gifts are immense. Thank you, thank you, thank you.

I happened upon Stacey Blake at Champagne Formats thanks to the recommendations of two of my author friends, and I'm so happy I did. You've done beautiful work with my book and have allowed me to bring my story to the hands of its very anxious readers. Thank you!

If you haven't met Wendy and Claire at *Bare Naked Words*, I have to ask you what you're waiting for! For keeping me in the know about what process comes when and for being relentlessly persistent in promoting this book, I am so grateful! Now, take a load off, kick off your shoes and have some wine! You've earned it!

Finally, I give the utmost thanks to my boyband friends who have given me glimpses into your lives, allowing me to give my readers realism that most "fans" don't get to see. Being your friend is a treasure that I will always cherish but will never take for granted. I love you.

About the Author

Mel Henry has been an avid reader since stealing her first Harlequin from her mom's nightstand in second grade. Because some words were too big for her seven-year-old vocabulary, she took to writing her own stories (much to the relief of her teacher) and has been doing so ever since.

After having held various jobs in her life that brought her no satisfaction and only a piddly income, she decided to publish her first book. She figured being a starving artist instead of just starving sounded much more interesting. Being able to do it in her pajamas and without make-up are just perks to the job.

Living in Iowa with her husband and two teenaged daughters, Mel's an avid cook (sometimes by choice), seasoned traveler (always by choice), and a hardcore warrior against chronic Lyme disease (definitely not by choice). She loves live theater, thunderstorms, and good tea. She loathes conspiracy theories, egotistical people, and sushi.

She is currently collaborating with three other authors on a project, and has the foundation in place for her next series. In the meantime, you can find her current works on Amazon and other online booksellers.

Contact Mel:

Website: http://mellysramblings.blogspot.com
Facebook: http://www.facebook.com/MelHenryAuthor
Twitter: http://twitter.com/Mel_Henry
Email: mel.henry@ymail.com

Other Books

TIME AFTER TIME SERIES

Distance and Time

Better in Time

Made in the USA
Columbia, SC
31 January 2023

11330060R00180